A M

leisure & culture DUNDEE

Working in Partnership

ABOUT THE AUTHOR

Helga Flatland is already one of Norway's most awarded and widely read authors. Born in Telemark, Norway, in 1984, she made her literary debut in 2010 with the novel *Stay If You Can, Leave If You Must*, for which she was awarded the Tarjei Vesaas' First Book Prize.

She has written four novels and a children's book and has won several other literary awards. Her fifth novel, *A Modern Family*, was published to wide acclaim in Norway in August 2017, and was a number-one bestseller. The rights have subsequently been sold across Europe and the novel has sold more than 100,000 copies.

ABOUT THE TRANSLATOR

Rosie Hedger was born in Scotland and completed her MA (Hons) in Scandinavian Studies at the University of Edinburgh. She has lived and worked in Norway, Sweden and Denmark, and now lives in York where she works as a freelance translator. Rosie was a candidate in the British Centre for Literary Translation's mentoring scheme for Norwegian in 2012, mentored by Don Bartlett. She translated Agnes Ravatn's *The Bird Tribunal* for Orenda Books.

A Modern Family

Helga Flatland

Translated from the Norwegian by Rosie Hedger

**ORENDA
BOOKS**

Orenda Books
16 Carson Road
West Dulwich
London SE21 8HU
www.orendabooks.co.uk

First published in Norwegian as *En moderne familie* by Aschehoug Forlag in 2017
First published in English by Orenda Books in 2019
Copyright © Helga Flatland, 2017
English translation copyright © Rosie Hedger, 2019

A catalogue record for this book is available from the British Library.

ISBN 978-1-912374-45-8
eISBN 978-1-912374-46-5

This book has been translated with financial support from NORLA

Typeset in Garamond by MacGuru Ltd
Printed and bound by CPI Group (UK) Ltd, Croydon CR0 4YY

For sales and distribution, please contact: *info@orendabooks.co.uk*

LIV

The Alpine peaks resemble sharks' teeth, jutting upwards through the dense layer of cloud that enshrouds Central Europe as if the creature's jaws are eternally prepared to clamp down. The mountaintops force the wind in various directions, pulling at the plane from all angles, and we're so small here, all in a row, the backs of the heads in front of me shuddering in unison.

More than half the population on the ground below us believes it's OK to raise a hand to their children, I think to myself, and for a moment my eyes seek out my own children; but they're hidden from view, seated four rows in front of me. Beside them, Olaf rests his head against the cabin wall. In front of him I spy Ellen's blonde hair, and between the seats I can see that Mum is sleeping, her head resting on Ellen's shoulder. Dad wanders along the aisle between the rows of seats, wearing his new Bose headphones around his neck. Did he wear them to the toilet? I feel a warm flicker of affection and smile at him, but I fail to catch his eye. He sits down beside Håkon, and I catch only glimpses of Dad's face, his high cheekbones and the tip of his nose, which has a faint blue hue about it from the glow of the laptop in front of him.

They could be anyone. We could be anyone.

◈

It's raining in Rome. Everyone is prepared for it; we've been checking the forecast every day for the past three weeks, and we've discussed it on the phone and via text message and in our family Facebook group, reassuring ourselves that it doesn't matter, that it's April, and April brings unpredictable weather, plus it's bound to be warmer than it is in Norway, and we're not going for the weather, anyway. Even so,

the mood at Gardermoen Airport, which was bathed in spring sunshine and close to a balmy 20°C, was noticeably better than it is at
Fiumicino Airport, where it is 13°C and raining. The mood may also
have something to do with a sense of anticlimax, an acknowledgement
that the tension and goodwill with which we greeted one another at
Gardermoen has dwindled over the course of the flight; the first leg
now over and done with, everybody's shoulders have relaxed ever so
slightly.

Having the others here, even at the airport, makes me feel intruded
upon. I try to catch Olaf's eye, to seek some confirmation that he feels
the same; Rome and all that surrounds it, everything that belongs to
it, is ours. Walking through the arrivals hall feels different this time; I
don't exhale in the same way I do when Olaf and I are here by ourselves,
I don't feel that same frisson of excitement. But Olaf is busy buying
train tickets for everyone, and I lament my own ingratitude, my self-
absorption. I make up for it by picking up Hedda, kissing her nose
and asking if the plane's shaking scared her. She squirms free, no doubt
hyper after munching her way through the biscuits and chocolate that
Olaf wasn't supposed to deploy in anything other than an absolute
emergency.

We're due to spend two days in Rome before leaving for Olaf's
brother's house, which is located in a small town on the coast. Two
days is both far too brief and far too long a stay, I think to myself for
the first time, and I see both my own little family – the one I've created
with Olaf – and the one that I've come from, with new eyes.

◈

Dad turns seventy in four days' time. Last year, during his birthday
meal, he called for silence and announced that the following year's
birthday gift to himself and the whole family would be a holiday – his
treat. We could go anywhere, he declared, turning to Hedda, who was
four years old at the time: 'We could even go all the way to *Africa*!'

The idea itself, the manner of its announcement and his almost frenzied disposition in the months leading up to that night were so out of character that Ellen sent me lists of brain-tumour symptoms on a daily basis for quite some time afterwards. It's probably just a reaction to the fact that he'll soon be turning seventy, Olaf said. But Ellen and I were having none of it: he's not the kind to make a fuss about his age. He's always poked fun at people who create a crisis when their birthday comes around – the kind who compensate with over-the-top reactions. They're using their age as an excuse, he's always said. They're really making a fuss about something else. But Dad didn't seem ill, and he didn't seem to be in the midst of any kind of crisis. And our concerns about him weren't so overwhelming that they outweighed our pleasure at being treated to a holiday, so Ellen and I let it go.

We haven't been on holiday together for what must be twenty years now, not since the days when the concept of 'family' extended no further than Ellen, Håkon, Mum, Dad and myself. Occasionally we've ensured that our stays in the family cabin have overlapped, with Mum and Dad and Håkon, and maybe even Ellen, staying on for an extra few days before Olaf, the children and I are given the run of the place, but this kind of trip – an organised *pack-your-bags-and-off-we-go* kind of trip – we haven't embarked on since I was in my early twenties, and Ellen and Håkon and I found ourselves piled in the back of a rental car in Provence.

I don't recall us being quite so distant back then, not like we are now. Moving away from Oslo and out of the house in Tåsen, leaving behind the familiar framework, with its fixed patterns, conversations, gatherings, places at the table, it's done something to the family dynamic; nobody knows quite how to act, how to adapt, which role is theirs to take. Maybe it also has something to do with the fact that we're three adults on holiday with our parents; we're half grown, yet still their children.

The Africa idea was quickly vetoed – by everyone but Hedda, that is – and it was actually Olaf who suggested Italy, saying that we could stay in his brother's house there. Olaf is careful never to find himself in anybody's debt, and the thought of Dad paying for a holiday for him and his children very quickly became too much to bear. You can't offer him money, I said when Olaf suggested we pay our own way, it'd be condescending. Liv and I really want to show you the Italy that we've come to know, Olaf told Mum and Dad. Perhaps we could combine that with your seventieth birthday celebrations?

◆

We're far too big for Italy. Big and white and blond, we barely fit around the table at the restaurant that evening. The furniture and interiors have been designed with trim little Italians in mind, not for Dad and Håkon, both almost six feet, four inches tall, not for such long arms and legs; not for us. We cram ourselves into our chairs, all elbows and knees, too many joints jostling for room. Ellen and Håkon squabble over the available space, suddenly teenagers all over again. I recall the way we identified the seams between the seat cushions in the back of the car, treating them as border lines – even the slightest hint of coat flap crossing a seam was forbidden. The air around us was subject to the same restrictions. Håkon was only three at the time, but he grew up with sisters and with clearly defined lines in the car, in the tent and at the dining table – and in life in general, really – lines that laid down the ground rules.

Sitting beside us is an Italian family. There are more of them than there are of us, but, as Håkon points out, they're seated around a smaller table, all making their way through one dish after another, just like Olaf and I did on our first trip to Rome. We'd told the waiter that we wanted to order the same as the family at the table next to us. I spent the following week gazing at large Italian families sitting down to eat together for several hours every evening – children and grandparents, loud and prone to gesticulation, just like in the films, and I missed my own family, though I knew even then that it wouldn't be the same if they were there. Here. But now they *are* here; now *we're* here, all of us seated around the same table: Mum, Dad, Ellen, Ellen's boyfriend Simen, Agnar and Hedda, Olaf and me – and Håkon.

I glance over at Dad sitting at the head of the table, and it strikes me that we're sitting exactly where we sit when we're at our parents' house. Dad always sits at the head of the table, with Mum to his right and me beside her, and Håkon across from Mum with Ellen by his side. Other later additions to the family – partners, Agnar, Hedda – have had to organise themselves around us; I don't think we've even given it a single thought. The only person ever to initiate any kind of silent protest is Simen; on the few occasions he's joined us for family gatherings, he's practically launched himself at the seat beside Ellen – Håkon's place at the table – draping an arm across the back of her chair and firmly clinging to his spot until everyone else has taken a seat.

Dad has thick grey hair, and even though pictures from when I was little show him with the dark hair he once had, I can only just recall it – in my memories, he always has the same grey hair he has now. He locks eyes with me and smiles, and I wonder what he's thinking about, if he's happy, if things are how he imagined they would be. Perhaps he hasn't imagined them at all. He tends not to predict whether things will be one way or the other, but he's always commented on my own tendency to do so: You have to try to accept things as they are, Liv, he would tell me when I was young and shedding anguished tears over holidays, handball matches or school assignments that hadn't gone as I'd expected, finding it impossible to explain to Dad just how critical it was that they should unfold exactly as I'd anticipated; any action or accomplishment, great or small, had to follow a predictable course to prevent things from becoming chaotic and intangible. But you can't plan life in that kind of detail, Dad said, you need to accept that you can't always control things.

Now he's leaning over to Mum. The hearing in his right ear – the ear that's always on Mum's side at the dinner table – isn't what it once was, and she lifts a hand to create a buffer between her words and the clamour of the restaurant. Or perhaps it's the other way around. Dad doesn't look at her; he smiles and nods slightly.

'So, have you made up your minds?' he asks loudly, looking out across the table before Mum has lowered her hand. He brandishes the menu.

Scarcely two minutes have gone by since the menus were handed out to us, and he hasn't yet opened his own.

'We should probably start by ordering some wine,' Mum says.

Dad doesn't respond to this. He studies his menu carefully. She leans over to his hard-of-hearing side and repeats herself, and he nods yet again without saying a word, just looking down. Mum smiles, but not at him, not at any of us. She opens the wine list.

◈

We don't have to spend every waking moment together, Mum said as we planned our two-day stay in Rome, and Håkon pointed out that nobody else felt the need to visit the MAXXI Museum. The *need*, Mum repeated. It's hardly a *need*. You're making it out to be as fundamental as eating. It's not a *need*, but a *desire*, and I think it's worth making time for. And even though Håkon and Ellen were both there too, as usual I felt that her words were aimed at me, that there was an underlying message that was somehow critical, in this case a dig at the fact that Olaf and I had holidayed in Rome on several occasions without ever having visited a single art gallery. In truth, it was an attack on our entire approach to going on holiday, to raising our children, to living our lives – an attack of the kind that hits me just the same each and every time, the kind I'm so used to that I'm incapable of forming concrete thoughts about it; there is only a stab of emotion that is preserved in my memory, telling me there's something I need to protect myself against. Rome itself is a museum, I replied hastily. There's so much else to see, it seems a bit unnecessary to me. She smiled condescendingly, as she always does whenever she sees through my argument or when I do something she describes as precocious, even to this day. Don't be so precocious, she says, and I forget every single time that I'm a grown woman in my forties.

Of course, we don't have to spend every waking moment together, she repeated, then looked at us to assess the impact of her words, and now, as we stand trapped in a throng of Japanese tourists milling around outside the Colosseum, I feel certain that Ellen and Håkon share my regret at having passed up going to the art gallery with Mum.

Dad has gone to the Vatican by himself. He didn't ask if anyone wanted to join him, instead simply announcing over breakfast that it was what he planned to do today. There's something not quite right about it all, I said to Olaf after breakfast. Something isn't quite right between them. You can see it too, I insisted, but I wasn't sure what exactly it was that I was seeing. On the one hand they were being nicer to one another than they had been in a long time – teasing one another, laughing emphatically at one another's anecdotes and engaging in topics of conversation brought up by the other as if their take on things was original and fresh, or as if they were seeing their arguments in a new light, perhaps. On the other hand, there was a noticeable distance between them, a lack of intimacy.

Olaf told me not to spend so much time focusing on them. We're on holiday too, you know, he said. And anyway, scrutinising their every move isn't likely to change anything. That's hardly what I'm doing, I replied, and Olaf laughed.

❖

Agnar insists on queuing to enter the Colosseum. We can't see where the queue begins or ends; it'll take several hours. Ellen and Håkon laugh and shake their heads, saying they'd rather sit in the café we walked past just across the way. I look at Olaf, who shrugs wearily.

'I can go on my own,' Agnar says.

'Are you mad? I don't think so,' I reply, almost without thinking.

Agnar looks at Olaf.

'It's not that bad an idea, surely,' Olaf says.

'It's a terrible idea, Olaf,' I tell him.

Agnar has only just turned fourteen, and I think he's a little immature for his age. Olaf doesn't think we have anything to worry about, but Agnar still looks upon most situations with the childish expectation that everything will naturally work out just as it should, giving no thought to the consequences, driven only by impulse. He always regrets things afterwards, and is wracked with anguish when he realises how worried Olaf and I have been when he's come home an hour later than planned without ever picking up his phone, for example – but then the entire situation plays out in exactly the same way just a few days later. We've told him it's self-centred, that he needs to buck up his ideas, that we need to be able to trust him. But at the same time, I know it's nothing to do with trust – he doesn't do it on purpose, as he himself points out. When I'm in the middle of something, I just forget, he tells us. He forgets absolutely everything else too. I know that and I understand it, but Olaf and I are at a loss as to how we should handle the situation. Olaf sees a little too much of himself in Agnar, and is convinced that the best course of action is for us to give him more freedom, not less. Back at the kitchen table in Oslo, four days before leaving, sitting across from 'Angst-ridden Agnar', as Olaf has taken to calling him on the days following our confrontations, those days when Agnar can't do enough for us – making coffee and breakfast and offering to look after Hedda and do any number of other lovely favours – I was open to testing this approach.

But not here, not in Rome. Come on, Olaf, I try to convey with a look in his direction.

'I've got my phone,' Agnar says.

'Which you only ever answer when it suits you,' I say. 'Better that I come with you instead.' I can't deny him the chance to go inside the Colosseum when he's showing such enthusiasm. Over the past few years he's developed an interest in history and architecture that has taken us by surprise, and when I told him we'd be going to Rome, his eyes shone.

'No, you don't have to do that, I *want* to go by myself,' Agnar says, fidgeting with impatience, nervously playing with his left ear, just like Håkon does in stressful situations.

'It's not about what you *want*, it's about what you're capable of,' I tell him.

Hedda tugs at my hand – she wants to sit down on the filthy tarmac.

I pull her up again and she starts to whinge, hanging from my arm like a monkey, my shoulder aching.

'He's capable. Look, this is what we'll do,' Olaf says, and takes both of Agnar's shoulders in his hands, looking him directly in the eye. 'You've got two hours. That gives you until three o'clock. That means if you haven't made it in by then, you have to leave the queue. At three o'clock, we'll meet at the café just up there,' Olaf says, pointing at the café towards which Håkon and Ellen are headed.

Agnar nods, almost paralysed, not daring to look at me for fear that I'll ruin things with my objections. But Olaf and I have made a virtually unbreakable pact not to disagree with one another in front of the children, to take a consistent and coordinated approach to their upbringing, to rules and boundaries, so I can do nothing but nod. I'm proud of him, too – the fact that he's so persistent in his interest in things to which other fourteen-year-olds wouldn't give a second thought – and I wish that Mum were here to see it.

Olaf checks that Agnar's phone is fully charged, gives him money to keep in his pocket, with instructions not to retrieve it until it's time to pay, and tells him that he has to check the time every ten minutes, that this is a test, the kind he needs to pass if he really wants the freedom he's been craving all this time. Has Agnar understood?

'Every ten minutes. Three o'clock. Money. Café. Message received!' Agnar says, and smiles his lovely smile, the one that lights up his soft, innocent face – the kind of face that would be a dream for any child kidnapper or paedophile. I feel sick and anxious as I watch him disappear into the crowd.

❖

Olaf takes Hedda to a playpark and I make my way to the café, looking back over my shoulder every ten steps to see if I can spot Agnar in the queue. I can't remember what I was like at fourteen but feel fairly certain that I'd never have suggested going off on my own in a foreign city.

Håkon and Ellen are sitting at the edge of a terrace with a view of the Colosseum. Simen has decided to have a lie-in and meet us for lunch instead. His approach to holidays is unthinkable in our family – the idea of not getting out and about, not *doing* something. Holidays are about sleeping late for me, Simen warned us at dinner the previous night. Dad's smile was strained. I imagine that Simen is also the type to park himself in front of the television on a Friday night when the weather is nice, something which is physically impossible for myself and Håkon and Ellen. Even now, as an adult, I feel guilty about doing anything other than making the most of any good weather we get, something that Dad established as a rule and imprinted upon us every sunny Saturday and Sunday from the day we were born.

Håkon has ordered a bottle of red wine; I ask the waiter to bring me a glass. Ellen covers her glass with her hand when he comes to pour some for her.

'I'm halfway through another course of antibiotics,' she says; she's been plagued by recurring urinary tract infections.

'You must be contributing more than your fair share to global antibiotic resistance, the way you get through those things,' Håkon says. 'Maybe you should try drinking more cranberry juice.'

'It's interesting to hear that you know so much about urinary tract infections, Håkon. Is there any subject you're *not* an expert on? Anything you *don't* have an opinion on?' Ellen retorts with a smile, rolling her eyes.

Their bickering makes me feel calmer, but I'm aware of my heart hammering inside my chest. My gaze is locked on the crowds of tourists, Agnar no doubt milling among them, unable to find his way. I take a large sip of wine, close my eyes and swallow. For a moment I envy Ellen and Håkon, sitting there entirely devoid of responsibility, free, seeking nothing but the sun, which peeks through the thin layer of cloud that lingers above us.

It's not often we're together, just the three of us. It's only since Håkon got older that we occasionally meet up for a beer or dinner, Ellen and I always taking the initiative. Ellen is two years younger than

I am, and Håkon is eight years younger than Ellen – he turned thirty just a few weeks ago. It's only in the past few years that he's started getting in touch with us, that the distance between us has felt less stark than it did when he was ten and I was twenty, and we've come to know one another in a different way, as adults – even though the sense of hierarchy is still tangible. I feel like he and Ellen have a very different relationship; they spend more time together and are in touch with one another more often than with me. I have the sense that they feel they've got more in common, and in fact there's something in that: they both look like Mum, they have her blonde hair and big eyes. Ellen shares Mum's curvaceous figure too – she's soft and plump in a graceful, attractive way, unlike me. My body has always been thin, almost angular.

I'd love to have swapped places with her; I'd love to have Ellen's body. I still remember how awful it was when she had more shape about her at fourteen than I did at sixteen – bigger boobs, the works. I recall the way the boys in my class would ring the house to speak to her. I was furious with her, wrote in my diaries that I hated her and listed a hundred reasons why: that she whined, that she was clingy, a brat. When she had a boyfriend before me – a boy who used to sit with us at the dinner table and play with her hair – I told Mum that I wanted to move out. I made every argument possible, without mentioning Ellen, but I realised afterwards that Mum must have seen through it all. I wrote in my diary that Mum took me out to various places, that the two of us went to see Grandma and Grandad, had dinner out, went to the cinema, that she spent a lot of time with me without inviting Ellen. I only ever seemed to mention all this in passing, though, perhaps alongside a comment or short review of the film we went to see. I didn't seem to be reflecting on or appreciating Mum's obvious efforts at the time, or perhaps it was just too embarrassing, even in my own diary, to seek sympathy for the fact that I had a younger sister who was much more successful than I was in every single way.

I still feel tiny glimmers of that shameful, overwhelming envy. It flares up in me when I see the looks she attracts as we walk down the street or sit together in a café, when I see pictures of us in our younger years, or worst of all, when I see the way she talks to Olaf sometimes – no, in fact, it's the other way around: the way *he* talks to *her*. I've never asked him about it, even though the most banal questions hound me with a child-ish intensity: Do you think she's prettier than I am? Would you choose her if you could? Even during our most serious arguments, when I almost lose control over what I'm doing or saying, still I keep these ques-tions to myself. I've longed to scream them at him, particularly during our early days together, but I've always caught myself in time, instead singling out a colleague or friend of his: Don't think I can't see the way you look at her, I've shouted, the way you light up around her. Do you really think you've got a chance? Do you really think she'd be interested in *you*? It's so petty and so shameful, but it beats the alternative.

Ellen and I became good friends in our early twenties. When I met Olaf, I found that Ellen filled a new role in my life. All of a sudden, she was someone I could confide in – she became a person, a sister, someone close to me, not simply a manifestation of everything I envied and could never be. I had been studying journalism and living in Major-stua with a friend while Ellen had continued to live at home. The year after I moved out, I don't think we saw each other at all, beyond the usual family get-togethers. All I remember is how lovely it was to be away from her, not to see myself reflected in Ellen every morning, to make friends who didn't know her. Then I met Olaf, and my ambiva-lent feelings towards her suddenly seemed excessive and childish, and she and I grew closer. When Agnar and Hedda were born, those old feelings became nothing but the faintest of flickers, reminding me of how things used to be.

◆

After two and a half glasses of wine and enough time in the sun to leave the tip of my nose tingling with sunburn, I feel more relaxed. I'm pleased that Olaf took control of the situation, pleased that Agnar got to see the Colosseum, that he has parents who give him the space he needs to learn that freedom comes with responsibility. I feel pleased to be sitting with my brother and sister in a tourist café in Rome as our mother peruses Italian contemporary art and our father wanders around the Vatican.

I don't dare mention my concern for Agnar again, not after Ellen and Håkon had looked so perplexed when I'd told them how stressed I was feeling before I'd even sat down. We've had long discussions about this in the past and I know that Håkon thinks I'm overprotective, that the children are subjected to too many rules and that I have too many anxieties as a result of it all. Ellen is fascinated by the way we give our children so much support, as she's commented somewhat sarcastically several times, though she's not even bothered to state her feelings outright this past year – she's simply withdrawn from the conversation whenever we've started talking about bringing up children. And even though I understand what she's saying, that we're part of a bigger trend, I don't know how I could possibly do things any differently. If I refuse to do all of those things that are expected of parents these days, it would only harm Agnar and Hedda, they'd find themselves outsiders.

'It's almost half two,' Ellen says, interrupting Håkon's reflections on the fact that we perceive Italian families to be large, when in fact families here now have just over one child on average.

'Beyond the fact that it says something about recession and family policies that aren't fit for purpose, it's not all that catastrophic in itself. Having lots of children shouldn't be something to aim for. Quite the opposite, in fact,' he says. 'The world is overpopulated as things are.'

Ellen talks over him as he utters the last few words, loudly parodying Mum, who, regardless of whether anyone has asked, has a habit of checking the time before announcing it to all and sundry.

We've teased her incessantly about it and it's become an inside joke between Håkon, Ellen and me, and even with Olaf, Agnar and myself. All the same, her declarations have a steadfast quality about them, neutral and informative. Even though we imitate Mum's tone in jest, Håkon, Ellen and I have started declaring the time to one another and to others outside of the family, giving us something to say when things go quiet, providing a neat way of bringing social gatherings to a close, or simply taking the form of a snippet of information to share.

I laugh at Ellen. Her impersonations are better than anyone else's I know; there's something about her ability to observe and imitate the tiniest of gestures, her mimicry; the slightest toss of the head or change to her expression and suddenly she is transformed into Mum, Grandma, a friend or some well-known politician or actor.

'Thank you,' I say.

'God, relax will you, he's fourteen,' Håkon says.

We suddenly become aware that Ellen's reminder of the time was an attempt to put my mind at ease, a point in common, a shared reference. I wonder how much of it is genetic, if we're programmed in the same way, if that's why we share this intuitive understanding of and for one another, or if it's simply a learned behaviour, a way of thinking, speaking, making associations, concluding matters. Either way, Ellen, Håkon and I share these connections, unspoken and unceasing, irrespective of time or place.

Back when I was a journalist, recently graduated and working freelance for a women's magazine, I researched and wrote a piece on twins separated at birth. However, unlike the usual tales of such cases, my article focused on a pair of identical twins who looked the same, sounded the same when they spoke and had the same mannerisms, but who lived entirely different lives, making entirely different decisions and holding very different values – one voted for left-wing parties while the other held right-wing beliefs, they had no common interests and they didn't share one another's taste in food, music or films; when it came down to it, there were no similarities between them beyond their physical appearance. Neither of them felt like half of one whole, they'd never felt as if they were missing a brother they'd had no idea existed throughout childhood, as I had so often read in stories of this nature, and they were completely unable to guess what the other might be thinking or to complete one another's sentences.

My editor didn't want the story, didn't think there was anything sensational or fascinating about it; she wanted to hear the opposite, in fact, telling me that it would have been far more interesting if they had made the same decisions, liked the same foods and did finish one another's sentences. I have a sneaking suspicion she was an only child.

◈

Agnar strolls in our direction at ten past three, and I have to restrain myself from roaring every thought that has run through my mind over the past ten minutes at him, because Olaf puts an arm around him and praises him, hasn't he done well, Liv? And he seems to have grown a foot taller from the experience, he looks proud and mature, his back as straight as a ruler. So instead I embrace him, kissing his forehead and cupping my hands around his face; he still has such soft, round cheeks. Only a few pimples around his nose testify to the fact that the transition from childhood to adulthood has begun.

'He has,' I say, smiling. 'You've done brilliantly. Did you have fun?'

I almost regret asking the question when Agnar regales me with a breakdown of the Colosseum in minute detail, but his talking continues until we reach the hotel, and I'm able to lean my head against the window of the taxi, Olaf squeezing my hand as we drive past the hotel we've stayed in on numerous occasions. I squeeze back and stroke the back of his hand with my thumb, suddenly excited about the days to come, leaving Rome, Olaf on a sunbed beside me with a book in his hands, watching Hedda and Agnar swimming in the pool – and the rest of the family buzzing around me, as I've pictured it while sitting in my office in Oslo, longing for the holiday to arrive. For once I've managed to convince myself that even if only half of what I'm imagining comes to fruition, I'll be content.

◈

We've divided ourselves up between three cars and drive out of Rome in convoy: Olaf, the children and me in the first car, Simen and Ellen in the second, and Mum, Dad and Håkon in the third. Despite the fact that Olaf drives unforgivably slowly in the impatient Italian traffic, Mum still fails to follow us at the roundabout; she takes the wrong exit and I watch as their car disappears in the throng of vehicles behind us.

I tell Olaf we'll have to stop or turn around, but the road takes us onto a three-lane motorway with cars on all sides and we're forced to carry on. I call Dad.

'Hello, Sverre speaking,' Dad says, as he always does when he answers the phone, even after getting a mobile that allows him to see who's calling him.

More than once I've pointed out the absurdity of answering in the same manner when he can see that it's me or someone else he knows – certainly when he's likely to have a fair idea of who's going to be on the other end of the phone – but he believes that it's standard etiquette to state one's name when you pick up the telephone, regardless of the circumstances.

'Hi, you've gone the wrong way,' I say.

'Isn't that you in front of us?' Dad asks.

'No, you took the wrong turn-off at the roundabout,' I tell him.

'I see, and where are you now?' Dad asks calmly.

'Where are we? I don't know, Dad, we're on our way out of Rome. You need to tell Mum to turn around and make her way back to the roundabout and then take the third exit. Then you'll need to follow the satnav.'

'It's not working,' Dad says. 'Liv says we need to turn around,' I hear him relay to Mum, and I can't hear her response.

'It does, Olaf set it up before we set off,' I tell him. 'Can you pass it to Håkon and ask him to sort it out for you?'

'He's asleep,' Dad says, and I hear such a loud hooting sound from outside their car that I'm forced to hold the phone away from my ear. Mum shouts something or other.

'For heaven's sake, wake him up,' I say. 'You need your satnav, we'll wait for you along the way once we find somewhere to pull over. Call me when you come off at the big roundabout.'

'The satnav doesn't work, as I said, but we'll manage,' Dad says, and it's clear that he's not going to wake Håkon, both out of a sense of pride – he's generally unwilling to ask for help, particularly where technology is concerned – and also out of consideration for Håkon; if he's tired, he should be allowed to sleep.

Both he and Mum lost a little of their hearts to Håkon, as Mum likes to say, as Håkon was born with a heart condition and they were led to believe he wouldn't survive for more than a few weeks. I remember it well, his tiny body inside the incubator, all of the leads making him look like some sort of extra-terrestrial.

When I was on the maternity ward after Agnar was born, I thought about Mum a lot, what it must have been like for her to lie there as I did then, only without her baby by her side, what it must have felt like to know that he was all alone elsewhere in the large, complex hospital building, a tiny hole in his tiny heart.

Ellen and I stayed with Grandma when Håkon was born, and Dad came the following day. He sat at the kitchen table and cried, almost totally unaware of Ellen and me, both standing there silently and watching him. I didn't know what to do with myself, he told Grandma, who held his hand as though he were a little child, you can't imagine what it was like, I spent all night running back and forth between the delivery room and intensive care, he said.

He and Mum took it in turns to stay at the hospital in the months that followed. Håkon had an operation, he changed colour and started squealing, and both Mum and Dad were so grateful for his wails that Ellen and I grew frustrated. Can't you make him be quiet, I said one night after they'd brought him home – Dad rocked a screaming Håkon in the living room, which was just under my bedroom, all with a blissful look on his face – and I remember him saying that at that moment, Håkon crying was to him the most beautiful sound in the world.

The fear that Håkon would die turned into certainty that he was a little bit different, a little more fragile, possibly a little more important than everyone else. Mum and Dad dealt with Håkon in a completely different way from how they did things with Ellen and me. They were told by the doctors that he might experience some developmental delays, that he might have learning difficulties or various other behavioural issues, but in spite of the fact that Håkon was a head taller and a shoulder's width broader than his classmates, even in primary school, or that he was able to read and write and count before he started school, or that he was almost exaggeratedly empathetic where others were concerned, Mum never stopped worrying about him, and almost refused to accept that he was entirely normal.

Instead it was Ellen who turned out to be dyslexic, a discovery that was made too late, something she still blames Mum and Dad for – because they spent all their time worrying about Håkon, she tells anyone who'll listen, and everyone just thought I was stupid. That's not true, nobody thought Ellen was stupid, it's something she's read about dyslexics somewhere and adopted for her own use to make a point, but it's true that it took a long time for her to be diagnosed, mostly because Ellen was so bright that she developed her own system for understanding words, managing to read just fine using her own method throughout primary school.

Håkon was also a sincerely longed-for third child. Mum and Dad had been trying for another baby ever since Ellen turned two, and even though both of them assured Ellen and me that they'd be delighted with the outcome regardless of the sex of the baby, I'm convinced they wanted a boy. There's nothing odd about that, it's just odd that they both insisted – even to one another, I'm sure – that they'd be just as happy if they were to have another girl.

When I fell pregnant with Hedda, I hoped she'd be a girl, and I was very open about that with everyone I spoke to. You can't say things like that, Liv, Mum told me. Why not? I replied. Someone would have to be exceedingly simple to fail to grasp the fact that I'll love my child regardless. But as things stand, I'd be happier with a girl, and I don't see the issue in saying so. I'm just glad you didn't end up having a boy who'd have had to go through life hearing about how you'd wished for a different child altogether, Mum said when it turned out I'd been expecting a girl all along. I replied that I hoped I'd never have such insecure, impetuous children, regardless of their sex.

Nobody knows why Mum and Dad had so much difficulty conceiving Håkon, why it took so many years and so many miscarriages, but Mum eventually sought help from a private clinic, where it was suggested that it might have something to do with a birth-related injury from when she'd had Ellen. A terrible delivery, as Mum always says, to Ellen's great irritation. Do you want me to be grateful or something? Ellen always asks her, followed by a squabble that is almost identical every time; they're so alike, and both equally stubborn, sometimes it's as if they're competing over something that nobody else could ever comprehend.

Håkon was a sorely wanted child, in any case, and remains so. He still acts like a child in the family context, assuming the role of the youngest, a hapless youth, sprawling out on the sofa while the rest of us cook meals, leaving the table without clearing his plate, sitting in company with his headphones on and his laptop out in the middle of the living room, and it wasn't so long ago that he would still take his washing home to Mum and Dad – and that only stopped after his most recent girlfriend made a point of mentioning it to him. When it's just Ellen, Håkon and me, he's totally different, a grown man who partici-pates in adult conversation and has his own adult issues to deal with.

But sitting in the back seat of Mum and Dad's car as they drive through Italy, as far as Dad is concerned he needs his sleep, in spite of everything going on around him, and I end the conversation without mentioning the satnav or offering to wait for them again.

◈

Olaf's brother's house is on a small hill in a medium-sized coastal town on the Riviera. We drive part of the way alongside the Mediter-ranean Sea, which sparkles turquoise in the sunshine, and part of the way further up in the dry, olive-brown mountains, passing through tiny villages where it seems that time has stood still, even though Olaf thinks I'm narrow-minded to say so.

'What do you know about it?' he asks. 'You don't know anything about her, or her life,' he continues, pointing at an old lady dressed in black sitting on a stool outside her home, seemingly doing nothing at all.

I don't respond. Instead I turn to Hedda and Agnar in the back of the car, each looking out of their own window.

'Just think, people live out here,' I say to them.

Mum always used to say that to us if we drove past places that seemed abandoned or uninhabitable in our eyes, whether we were at home in Norway or abroad. I remember one area of Portugal in particular; we'd rented a car and had driven up into the hills by the Algarve. I might have been fourteen at the time. We had driven along endless narrow, winding country roads; it was so hot that the heat flickered in the air just above the surface of the road ahead of us, and Ellen and I were stunned when Dad told us quite seriously that we could have fried an egg on the asphalt. We drove through a small village consisting of ten or twelve houses, a small square and a petrol station where Dad stopped to fill up. The station resembled a little shanty hut more than anything else, the signs and pumps reddish-brown with rust. Outside, a man sat in the patch of shade offered by a small parasol, getting up as we pulled in. He smiled, Ellen said afterwards that he'd only had one tooth, and he filled the car with petrol for Dad even though Dad would have preferred to have done it himself, and when we drove away afterwards, he stood there and watched us go. Ellen and I turned and looked at him through the back window as he grew smaller and smaller. Just think, people live out here, Mum said, as usual, and suddenly I understood what she meant. I felt a surge of overwhelming sympathy for the man who had to remain here, out in the wilderness somewhere in Portugal, outside a petrol station; this was actually his life. I spent the rest of the holiday thinking about him, burdened with a sense of guilt as I went about my daily activities. Back at the hotel a few days later, I asked Mum if she thought he had a family. She couldn't remember him at first, and I started to cry as I explained who I was talking about, the lonely man with no teeth from the petrol station, who no doubt sat there day in and day out, no family or friends or money, no life at all. Oh, *him*.

My love, Mum said, smiling at me, he'd probably find our life in Oslo unbearably tiresome and hectic. We needn't pity those who don't live life exactly the way we do.

Neither Agnar nor Hedda appear to have any particular reaction to the same phrase. Agnar is mostly busy explaining to us all about the algae that gives the Mediterranean Sea its azure-blue colour, and Hedda blinks, nodding off. I wonder if it's worth the effort required to try to keep her awake until bedtime, to avoid her disturbing and delaying the relaxing evening I've imagined awaits me, or if I should just let her sleep. She nods off before I make up my mind, and I don't say anything to Olaf, who is usually more concerned with the children's sleeping habits than I am.

❖

After four hours in the car, Olaf turns into a flagstone driveway some way up the mountainside, the sun now low in the sky, hovering just above the sea. I can't see the house for all the vegetation around our parking space, but I catch sight of a small set of steps hidden among the greenery and Hedda and Agnar disappear up them, running off the long car journey. Olaf flashes me an expectant, self-assured smile. I follow them, emerging on a south-facing terrace with a view of the small town in its entirety, and the distant horizon beyond that. Agnar and Hedda shriek with delight at the pool that juts out slightly over the edge, and I feel my own tingle of childish glee at the pale-blue chlorinated water, even though the Mediterranean lies just beneath us, tranquil and inviting.

The others join us up on the terrace. Olaf opens the glass double doors leading into the house, we make our way into a large kitchen with red terracotta tiles and open shelves and everybody goes off in their own direction, exploring the large house that Olaf has never suggested is anything more than a small holiday home he allowed his brother to inherit when their parents died several years ago – I hear Ellen's shriek of delight and Dad's murmurs of approval. Mum follows me into the largest bedroom, a southwest-facing room with a fresco painted on the ceiling; it smells of fabric softener and the sea. She stands at the window saying nothing, her hair lustrous in the light of the red sun, and for a moment I find myself worrying that she thinks it's too garish, too extravagant and vulgar, but then she smiles at me.

'What a place,' she says, and I think she means it in a good way, running her hand along the wide windowsill.

'Yes, I had no idea it was so spacious,' I say. 'It almost makes me a little bitter to think that Olaf passed it up.'

'It didn't look quite like this when his brother inherited it, though, I was under the impression he'd spent years doing it up,' Mum says.

I wonder when she and Olaf talked about it, he's never told me all that much about the place.

'Yes, well, still,' I say.

'I think you ought to be glad you don't own it; imagine the upkeep,' Mum says. She sees upkeep everywhere she looks, in every house or cabin Ellen and I have ever considered buying. No, she'd say, just think of the upkeep, her conscience no doubt weighing on her over all the upkeep she neglected to undertake in the cabin in Lillesand that she inherited.

'I'm just glad that Olaf wanted his brother to have it, to be honest, glad that it didn't turn into some kind of ugly inheritance fall-out,' I tell her, and I mean it.

'Yes, that's understandable,' Mum says, and her response harks back to a conversation that's been had several times now, between her and me but also with the family as a whole, about the incomprehensible nature of fall-outs over inheritance that go on for so long that people stop talking to one another, about the way in which material possessions can tear emotional bonds to shreds, trumping memories and genes and any sense of belonging.

Olaf, who had been in the middle of dividing his parents' assets when one of these conversations had unfolded, had argued that things weren't as simple as all that, that material possessions can become metaphors for suppressed emotions, or for fair or unfair treatment, and that these things often only come to light under such circumstances. I don't know if he felt that way about his own younger brother, I don't think he did. I think the reason he allowed his brother to have the house in Italy at market value was to do with the fact that he didn't really want it, but I believe it was also a consequence of his exaggerated and sometimes unnecessary concern for his brother, as well as the fact that Olaf didn't wish to owe him anything, as was his wont, not even in the long run. Anyway, we've got enough money, he said, and he's right, we do, but so does his brother, I think to myself as I stand here, and I feel embarrassed at the sudden stab of jealousy I feel, just as I always do – our family isn't preoccupied with material things, and certainly not with money.

I've always felt certain that when the day comes to split the inheritance we receive from our parents, Ellen, Håkon and I will agree to divide everything equally between us, and that anything that doesn't lend itself to being split in such a way will be shared out fairly, that we'll be generous with one another. Olaf has challenged me on this assumption: What if Håkon wants the cabin in Lillesand? He doesn't want the cabin in Lillesand, I've replied, and I know that's the case, he'd rather have Grandma and Grandad's cabin in Vindeggen. But what *if,* Olaf insists, and I tell him that we'll find a solution if that's the case, but I know that the only solution is that it's passed on to me, it's quite simply unthinkable that it should go to Håkon or Ellen, and I feel the same way now, as Mum and Dad grow older, it's unthinkable that Ellen or Håkon should receive any more than me, that they should emerge from things more favourably than I do.

'I'm so glad we've come away like this,' Mum says all of a sudden on her way out of the room, stopping before she reaches the door, standing in front of me, her expression grave.

I smile at her.

'That's good,' I say. 'I feel the same.'

She wraps her arms around me and hugs me. We're exactly the same height, but her body is softer than mine, plumper and warmer, which makes her hugs some of the softest and most soothing I can imagine.

'You're not dying, are you?' I mumble into her hair, as we often say when one of us gets overly sentimental, only ever half-joking.

Mum laughs and lets me go.

'No, I'm not dying.'

◈

Agnar and Hedda are allowed to go for a swim in the pool before bed. Dad joins them. I sit on the terrace and watch as they play, certain that Dad is having at least as much fun as the children, remembering the way he always played with us, too. He did things properly, took our games seriously. Whenever we visited Grandma and Grandad on their farm when we were little, we would build small colonies of dens on their land made with hay bales after threshing. All the kids in the village would be there, and there were always very clear agreements in place about how the game should unfold – which part was the designated kitchen, living room, sofa, who our chief was and who'd be our slave, and which of us were the robbers. Dad turned up one evening and everyone was convinced he'd come to fetch us in for the evening, but instead he asked if he could play with us. I felt embarrassment and pride all at once, but I soon forgot that Dad was Dad because he engaged so readily in our play – and did nothing at all to try to let the others win.

Håkon comes out and sits down beside me. I often think about how different our childhoods have been and wonder how it's affected us. Ellen and I share the same memories, the same references, the same rules. Håkon has something else entirely to relate to, he's grown up differently, almost all by himself, and in a different decade.

Mum, Ellen, Simen and Olaf are talking in the kitchen, I can't hear what they're saying but I catch Ellen laughing out loud. After a short while she emerges with a plate of olives, ham and cheese and some wine, placing everything on the table and sitting down with us. Simen comes over and wraps his arms around her from behind, kissing her neck a few times and making a grunting sound; I'm usually embarrassed by just how physical they are with one another in front of us all, but it doesn't bother me this time.

Olaf calls out to the children, pointing at his watch emphatically.

'We had a deal, Agnar,' he shouts.

'Don't listen to him,' Dad chips in, to Agnar and Hedda's great delight.

I turn around and look for Mum, but she's no longer in the kitchen. 'Where's Mum?' I ask.

'She went to lie down for a bit,' Olaf says.

'No, she went for a walk,' Håkon says.

'By herself?' I ask, an unnecessary question since everyone else is here, but I feel uneasy: it's so typical of her to feel the need to do something demonstrably different from whatever it is everyone else is doing together.

Nobody says a word, and nobody looks worried, so I make up my mind to think no more about it, try to follow Olaf's advice that I should spend less time worrying about others, their moods, keeping an eye on whoever might be feeling a certain way and when. It serves no purpose, he tells me, and of course he's right. It's a hard habit to break, because I'm so accustomed to keeping an eye on Mum, watching for even the slightest change in her expression; I can see the tiniest wrinkle appear at the corner of her mouth when she's feeling frustrated or resigned, the tiny lift in her brow when she's worried, I can see it in her eyes when she's happy. I've often thought that I'd be the only one who could communicate with her if she had a stroke and lost the ability to speak, the only one who would really understand her, so committed to memory is my interpretation, so automatic, that I barely have to see her to know her temperament at that moment.

She returns after half an hour, just as I'm putting Hedda to bed, and comes in to say goodnight to her granddaughter. She looks as if she's been crying, and it takes every effort not to probe, not to ponder, instead forcing my attention back to old farmer Pettson and his cat Findus, the one book that Hedda elected to bring with her on holiday.

◆

The crickets wake me the following morning with their intense song, and I remember Agnar explaining to me once that the distinctive sound I'm hearing isn't, in fact, a song, but a noise created when the males rub their wings together to attract the females for mating. I look over at Olaf, lying on his back with his hands crossed beneath his head as if caught mid-pose. I turn towards him and lay my palm flat on his chest, the tips of my fingers brushing the delicate hollow of his neck, which quivers momentarily with every heartbeat. I've always found a sense of security in the rhythm of breath and the thud of a heartbeat.

My touch doesn't wake him and I wonder if I should rouse him properly so we can have sex before Hedda wakes up, as I've imagined we might while sitting back at home in Oslo, daydreaming about long mornings with plenty of time at our disposal, a gentle breeze and sunlight that darts and flickers through rippling white curtains, just Olaf and me, but then I remember Mum and Dad, that today is Dad's seventieth birthday. I kiss Olaf softly on the neck instead, he wakes up and shifts his arm, which must be dead from the loss of blood flow, then wraps it around me and pulls me close.

'I wondered about waking you up so we could have a bit of fun, if you know what I mean,' I tell him. 'But then I remembered it's Dad's birthday.'

Olaf opens his eyes, looks down at me and laughs.

'So instead you decided to wake me up to tell me that?' he says.

I nod, smiling. It was years before I would have sex with Olaf when Mum and Dad were in the same house or cabin, or even in the same hotel, even when their room was miles away from our own. Their presence is equally strong regardless of how many metres of concrete or brick walls might separate us. I had to give myself a few years after we got together, waiting until we spent a whole summer with my parents at the cabin. But I still find it uncomfortable, I can't relax or keep from thinking about them – and worst of all is the thought that *they* probably think we're having sex. Olaf doesn't get it. We're adults, we're married, he says, we've got two children. I can't explain it, but it feels invasive and embarrassing that they might think of me or look at me in that way.

'Well, then, we'll have to find another way to celebrate your dad,' Olaf says.

◈

Dad has a lie-in for once; I know how difficult it is for him to stay in bed long enough for Hedda and Agnar to have the fun of waking him with their rendition of 'Happy Birthday', and I'm grateful to him.

He's usually up by six every day for a run, says it has a knock-on effect on his whole day if he doesn't fit it in. He's having issues with his left knee after so many years spent running on asphalt and was disproportionately upset by the doctor's advice, which was that he should have an operation; he talked about it for weeks, refused to stop running, and got to the point of hobbling past Voldsløkka Stadium before agreeing to take a break for a few weeks. Now he wears a support bandage under his running leggings, refuses to see the doctor again even when his knee puffs up like a football, and we've given up nagging him about it. If he wants to wear out his knee, he can go right ahead, Mum says, but she also seems conspicuously lacking in motivation to make him see that he either needs to give up running or have the operation – or, as is the most likely scenario, both.

Mum is in the kitchen whisking pancake batter, and it's obvious she's been awake for some time – she's been out and come back with berries and coffee and juice, which she's left sitting on the countertop. We always have pancakes for breakfast on birthdays, it's one of Mum's traditions, and something I've carried on with my own family. I can't remember ever asking Olaf how he celebrated birthdays in his family, I realise now as I watch Mum standing over the pancake batter, just as she has every birthday morning since the day I was born, and possibly even further back than that. She and Dad still have pancakes for breakfast on our birthdays, even though it's almost ten years since the last of us flew the nest.

She seems happy, energetic at least; yesterday's mood has lifted and I feel relieved.

'Happy unbirthday,' I say.

'Likewise,' she says, smiling. 'Would you mind doing the blueberries?'

'It's alright, I'll do it,' Ellen says, appearing from behind me. 'Liv's developed an acute phobia of sugar since having children.'

I do my best to laugh, but it comes out as more of a splutter. Ellen gives me a brief smile as she pours sugar into a bowl, mashing the blueberries with a fork and mixing it all together.

'Look at this, Hedda, do you want to try some?' she asks, without looking at me. Hedda is drawing at the kitchen table.

Hedda nods. Ellen pours a little of the jam into a bowl then gives Hedda a spoon without saying anything further to either of us. Hedda picks up the bowl, brings it to her lips and slurps up the reddish-blue jam. I hear the sugar crunching between her tiny teeth. I say nothing; it would only lead to a discussion of the way Olaf and I are bringing up the children, which Ellen and Mum often gently ridicule. Has Agnar remembered to go to the toilet today? Ellen asked me a few weeks ago when we were having Sunday dinner at Mum and Dad's, for instance. We were about to go home, and I called out to Agnar to remind him that he had football training the next day, trying to tear him away from the game he was playing with Dad. Mum burst out laughing at Ellen's comment. Oh Liv, I don't mean it unkindly, she said when she noticed that I wasn't laughing. But you have to admit that Ellen has a point. You have such tight control over them. It's not necessarily a bad thing, it's just so different from the way that you were brought up yourself – you were all so much more independent, and I couldn't have given you all the attention that you and Olaf give the children. I bit my tongue to keep myself from commenting that it probably had more to do with her own self-interest, nodding instead. I knew what was coming: children nowadays have a different status to the previous generation, their needs are too much in focus, they're tiny consumers with enormous demands. And their parents are at their beck and call, desperate to make them *happy* at the age of three, terrified of the consequences of the slightest misstep. I don't think I ever wondered if you lot were happy as children, Mum continued – but it doesn't seem to have done you all any harm.

◈

Ellen and I make our way into town with a shopping list written by Mum in order to buy some things for dinner. Ellen laughed when Mum pulled it out. Honestly, she said, we've been discussing this meal for a month now, I think Liv and I can manage the shopping. Mum was offended and asked if there was something wrong with her taking an interest in the details when her husband of forty years was on the verge of turning seventy and had treated his entire family to a holiday, no less. Ellen replied that she was equally concerned with the details of the party intended to celebrate her father of thirty-eight years, but I pulled her away before she had the chance to initiate a full-blown argument, slipping Mum's shopping list into my pocket on the way.

As I have to wait for Ellen, who's wandered off to buy herself a handbag she spotted in the window of a shop we drove past, I sit down in a small square and order myself an espresso. I indulge in the first of fifteen carefully planned holiday cigarettes. I take out Mum's list, her handwriting so distinctive, the letters almost like musical notes, long strokes and small loops, and the image of them resonates somewhere in my memory. I haven't seen her handwriting for a long time and it reminds me of her diary, which I furtively read back at the age of seventeen or eighteen. It must have been one of several she'd had, there was no beginning and no end, but it lay alone inside the drawer of her bedside table. It was several years old, and I don't know why it was there, perhaps she'd been looking back on it one evening, and now I wonder if she was looking for something. I'd been entirely consumed by it at the time, getting to know her in a new light – even to this day I don't regret having read it, because while seventeen-year-old me obviously knew that Mum and Dad had lived a life together before I'd come along, before Ellen and before Håkon, before what would become the virtually perpetual state of being that was *us*, there was something else there. I read about the time before all that, before and after she met Dad; it was like reading a novel, and what struck me most about it – and what has stayed with me until this day – was just how mature and refined she was at the age of nineteen. Reading her diary at the age of seventeen, she seemed so much older than me, and now, sitting in a square in Italy as a forty-year-old and recalling the mood and concrete formulations within her writing, I still think she seems older and wiser than I am even now. It is as if she had a greater sense of perspective, greater control.

◆

She and Dad met at an event back when they were both at university, I think it was some sort of political debate. Mum wrote a long and detailed diary entry about how they came to be a couple, each day a novella in its own right, with a beginning, a twist in the tale and a conclusion. She describes Dad in great detail, how he was so tall he had to stoop to fit through the doorway into the kitchen, the way he walked and stood, his voice, his laugh. I remember the way he seemed familiar to me in her descriptions, but I simultaneously felt alienated by her analyses and appraisals of him. She depicts them both as being much too philosophical and intentional considering their young age at the time, but I doubt that either of them has ever thought or spoken in the way she describes – it is as if they were two proper, grown-up adults who met and made the very deliberate decision to couple up. Mum must have made that decision, at any rate, though I could never understand why it was so important for her; she was pretty and intelligent and strong and capable, as Dad has always said. My diametrical opposite, he says. He's just showing off, Mum says, looking pleased, and always adds that there was no shortage of girls hanging around him at any time. That was the guitar, Dad says.

Mum writes nothing about the dissimilarities between them early on, instead concentrating on how well suited they are. They think the same way, their take on things and their ambitions and their values are the same, they're both politically unconvinced, as she's put it – something rooted, no doubt, in the same decision paralysis that I've inherited from them both – with the exception of the fact that they are both passionately opposed to US intervention in Vietnam. On the pages that follow, she plays out arguments, some concerning Dad, some more general, sticking in articles about the war and the Viet Cong, various sections underlined or circled. After this she writes mostly about the two of them, filling almost an entire diary before reaching the point that they agree to become a couple, even though in reality it takes no more than a few weeks.

She also lies quite openly in her diary entries, as if they were written for others: trivial little fabrications, such as when she describes herself as being 'often out on my skis, I love being outdoors, and I was so pleased when Sverre suggested we head out for a day's cross-country skiing together next Sunday'. Mum hates skiing, she always has, she's taken every opportunity to remind the world of that fact, as if making some sort of protest against something nobody quite understands. I can count on one hand the number of ski trips she's joined us on, but she's always been very proud of Dad's talent, often boasting about it in company, noting how many miles he got under his belt on a recent cross-country trip, or drawing attention to his latest piece of kit.

Towards the end, Mum mentions their dissimilarities, but only ever paints these in a positive light. The fact she needs someone who can lighten her mood, give her the lift she might need, someone with the ability to 'laugh when she cries and shout when she whispers'. I can't say I've ever heard my mother whisper, her voice is louder than most, but it's one of many metaphors to be found in her writing – she was trying to take a literary approach, I've since thought to myself, the very opposite of my own muddled, frenzied, loved-up, awkward diaries, which I only ever used as an outlet to vent about life, the only place I allowed myself to relinquish control. Her diary seems to have been written for someone else, perhaps for Dad, perhaps for me, but she is the less recognisable of the two of them, and I still wonder if that comes from a lack of insight, or if I don't know her as well as I might think.

She fills a whole book with her reflections on him and them, chronicling everything they do and discuss, and then, eventually, at the bottom of one page, after an evening on which Dad apparently held forth on The Who's 'My Generation' for quite some time – described in great detail in Mum's entry – she's written: I'm overwhelmed.

I remember feeling that there was something scary and unfamiliar yet simultaneously reassuring in her words.

◈

We return to the house with four carrier bags of food. Mum eyes the bags with a look of surprise that borders on disapproval, as if she suspects us of having bought much more than whatever she had written on her list. We have, of course, since Ellen and I know that Mum always underestimates how much we all eat. It's better than throwing food away, she always says, and it's not as if anybody ever goes hungry. No, but there always ought to be a little bit of something left over, Ellen has said. Just think of the children in Africa, Håkon has teased, and Mum has always taken his words at face value. Long live Generation Irony, he says.

Mum has devised the menu with some input from Dad, who has requested authentic Italian fare, and so we're making bruschetta, spaghetti vongole, saltimbocca and tiramisu. Ellen and I have discussed how to time the dishes in such a way that nobody needs to be standing in the kitchen while everyone else is eating, and we get started on chopping onions and cleaning the shellfish. Mum stops us in our tracks, telling us she doesn't need any more help.

'Help?' Ellen says.

'With the cooking,' Mum replies.

'But we're going to do it together,' Ellen says.

'There's no need,' Mum says. 'I'd rather do it by myself, actually. But you can lay the table.'

I don't know what to say, I don't know why Mum has decided all of a sudden that the meal we've been planning together will be prepared by her and her alone. I try to read her expression, but she's beyond my reach somehow, not angry, just efficient, and she still seems happy enough, or at least friendly, and there doesn't seem to be anything more significant concealed behind her words.

'But seriously, Mum, it's coming up for five o'clock; you don't have time to do all of this yourself.'

'Ellen and I can take care of the tiramisu, at the very least,' I say, mostly to lend some support to Ellen, who is biting her lip in frustration.

'Can't I be allowed to take care of this one meal for Sverre?' Mum replies, not calling him Dad as she usually does.

Ellen shrugs. She makes her way out of the kitchen and over to Håkon and Olaf, each laid out on their own sun lounger, reading.

'Have it your way,' she says as she leaves.

I look at Mum inquisitively, allowing the opportunity for her to explain things now that Ellen has left the room, but she looks away, instead placing the veal steaks on the wooden chopping board Ellen retrieved from a cupboard and covering them with cling film before beating them flat with intense concentration and a series of heavy pounds.

◈

It's warm enough that we decide to set the long oak table on the terrace for dinner. Agnar comes over, wondering if there's anything he can do to help, and I'm pleased that he's taking the initiative and make him responsible for folding napkins and dressing the table. I regret my decision when he returns with an abundance of bougainvillea cuttings taken from the tree around the back of the house, the one Olaf's brother always boasts about, strewing them grandly over the white linen tablecloth. I imagine the clouds of invisible pollen and miniscule larvae being dispersed across the table, the crockery and cutlery, but I say nothing, because Agnar looks at me as if he can read my mind

– or perhaps he's just grown used to me correcting and commenting on everything he ever does, I think to myself – and I smile instead.

'That's lovely with the purple against the white,' I say, nodding encouragingly, clasping my hands together behind my back to keep myself from adjusting the napkins he's folded according to instructions he saw in a YouTube video, which he can't possibly have executed properly, but which he's spent the last hour working on all the same.

I know I need to refrain from constantly remarking on everything he does, to stop watching him all the time, as Olaf says, and I'm trying, but much of the time I disagree that I should keep my thoughts to myself, given that he'd miss out on so many things that he really ought to learn. I don't know how you manage to strike that balance, I tell Olaf, I feel compelled to teach him what I know. But he needs to learn some things for himself, Olaf says, he has to find out in his own way. And in that respect Olaf is better than I am, he always has been better at standing on the sidelines and watching Agnar mend a puncture with gaffer tape in spite of any warnings to the contrary, or balance an impossible number of plates and glasses to avoid having to go back and forth between the table and the kitchen more than once, or spend all of his pocket money on some incomprehensible and useless piece of tat, the type that falls apart after two days, seemingly without exception. He experiences the consequences, that's the best lesson of all, Olaf says, and I agree to an extent, but I rarely pass this test of patience.

It stems from the fact that Mum has always done the same thing, I tell Olaf, she can't leave anything alone, but unlike her, I do at least have some sense of insight into my own behaviour. She criticises me for being controlling where my children are concerned, but she has no grasp of the fact that her own comments have been – and still are – at least as controlling, I tell him. It's true that Mum often remarks on things, but she does so very differently: she's much subtler than I am, of course, and somehow thinks that makes things very different. She doesn't realise that it's precisely the subtle nature of her comments that make things so much worse, that the opportunity for misinterpretation increases exponentially and can easily make me think – with good reason or otherwise – that a comment on a shirt I'm wearing is *actually* intended as a comment on my entire personality and every decision I've ever made.

I'll never be like this with my children, Agnar often shouts at Olaf and me when he loses his temper: I'll never be this unfair. I'll actually make the effort to *understand* my kids! It hurts to hear him say those things, mostly because I know that I felt the same way when I was his age, and beyond that age too, perhaps I still do, and I also know how impossible it's turned out to be. I've spoken to Olaf about it, that perhaps it's more difficult to change the little things you've promised yourself you won't emulate. In a way, it seems easier to avoid following in your parents' footsteps if you've suffered something much more traumatic, if you've been subjected to a greater betrayal. The little faults are the ones you fail to discover, I say, at least until long afterwards and only then within the wider framework of life. I don't know how to change that. I don't want to be like Mum was with me, I don't want to be quite so critical of Agnar and Hedda, I don't want them to feel that the world is tumbling down around them just because I'm unhappy, or that their emotional lives should be dictated by my own. Olaf thinks I'm exaggerating and that I ought to be grateful to my parents, that it's a typical example of a first-world problem, having a mother be *too* attentive. He's always been fond of my family, Mum and Dad, Ellen and Håkon; he's enjoyed a much closer bond with them than with his own family in recent years. He thinks, in contrast to me, that Mum is liberatingly direct, Dad is modest and doesn't take himself too seriously, and that there's something about our family that he's always felt was missing in his own – a sense of freedom and open-mindedness, as he put it on one of the first occasions he spent with us all. I was pleased, felt that I was able to see my family in a new light through Olaf's eyes, and I understood what he meant. I still do, and I sometimes feel overwhelmed with gratitude when I think of them, of us, but then I become exasperated or distracted by something I think or feel when I'm with one of them. But that's just how things are, Olaf says, those are the little things, and every family has its own peculiarities, as your mother says.

◈

I call for silence and stand up. Smile, clear my throat, feel my cheeks grow warm. It always feels uncomfortable adopting a formal tone when it's just family, a change of scene and role that feels unnatural, transparent. I become aware of the fact that my hands are shaking, remember an old piece of advice from Ellen about pulling both sides of the piece of paper to engage one's muscles and make the paper stiffer. I sweep my gaze over everyone seated around the table before allowing it to rest on Dad.

'Dear Dad,' I begin, and at once his eyes start to shine.

Håkon, Ellen and I agreed a few months ago that I would make a speech as the eldest of us siblings, and that they would chip in while I put it together. Neither of them chipped in with anything other than the odd answer to a question from me, assuming as usual that it would get done with me at the helm. This time around I didn't actually mind, I want to make a speech of my own for Dad, written in my words and without too much interference. I've worked on it a lot over the past few months, and it's forced me to think through my relationship with my father. I was initially so overwhelmed with thoughts, ideas and ways of wording things that I felt I ought to limit myself, to draw out the most important elements and weave a consistent thread. As I sat down to write, however, nothing seemed adequate, nothing was sufficient to express what I wanted to say to him, everything fell flat on paper, it sounded so banal, everything seemed overstated – I felt embarrassed when I attempted to read my words aloud. What's more, Mum's voice filtered through, even as I penned the first word, and where I'd imagined her gazing approvingly during the planning stage, I was now only able to envisage her raised eyebrows and the small wrinkles that gather around her mouth – as if in feigned surprise that something can be quite so bad, combined with an obvious effort not to laugh.

You spend too much time thinking about yourself, Ellen told me when I finally asked her for some advice. People who spend too much time thinking about themselves when they're giving a speech are the worst, always wondering how they're coming across and what people think about them, she continued. Your job is to focus on *Dad*, how you portray him, what you want others to think of *him*. That has to be your starting point. That was my starting point, I tell her, but maybe that got lost somewhere along the way. You got lost in *yourself* along the way, Ellen replied, laughing. She works as an advisor and speech-writer, and now, standing in front of her and the others, it seems obvious that it ought to have been her who made this speech.

I carry on, holding Dad's gaze.

'Happy birthday. When I told Hedda a few weeks ago that we were going to celebrate your birthday, she asked how old you were going to be. I told her you'd be turning seventy. Is that less than a hundred? she asked me. It is, I replied. She thought for a moment and then, with slight disappointment in her voice, said: So he's not really that old at all,' I say, and Dad chuckles with delight.

'Even though the reasoning behind her conclusion is a little different from my own, I agree with her. For me, you're ageless, you're Dad, just as you were twenty years ago, thirty years ago, and as you are now, a constant in my life,' I continue.

I pause for a moment. Everyone is looking at me apart from Mum, who's looking down at the table and nodding. Ellen smiles and gives me the thumbs up, and I exhale. We've been sitting at the table for an hour already, we've had our bruschetta and our pasta, the sun has just set, and for this brief quarter of an hour, dusk will surround us. Ellen, Håkon and Olaf's faces, all of them sitting with their backs to the sea and the sunset, shine golden in the light of the candles that Agnar has arranged in a sort of heart shape in the middle of the table, while Mum, Simen, Agnar and Dad's foreheads and cheeks are pink, whether as a result of sunburn or the reflection of the red sky opposite them. The smell of meat and garlic emanates from the open kitchen doors, while the scent of pine and lavender fills the air around us.

I tell Dad things I've never told him before – about him, about the way I see him, the way I think about him and us. I talk about how unusually present he was when Ellen and I were young, about the feeling that I was being taken seriously, regardless of what I had to tell him, both as a child and as an adult, and about the fact that in spite of his manner of listening – seemingly entirely without interest, distanced and often accompanied by fidgeting with his glasses, pocket knife or whatever else he has to hand – nobody else takes in quite as much as he does, both in terms of what's being said but also what is left unsaid, that nobody else responds with such insight. I talk about how he handled Håkon, whose curiosity stretched far beyond that of any ordinary four-year-old, who asked why this or that or the other was the way it was until everybody else, including Mum, were so bored they wanted to explode. Dad, on the other hand, took almost all of his questions seriously, leafing through encyclopaedia and dismantling the radio for demonstration purposes.

I sneak the briefest of glances at Ellen, who no doubt feels that I'm not focusing on Dad's personality, but rather on the fact that Håkon was showered with more time and attention and material possessions than she and I had enjoyed, but I disagree: the way Dad has listened, responded, treated us as being deserving of his attention, these things have been the same for all three of us.

I'm careful to include Mum too.

'It's hard, if not impossible, to talk about Dad without mentioning you, Mum,' I say, looking at her. 'Even though you are two very different individuals, you are a unit in our eyes, and each other's. The way you complement one another, the way you cooperate, the way you demonstrate the values of respect and love – all while giving each other necessary space – is something that I've always strived for in my own marriage,' I say, and Olaf laughs.

'Some might suggest I've tried to follow your example with a little *too* much gusto,' I add, improvising slightly and smiling at Olaf. 'But still, the two of you are a formidable act to follow. It is said that women choose men who remind them of their fathers, often with a certain degree of irony, but I can honestly say that I have sought – and found – a man like you, Dad, because for me you represent the very best there is, in every way imaginable.'

Dad smiles, moved by my words, Mum looks down at her plate. I raise my voice and read on, ending with a poem by Halldis Moren Vesaas, a choice that I'm sure Mum silently judges me for making.

'Cheers, Dad,' I conclude. 'And many happy returns.'

◈

After finishing our saltimbocca and hearing Dad declare it the finest meal he's eaten in all seventy years of his life, an expectant silence falls. Everyone is waiting for Mum to call for everyone's attention, and nobody else dares to do so before she's had the chance. I know that Olaf has been considering speaking, not giving a long speech or any-thing, he said before we left, but I feel it would be right for me to say something. It's an impulse he seldom stifles; he loves speeches, espe-cially giving them, and he doesn't take himself too seriously; overall, I think it's more about having the opportunity for someone – Olaf, in particular – to say things they might not usually say. An opportunity to pay the kind of compliments that are difficult to weave into normal conversation or convey through a pat on the shoulder. I know that Olaf takes advantage of every opportunity to say a few words to his employees, whether on their last day at work or on their birthday, not to mention at Christmas, when the speeches he practises at home grow longer and longer with each passing year. But he's so good at it that it's envy-inducing, and on my fortieth birthday he gave a speech more touching than the one Crown Prince Haakon famously gave on the day he married Mette-Marit, as one of my friends put it at the time. Ellen even asked if she could take elements from it to use in a pro-fessional context after the event. This did nothing to hamper Olaf's desire to hold forth for an audience.

Nobody gets up to clear the dinner plates from the table, we start to chat idly, and Olaf looks at me; he thinks that Mum ought to speak first, he can't say anything before she does, things have to take place in the correct order. I shrug. Dad is the only one who doesn't seem to have noticed the atmosphere, he's busy discussing Pokémon Go with Agnar;

they've been enthusiastically hunting down numerous Pokémon over the past few months, and both made some valuable additions to their flocks while taking in the sights in Rome. Suddenly I feel uncertain about the motivation behind Dad's trip to the Vatican and Agnar's visit to the Colosseum, but I have no chance to think any more about it as Mum finally clears her throat.

'Sverre already knows this, but I can tell you all, in case you're wondering, that I'm saving my speech for the party Sverre will be having in Oslo once we get home,' she says.

Dad picks at a red wine stain on his shirt and nods. We sit in silence for a few seconds. Olaf prepares to lift his fork to his glass, but Ellen beats him to it.

'But why?' she asks.

'What do you mean, why?' Mum replies.

'Why don't you want to say a few words now?'

'I just told you that I'll be doing it at the party when we get back,' Mum says.

'Can't you do it at both?' Ellen asks.

She holds Mum's gaze for a long moment, unnaturally long, and I notice her summoning her reserves of concentration and strength to prevent her gaze from faltering. I realise that I'm not the only one to have picked up on the atmosphere between Mum and Dad, that Ellen has noticed it too. It hadn't occurred to me that she might have caught the glances, the words exchanged, the inexplicable glimpses that suggest something has changed between them. I'm almost disappointed, if relieved, that I'm not alone in having observed it.

Simen, who isn't accustomed to the social conventions within our family, who still can't distinguish a joke from a comment made in all seriousness, who isn't attuned to the nuances in expression and tone, laughs at what he believes to be Ellen's joke – a joke that has fallen very flat, if anything – about Mum giving her speech on both occasions. He's used to the clamour of us teasing one another, used to seeing a direct, confrontational spirit abound without us ever resorting to arguments, used to the fact that we might burst out laughing at the merest shared reference in the midst of an animated discussion. Even though they've been together for more than a year, he's too new to this to realise that Ellen's tone has changed, it's filled with subtext. Defiant, angry, perhaps even scared.

'Don't joke about it, Ellen,' Mum tells her, but her expression gives away the fact that she's all too aware Ellen isn't joking.

'You were the one who insisted earlier on today that this was *your* celebration for Dad, surely it's a natural part of any celebration to say a few words to your husband of forty years,' Ellen says, imitating Mum for the last part of the sentence, Simen chuckling all the while, and I feel the urge to punch him.

'Enough now,' Mum says. 'I'll make my speech in Oslo.'

She gets up and starts stacking dirty plates. I feel a mixture of hope and fear that the conversation might end here, that Ellen might give in.

'What's really going on here?' Ellen asks.

Mum stops and sets the plates down on the table abruptly. They clatter menacingly, and Olaf snatches a concerned glance at his brother's crockery, but the plates appear to have held their own better than Mum under the circumstances.

'Is it really so strange that I'm not giving a speech for Sverre this evening? That I choose not to stand up in front of you all and repeat the same things you've heard on every birthday leading up to this one, rather than to give a proper speech in front of his friends and colleagues at a big party in just a week's time?'

'It's strange for you, of all people, to choose not to say anything to *Dad* on this particular birthday, given that you make a speech on every other birthday, yes,' Ellen says.

Mum doesn't always give full speeches, but she does always say a few words on our birthdays. In the case of Ellen, Håkon and me, she usually tells the story of our birth, our little quirks – I was born with a squashed left ear, for instance, which Dad spent many an hour rolling flat so that it would take the correct shape – or what we were like as babies – I cried a lot, Ellen was worryingly quiet, Håkon had his heart defect – and how we assumed our different roles within the family in such a way that it seemed they had been waiting for no one but us to come along. There are slight differences from year to year, and Mum always adds something from the year that has passed. If we aren't together on our birthdays for whatever reason, she sends the same story via text. With Dad, she talks each year about how they met, a highly edited version of the events I read about in her diaries, always far more romantic.

'You've been off with us ever since we got here,' Ellen says before Mum has a chance to reply. 'Can't you just answer the question, rather than making such obvious hints all the time? What's wrong?'

I hold my breath. I don't realise I'm doing it until I feel my heart hammering inside my chest.

Mum keeps opening her mouth as if to say something, but no words come out. Eventually she turns to Dad.

'Do you have anything you want to say about all this, Sverre?' she says.

They stare at one another for a few long seconds. I can't read their expressions. Dad is the first to look away, turning to Ellen, Håkon and me, ironing out the tablecloth on either side of his plate with the palms of his hands, hesitating slightly, then laying both hands flat on the table and letting his shoulders drop.

'We've decided to get a divorce,' Dad says.

Mum flinches almost as if he'd struck her; it's clear that wasn't what she had expected him to say.

Initially I respond more to Mum's reaction than to what Dad has said, she suddenly looks so small and scared. I look at Ellen and Håkon, feel the immediate need to protect them both, want them to leave the table, the conversation, want to tell them that I'll sort all of this out. And yet I remain where I am, silent. Mum sits back down.

'Well, it's probably just as well that you told them,' she says to Dad. 'But it's not as dramatic as it sounds,' she says, looking at me.

'How on earth can it be *less* dramatic? Are you *not* getting divorced?' Ellen asks before I have a chance to say anything, as if she has suddenly transformed into an obstinate teenager.

Mum throws a hand out in Dad's direction with a resigned look on her face, as if passing the matter on for him to deal with.

'Yes, we're divorcing. But it's difficult to explain. We're going to sort things out and work out something between us, tie things up. It certainly hasn't been an easy decision.'

Ellen looks at me, seeking out somebody to hold responsible.

'We've put a lot of thought into this. We both feel an emptiness, a sense that we've taken everything we possibly can from one another and from our marriage,' Dad continues. 'We just no longer see a future together.'

'Did you know about this?' Ellen asks me.

'No,' I tell her, looking over at Mum.

'We've talked it through again and again, tried to find some sort of solution, but it's quite simple, when it comes down to it: we've grown apart,' she says.

I try making eye contact with Håkon, but he's staring at the table. Agnar was allowed to leave the table after dinner and is sitting on a sun lounger just a few metres away wearing his headphones, he can't hear any of what's going on. Fortunately, Hedda went to bed hours ago.

'We're going to try to work things out between us, they haven't been right for years now. I've tried talking to you all about it,' Dad says.

'Not to me you haven't,' Håkon says.

Not to me either, as far as I can recall. Silence falls. Mum and Dad look like two shamefaced children, and it pains me to see them. I automatically reach out to take Dad's hand and squeeze it, but I let go as soon as I catch Mum's gaze upon us and see the way her hand smooths the tablecloth, nervous, alone. I can't control my thoughts, they leap from one scenario to the next: thoughts of how I might go about explaining this to Agnar and Hedda, images of Dad moving boxes of his things out of the family home, or perhaps Mum will be the one to move, the house in Tåsen without Mum's armchair in the corner of the room, the prospect of who we'll invite over for Christmas, I'm a child all over again.

Suddenly Ellen doubles up. Her laughter sounds genuine.

'Grown apart? Future? Seriously, you're seventy years old!'

ELLEN

The meat is bloody, the red liquid seeps out from between the fibres of the veal fillet as my fork pierces the steak's crust. I do my best not to compare it to the blood I awoke to this morning, large streaks of red staining the bedsheets and my underwear and my thighs. My body is trying to make a point, I told Simen as I pulled off the bedsheets while he still lay in the bed. Don't even bother trying, that's what it's saying, I'm here to show you that the more you hope, the more unequivocally I'll refuse you, tell you no, not a bloody chance of it, I muttered quickly under my breath. I didn't cry this time, not like last month.

◈

Last month, twenty-nine days ago, we awoke to cloud cover and cold rain in Oslo.

The beams of sunlight that shone through the window and illuminated my body as I showered this morning, the scent of the sea and the slightly spicy fragrance of our natural surroundings here in Italy made this setback slightly easier to deal with. It's Dad's birthday, after all, I said to Simen after the blood and my initial reaction to its appearance had washed away down the plughole. Either way, I have to pretend as if nothing's amiss, I just have to suppress it. Yes, he replied, we just have to make the best of the day ahead; he held me close, a long embrace, and I felt as if I could smell the disappointment where my head rested at the hollow of his neck.

I extricated myself from his embrace and left the room without looking at him, making my way to the kitchen where Hedda was the first to meet my gaze. I tried to avoid eye contact, did my best not to lose my composure because she's always reminded me of what I don't have; over the past year I've felt myself on the verge of being so furious with Hedda that I don't know what to do with myself; it comes out of nowhere, sudden and explosive, and I can do nothing but remove myself from the situation. It's totally unacceptable, I haven't even mentioned it to Simen, I realise how unfair and petty and embarrassing it is. Today I chose to make jam for her instead, mostly to have a dig at Liv, exaggerating the sweetness, which Liv and Olaf seem more afraid of than anything else in life. And for once it helped to be close to her, to stroke Hedda's smooth hair, her soft skin, to see her so thrilled with the jam that was so sweet it was virtually inedible, the jam I'd made just for her.

❖

It also helped to spend five thousand kroner on a handbag, leaving my conscience to busy itself with something else altogether. It helped to leave Simen back at the house with my family, and it helped knowing that he'd spend his morning playing in the pool with Agnar and Hedda – the easy way out, but even so. It helped to stroll around the square in the old town, to buy meat and vegetables with Liv, it helped to talk about anything else, about dinner, about the fact that Dad was turning seventy. I used to wonder what he'd look like when he was old, back when I was a girl, Liv said. How he'd look when he was seventy, you know, because that would make him *ancient*. Maybe I didn't even imagine he'd live that long, she continued. But it turns out he's just the same as he ever was.

I don't agree that Dad is the same, he's become an amplified version of himself – a caricature, in a way, as I attempted to explain to Simen before we left for Italy. Most people are like that, Simen said. They become parodies of themselves towards the end, whether they want to or not. I wonder why that is, I said, if it's because people are getting ready to kick the bucket and feel the need to leave a lasting impression of themselves before they disappear, maybe, to make sure those of us left behind remember them more distinctly. Simen laughed, I daren't imagine what you'll be like when you hit seventy, he said, you're already a caricature of yourself. But then, we all become more self-centred with age, so perhaps I won't even notice, he added.

Simen and I have been together for over a year now, and to this day I remain pathetically relieved whenever I hear him speak about a distant future that includes me, which depicts the two of us together. He's the only person who's created a fear that they might walk out on me; in previous relationships, there's always been a part of me that's hoped that the person I've been with would grow bored of things before I did; I've wished for less security in relationships rather than giving in to puppyish reliance and dependence. Now I'd love to feel more secure in my relationship with Simen, secure in the knowledge he'll stay with me in spite of my body's efforts to sabotage us, but Simen gives no guarantees.

I was surprised when he accepted the invitation to come to Italy with my family. I've never quite been able to tell whether he likes them or not, he always seems nervous and uncomfortable around them, he overcompensates and becomes boastful and envious when we're with them – particularly when Dad's around. I've tried joking about it, told him there's no need to compete with my father, if that's what he's trying to do, but it's one of the few things Simen won't laugh about, and it's clear he's not able to do so. Am I not allowed to touch you in front of your family? he's asked me in the past. Most of the time he has other plans when I ask him if he wants to come for dinner at Mum and Dad's, or to join in with any other activities that involve spending time with my family. I found it strange at first, past boyfriends have almost seemed keener than me to spend time with them, but after a while I realised that he probably felt the same way I did: I like Simen's family, but I prefer my own.

◈

But now he's here. Here with me and with them, in Italy, to celebrate Dad's seventieth birthday. I've noted the changes in my body throughout the trip, felt something attach itself within me and start to grow, I've felt the tenderness in my breasts, the nausea, I've lost my craving for coffee and I'm constantly needing to pee – all symptoms that occur in the early weeks of pregnancy according to everything I've read. I'd felt so certain this time around; perhaps in working to convince Simen – who's started to lose heart – I've managed to convince myself, too. Feel, go on, I've said to him, placing his hand on my breast, can you feel that it's bigger, swollen, almost? And then I've placed his hand on my lower abdomen, which has murmured encouragingly over the past couple of days.

Spending every month in wait is all-consuming. I remember almost nothing else of the past six months, nothing other than the waiting I've done. I know that I've done much more than that, that among other things I've written one of the most important speeches given by cabinet this year, a speech that is likely to have contributed towards the visible swing in the opinion polls in the week that followed, or that Simen and I celebrated our first Christmas together, or that we saw in the New Year in New York – where I was so touched when Simen pulled a tiny bottle of non-alcoholic champagne from his jacket pocket at midnight – that I've talked, visited, laughed with Mum, Dad, my brother and sister, my friends, that life has gone on as usual, but now that I think back on it, everything runs together into one, it all seems so unimportant, and all I can remember with any clarity is the waiting and the disappointment. A feeling swiftly followed by the fear that something might be wrong, the impossibility of it happening for me, the image of me sitting in a white room with Simen and a doctor in a white coat explaining to us that I'm the one with the problem – unfortunately your body is incompatible with the creation of life and is, therefore, redundant, faulty.

This image graces my retinas on a regular basis, more so in the past few months, in spite of Simen's efforts to be sympathetic – he tells me it's going to happen, that we can't get stressed out about it, that it's normal to try for much longer than we have. At the same time, I can see that he's been googling fertility issues, and last time I got my period, I saw that he'd searched *pregnancy* + *menopause* the following day. Simen is three years younger than I am. I'm thirty-eight, and it places an unspoken pressure on us, on me. We have to move quickly if we're going to start a family, before it's too late.

Even so, I know that I shouldn't get stressed about it; if there's anything you see repeated on every forum and website going, it's that pregnancy is far less likely to occur if the body is under stress. I've trawled mum forums I previously mocked, soaking up the details of every experience I can find that involves someone falling pregnant when they least expected it, it was only when I'd given up hope and started to relax that I finally fell pregnant, and so on and so forth. I feel embarrassed when I think about the plethora of advice I've picked up over the past year, how much of it I've stashed away, not to mention all of the strange positions I've slept in – all this even though I know that it's nonsense. Simen has laughed at me, and I've told him there's no harm in trying – but I've promised him that I'll see the doctor if it doesn't work out this time either.

◈

It's Dad's birthday and I've concealed the truth all day long, avoided acknowledging my thoughts, kept them at a distance, but after knocking back my first two alcoholic beverages of the holiday, two glasses of wine, my first in several months, all to Simen's apparent indifference, I can no longer keep my anger and sorrow in check. I haven't paid any attention to the conversation around the table, I don't know what we're talking about, though I've been half-listening to Liv's slightly long-winded, clichéd speech for Dad – she's finishing up now, looking at me with uncertainty, she's struggled so much with it that I haven't had the heart to do anything but smile approvingly, in spite of the fact that it goes against a definitive principle of mine: to give credit and praise only where they're due. I try to pull myself together, take a few large gulps of water, look at Simen, who's had more wine than I have and who's in excessively good humour, glance at Mum, who seems restless more than anything, wearing the same expectant expression she always assumes when the attention is focused on others. I direct my anger towards her, she's got no right to be so self-absorbed on today of all days, and when I hear that she has no intention of giving a speech for Dad, probably because she thinks Liv's spent too much time focusing on him instead of her, the fury burns in my chest.

'But why?' I ask, controlling my tone in the same way I've taught so many politicians to do.

Mum fixes her gaze on me, an experience I once found terrifying – condescending and corrective, bordering on contemptuous. I've always thought about the fact that I could never look at my own children that way, as if I truly despised them. I'm not afraid of it any more, it's just a play for power, an attempt to dominate, and I know that Mum doesn't despise me, that none of this is necessarily even about me at all.

'What do you mean, why?' she replies. 'As I said, I'll give a speech at home in Oslo.'

'You love saying a few words on occasions like this, can't you do both?' I ask, using the same controlled tone. 'Surely that's not too much to ask when it concerns your husband of forty years?' I add, imitating her voice, far too cheap a trick, but I don't care any more.

Simen laughs, as he always does when things get awkward. It's actually a surprisingly effective mechanism more often than not, it defuses the situation for most people, but not now, not for Mum and not for me. Nor does it have any effect on Liv, who's gone pale, no doubt furious that I've ruined Dad's birthday, and for a moment I consider giving up, letting things go. But then I see Dad's face, he looks so troubled that I let my anger take root there; it's for his sake that I allow my anger to flourish.

'That's enough, Ellen,' Mum hisses. 'What's wrong with you?'

'What's wrong with me?' I repeat loudly. 'What's wrong with *you*?'

Mum stares at me, looking as if she's about to say something before eventually depositing the plates she's collected on the table, where they land with a clatter.

Olaf and Simen jump. Liv looks as if she's about to burst into tears. Håkon is his usual silent self, staring at the table.

'If it's a speech you want, you could always do one yourself, isn't that what you do for a living?' Mum replies insistently.

Then it's almost as if she realises there are several of us around the table and she looks at the others, her expression softening, and adds:

'I just don't want to use up all my ideas in a speech that I want Sverre's friends and colleagues to hear in Oslo, and which you've all no doubt heard before.'

The way Mum has suddenly started referring to Dad by his name is just as significant as if I had started calling her Torill instead of Mum. I roll my eyes to show her how transparent and feeble I find her rhetoric.

'It's funny that you don't think Dad can bear to hear you say nice things twice, unless there's actually something else going on here,' I say.

Mum says nothing, staring hard at me with an expression that suggests I'm challenging destiny by disputing her preoccupation with herself, and in a way, it makes me even angrier to know that she's being granted the attention she craved all along.

'You've been acting strangely ever since we got here,' I say, unable to stop myself. 'What's going on?'

I don't actually know how Mum's been acting, I've barely paid any attention to her at all until now. The same can be said for the others, I've been so absorbed by my own hopes and expectations. But I imagine that I'm right, and that's good enough for me.

'I think I'd best let Sverre answer that one,' Mum says, suddenly calm, turning to look at Dad. 'Do you want to tell them what's wrong, Sverre?'

'We've decided to get a divorce,' Dad says, almost interrupting her in full flow, as if he's been impatiently waiting for an opportunity to speak the words aloud.

Everyone falls silent. Simen looks at me, sitting across the table from me for once, and as my eyes meet his, I reflect on the fact that it ought to have been me making a big announcement over dinner. I'm pregnant. We're having a baby. Yes, thank you. No, we didn't want to say anything until we knew for certain, no, it's not been easy. But happy birthday, Dad, you're going to be a grandfather again.

'It's not as dramatic as it sounds,' Mum says; she's sitting down again, and I feel the fury still surging towards her, towards Dad, towards the deep injustice of the situation, who do they think they are?

'It's not dramatic that you're getting divorced?' I say.

'We've tried everything, Ellen, you should know that, but we haven't managed to come up with a solution.'

You've got no idea about trying, I want to scream at her, even though I know that's not the case. I look at Dad, waiting to see something in his expression at any moment that might suggest he's joking, or that it's not all that serious, that they'll still be living together, at least. But he doesn't say that. Quite the opposite, in fact:

'There's nothing left for us in this marriage. No future.'

'Did you know about this?' I ask Liv. She looks just as she did as a child when she was afraid she'd done something wrong, her eyes wide, worried, her mouth half-open; there are a thousand versions of the same expression in her repertoire, so much inside her constantly seeking forgiveness without ever having done anything to require it.

Liv shakes her head in despair, undoubtedly wondering which of us she should save first.

'No,' she says. Nothing more.

'We didn't realise it ourselves until recently,' Mum says. 'We've quite simply grown apart.'

'Things haven't been working between us for many years now,' Dad says, and I wonder what exactly needs to work in a marriage when you're seventy years old, other than being able to look back and see that you've created something, something that Mum and Dad can both do with a certain degree of satisfaction in most areas of their lives. 'We've been over this several times.'

He looks at me. I wonder if he's referring to the conversation we had when we were out skiing earlier in the winter, when he told me that Mum wanted him to retire completely, but that Dad wanted to carry on working two days a week for as long as his colleagues would have him. Dad was an early adopter when it came to the possibilities offered by the internet, as he himself likes to put it, I think we were among the first people in the country to have internet in our home, all thanks to Dad's interest in technological developments. He's a trained mathematician and worked for a bank for many years, but as the nineties came to a close, he and a younger colleague designed an analytical tool that was bought by one of the largest international conglomerates for further development. Dad and his colleague were paid enough to start up their own company, which has since developed several analytical tools for search engine optimisation. Nowadays I get the feeling that Dad's knowledge is a little outdated, even though he'd never admit it, at least not to anybody but himself, but he represents the company's history. Robots can't replace personal experience, he always says – something that Håkon disagrees with, but so far there hasn't been a robot that has been able to fill Dad's shoes, and he continues to work as a consultant two days a week, which together with exercise lends his days a sense of purpose. Mum ought to be generous enough to under-stand that, he thought. I agreed with him. So, what does she want? I asked him. That's the thing, Dad said, I don't know what she wants. She can't be wanting us getting under each other's feet at home or going on meaningless holidays willy-nilly. But what does she have to say about it? I asked him. I haven't asked her, he said. You have to ask, I said, see how she pictures things, find out why it's so important to her that you stop working. She'll say it's for the sake of the grandchildren, he said, that we should be spending more time with them, that we don't have enough time these days to be with them as much as we'd like. I didn't say anything else, in spite of the explicit and unreasonable notion that Mum should be allowed to define what 'we' think on behalf of the two of them.

'Not with me you haven't,' Håkon says, interrupting my train of thought.

I stare at everyone around the table in turn, Dad, Mum, Liv, Olaf, Simen, Håkon. Simen is the only one to make eye contact with me, he looks hesitant then fleetingly pulls a face, his mouth and eyebrows summing up the entire situation, and I feel the urge to laugh. I chuckle loudly, furiously. I look at Mum and Dad.

'Grown apart? No future? Seriously, you're seventy years old,' I say.

Nobody says a word. I look at the plates Mum set down on the table

in front of her, realise that we haven't had any dessert yet, and I turn to
her, my gaze defiant, then look at Dad, wondering how they're planning on resolving this and salvaging the remainder of the celebrations.
I'm not going to help them, I cross my arms over my chest and stomach,
lean back. Liv clears her throat, obviously keen to say something, but
she's never been very gifted when it comes to conflict resolution and I
shake my head at her: don't help them out of this one.

Eventually Agnar saves them from the situation, wandering over to
the table having finished the computer game he's been playing with his
headphones on for the past hour, entirely unaware of the mood that
has descended – so like Olaf – and asking if we're going to be having
any cake soon.

'Yes! It's definitely time for cake,' Mum replies with exaggerated
resolve, getting up and taking the plates into the kitchen.

Agnar returns to his seat beside Dad, who rests an arm around the
back of his chair, and he and Mum both cling to Agnar for the rest of
the meal as if he were a lifebuoy.

◈

I wake to stomach cramps; the pain shoots down the right side of my
body. I didn't experience period pain until I was well over thirty, and at
first I was convinced I'd been struck down with appendicitis. I called
the out-of-hours clinic in the middle of the night and they put me on
with a charming doctor who, after asking me a number of questions,
was able to ascertain that I was experiencing menstrual cramps. I was
so embarrassed that I wanted to hang up then and there, but he clearly
had time on his hands, asking me if it was this painful every month.
I told him that I'd never called an out-of-hours clinic about it before
now and tried laughing it off, but he told me that it can be serious, that
lots of people experience so much pain that it makes them ill. When
he asked if I had children and I told him no, he informed me that
women in their thirties without children often experience stronger
cramps than they used to. I thanked him for his help and thought

no more about it, but over the past year the pain has been yet another reminder that I've put things off, taken them for granted, a reminder of what an idiotic, carefree life I've been living, and for that the pain feels like a warranted punishment.

I get up, make my way into the bathroom, take two paracetamol and step into the shower – I use the shower head to spray the warm water directly at my stomach in small circular motions. I rest my back against the tiled wall and cry, mourning the entire situation rather than any one particular trigger. Dinner tonight was like something from a clichéd Scandinavian noir, Simen said, laughing, after we'd gone to bed last night. I nodded. Aside from the lack of revelations, I said. Other than the fact that Mum and Dad have revealed themselves to be two old people who have convinced themselves that life has more to offer and who have decided to sacrifice their entire family in order to find themselves, I continued. Perhaps the revelations will come in time, Simen said, we don't know what's been going on between them. Nothing's been going on, I said, and I felt certain of that, nothing other than the fact that in one breath they talk of retirement, and in the next they do all they can to gloss over their age.

Mum retired from her role as editor at a publishing house when she turned sixty-seven, and she regretted the decision just four days after leaving, she says, as if her advancing years were within her control. She still does a little consultancy work for them now and then, as well as for some of the authors who refuse to let her go, as she often puts it with thinly veiled pride – though it's obviously true, given that they're on the phone to her with self-absorbed frequency. But as I stand there in the shower, I wonder if that might be the reason behind all this, if Mum simply has too much time on her hands, if she's bored and looking for something to fill that time, and if Dad isn't enough – if, perhaps, the verification and recognition and attention she received at work is missing from her life, and Dad and the rest of us aren't enough to replace that. It strikes me that maybe she misses the sense of achievement, that she's looking for something more meaningful than simply living out her days as a retiree who happens to be married to

Dad. Perhaps I might have had a better understanding of it two years ago, but now it's beyond my comprehension, it almost seems unjust, that she, with her children and grandchildren, should feel her life to be empty. The situation concerns Dad too, but it doesn't occur to me that he might have been the one to initiate the split; he still has so much going on that fills his life. Too much, Mum clearly thinks, and I wonder why she's been so preoccupied with the notion of him retiring.

They both went to bed – in the same room – after dinner. I wonder what they talked about when they were alone, if they said anything to one another at all. When Agnar could no longer be bothered to remain at the table, and Liv discovered – to her greatly exaggerated and projected horror – that it was two hours past his normal bedtime, he was whisked off to bed and the party quickly broke up. Liv started tidying up, as usual, always her first instinct when things get difficult, tidying and clinging to her routine, as she had with Agnar's bedtime. It's so important to her, she feels compelled to act in the way she does, and Håkon and I often joke about it, but not today. Simen and Olaf helped her tidy things away, and Håkon and I remained at the table. I felt even angrier that Mum and Dad had simply left the table and gone to bed, leaving the rest to us, angry that we had to respond to their decision without them present. Are you alright? I asked Håkon finally, didn't know what else to say. He chuckled under his breath and shrugged. Then Olaf and Simen returned and the three of them sat and talked about Italian football teams while I went to the kitchen to look for Liv. She was standing there, crying over a bowl of salad, and I couldn't help but laugh. Oh Liv, I said, putting my arm around her.

Liv has always been more dependent on Mum and Dad than I have, dependent on their recognition or acceptance of everything she's done, even as an adult. I remember the way she practically asked for permission to marry Olaf, the way she anxiously called me every day in the lead-up to biting the bullet and telling them that she and Olaf were planning a church wedding, as if it were the worst thing she could have done to them. Liv, I said, it's not Mum and Dad you're promising to have and hold, it's Olaf – maybe not so much for better as for worse, as far as he's concerned, I joked. It's alright for you, she said, you don't know what it's like. What what's like? I asked her. They've got such high expectations, such strong opinions about everything I do. That's not true, you're just as guilty of establishing these expectations, you expect their expectations, it's a vicious circle, I replied. I was twenty-six at the time, and I had no idea how much I would come to think about family, how important the concept would become to me twelve years on.

Imagine we never have children, I think to myself now, standing in the shower. That would make this the only family I have.

◈

In June, Simen and I buy our first flat together.

When we returned from Italy, minus one imagined pregnancy and two married parents, the property pages were the first thing I checked. I was convinced that Simen would be leaving me at any moment, that everything was more delicate than it had been before. I had sat next to Dad on the flight home, trying to encourage him to expand upon what had happened between him and Mum. Nothing in particular, he said. People think that these things emerge from one point in time, a particular event, something concrete, but this has been much slower and more gradual than all that, he said. I don't even know when it began. But you've been good together, I insisted. Of course we have, he said. But you can't get away from the fact that duty has trumped desire for a lot of that time, it's how I thought things were supposed to be. I turned to look at Liv, who was sitting a few seats behind us. She would have said that's true, that *is* how things are supposed to be, that's just life. I wish I could have said the same thing to Dad, persuaded him of that fact, but I was silent. I don't know, he continued, people enter into all sorts of contracts as part of various different relationships in life, but not every contract ought to last a lifetime when the conditions change. Which conditions? I asked him. Torill and I have both changed, we're not the same people we were when we first met, it shouldn't be assumed that we're still compatible.

They've never been compatible, I told Simen later. And I've thought about it before now, the way they perceive and approach the world in such entirely different ways. She's confrontational, intense and sensual while he is distant, logical, and emotional in ways she isn't. Neither do they have any shared interests beyond us, I said. They have, as Dad put it, quite literally entered into a contract, and both have held up their end of the bargain. Do you think they were ever in love? I asked Simen, knowing that he couldn't possibly answer that question, but the question itself was partly rhetorical to make him see the difference between them and us. I believe in relationships and families where the foundation is two people who love one another, rather than choosing to pair up with someone out of practical considerations or fear or anything else along those lines, I continued, attempting to reassure him.

Simen is *consumed* with the concept of family, with frameworks and clear-cut relationships. Everything should be as normal as it can be, unambiguous and orderly. He hates any kind of vaguery, as he puts it, and I'm not entirely certain what he means by that, but I'm fairly sure that a couple in their seventies in the throes of divorce rather comfortably falls within that category.

❖

Until now, we've lived in a flat he bought several years ago with his ex-girlfriend. Even though I've changed the furnishings and painted the walls, hung up my pictures and filled the drawers with my coffee cups and clothing, it still feels like her space, her screws in the walls, her wardrobe with the sliding doors, her kitchen cupboards. Jealousy is new to me, and I almost felt pleased to discover that this was where my petty envy and need for self-assertion came from. I mentioned it to Simen, not without a certain pride: You do realise how jealous it makes me feel to be living in a flat you two bought together, you have so many memories here, I don't know what you've done where. Even though Simen told me he understood where I was coming from, we remained there for a year after that conversation. We can't have children here,

I said to him six months ago. No, Simen agreed. I was the one who started looking at houses, though somewhat half-heartedly, because in spite of everything, moving house is one thing I detest.

The new flat is in St. Hanshaugen, on the fourth floor of a building with its own lift and a view over the park where mothers go jogging with babies in buggies. The flat itself has two bedrooms and a balcony. It went for almost a million kroner above the asking price, and even though Simen and I are both good earners, we took out a huge mortgage on the place, so high that it felt like an act of rebellion against Dad, who has always tried to teach Liv, Håkon and me about taking a responsible approach to financial affairs.

The process of purchasing the flat has occupied my mind; the expectations, hopes, disappointments; I've poured my feelings into ads, viewings, bids, losses, increased mortgages, more viewings, more bids, and then the eventual intoxicating victory, and now here we are. Simen and me. In our new flat, sitting at our new kitchen table – we had to buy furniture to suit the place – sharing a bottle of wine. There hasn't been the same pressure from Simen to avoid alcohol since returning from Italy, and even though that in itself worries me, it's too gloriously numbing to drink until I feel like stopping. It's all a load of nonsense anyway, I told Simen at the start, avoiding alcohol all month when I know I'm not pregnant. I can give up wine towards the end of my cycle, I suggested, still carefree. He asked if we shouldn't just leave it; after all, there wasn't any point in taking any chances, why would I risk it, surely it's better to be sure I'm doing all the right things? For the Baby, I mean, he said to me, and it was hard to argue against doing the best thing for the Baby. As if there were already a child to speak of. It's how we've talked about things ever since we started trying: always the Baby, with a capital B. Simen stopped drinking too, out of consideration for me, avoiding his favourite cheeses and cured meat at Christmas, all of which only served to increase the pressure on me. Eat, drink, please, I told him eventually, after our fourth failed attempt, have a big hunk of brie, I can't face the idea of you being unable to enjoy yourself. We're in this together, Simen said, still filled with a sense of misguided solidarity.

It's something of an anticlimax, I can't enjoy the new flat, the table, the wine or Simen, not as I'd imagined I would. Too much simmers beneath the surface, too much that needs to be aired, talked about, but something in me has changed – I don't have the energy for the fight. I can't face having to formulate the words. I don't even think it will help things; I no longer believe with such conviction that problems are better off being put into words, discussed and thereby rendered harmless. Liv has always thought me too confrontational, not everything needs to be talked about, she thinks, and maybe she's right, because now it seems that talking to Simen about the Baby – or lack thereof – and Mum and Dad's situation is more of a risk than it is reassuring.

'Shall we sit out on the balcony?' Simen asks.

It's raining, just as it has been ever since we got back, the air wet, the ground wet, Oslo sprawled before us, colourless and Eastern-Bloc-like.

'Do you think summer will ever come?' I ask Simen as we sit against the outer wall, protected from the rain by the balcony of the flat above us.

Simen sighs, no doubt seeing the metaphor within my question. He doesn't like metaphors, and avoids them as far as possible in everything he writes and says. He makes a good living teaching people working in industry and commerce to write well, and he's steadfast in his approach; simple is always best when it comes to technical terminology. Metaphors obscure things, he thinks. They can enrich things, I say. Sure, if you're writing fiction, he says, but not when you're striving to convey a clear message. There's been an inflation in the use of metaphors, Simen says, and I've pointed out that that's a metaphor in itself, that it's impossible to avoid them, even for him.

'I'm serious, though, I saw something recently about what the climate might be like in a few years' time, and in Norway we'll have neither summer *nor* winter,' I add.

'We'll still have summers and winters, even if there isn't as much snow or sunshine as there once was,' Simen said. 'The seasons are about more than just the weather.'

He leans his head back against the wall. Looks out across the park. I try to think of something else to say, something we can talk about, but there's nothing. I've never been good at small talk, and the worst thing I can imagine is the idea of having to make polite chitchat to disguise a profound silence, particularly with a partner. Take breaks, exploit the silence, I've often instructed the politicians I work with, it's nothing to be afraid of, it can often be a much more powerful tool than words. The silence between Simen and me is one I have no control over; it's new, and it's gaining ground.

◈

Mum texts me early in July, wondering if I'm going to the cabin this summer. She only asks about me, not about Simen, feeling a sudden need to underline the fact that everyone is an independent individual. Simen and I are going at the end of the month, I reply. I don't return the question, but she tells me anyway. I'm off to the mountains, she says. Her sister has a cabin in Telemark, and though it's not really all that many metres above sea level, Mum's entire side of the family is surprisingly imprecise in this regard, describing virtually anything that isn't situated along the coast as being in the mountains. I don't reply, feeling that everything she and Dad are doing at the moment is intended to prove a point. They're demonstrating that there's been a change. None of our traditions or routines are to be carried forward. I don't think that's what they're doing, Håkon said when I called him the other day. How else are they supposed to do things? The whole point is that things are *supposed* to be different from here on out, he said. I don't know, I told him, I just feel like they're rubbing it in all the time, they're being inconsiderate. Inconsiderate of you? Håkon asked. Of us, I said. Even though nobody else knows that Simen and I are trying for a baby, and even though I know it's unfair and childish of me for precisely that reason, I'm gripped by the sense that everyone should be more considerate of *my* needs. There are moments when I feel it's hugely unreasonable of Mum and Dad to separate now, of all times; do they really have to do this in the middle of everything I'm

struggling with, to impose this extra burden upon me? An insistent
sense of injustice often follows; they're rejecting their own family right
before my eyes, and just when I'm so desperate to have one of my own.
I always feel ashamed immediately after this occurs to me, ashamed of
my self-centred thoughts, but the anger remains within me, despite all
my attempts to force myself to think rationally.

Have you spoken to Liv? Mum asks me in a text message ten minutes
later, after receiving no reply from me. I roll my eyes at the phone, realising that this is what Mum had been wanting to know all along. *No,*
I reply, and ask her to call Liv herself. Mum is terrified of invading her
space, as she puts it, since Liv can be so emotional. She's tiptoed around
Liv for as long as I can remember, and she hasn't been anywhere near
as controlling with Liv as she can be with me, apparently under an
unspoken impression that I've needed clearer boundaries.

I haven't spoken to Liv or Håkon much since Italy; aside from
my brief chat with Håkon just a few days ago, I've hardly spoken to
anybody and the silence has gripped almost every inch of my body. For
the first time I feel as if nothing I have to say could change anything.
In a framed cartoon of me that hangs above the desk in the office is the
saying *Words matter!* It was a thirtieth birthday gift from an illustrator
friend, and he's drawn me with one long arm gesticulating wildly, a
finger pointing upwards, my mouth open and a stern expression on my
face. This is how my friends see me, I thought to myself with surprise.

As someone who judges people every day, given my age I've demonstrated an embarrassing inability to judge myself. I didn't realise that
I only ever revealed a few sides of myself to those around me, instead
wandering around believing others thought me to be as vulnerable
as I felt. It's because you look the way you do, nobody believes you
could possibly feel any weakness, my ex once told me. I didn't mean
it like that, he said when he realised I was angry, I just mean that you
don't have to compensate – you don't feel the need to smile and laugh
and hold back in situations where others do, he said. He didn't know
that I'd compensated for my appearance since I was a teenager, that
I'd worked hard to be taken seriously, spent thousands of kroner on

clothing that didn't accentuate my figure, that I'd dyed my hair darker, made myself reliable and serious and reflective, and worked twice as hard as most others around me to ensure that nobody could ever accuse me of getting something for nothing. We have to be careful not to be considered vulgar, Mum told me when I was fourteen years old and already well endowed in the chest department. She meant well, I see that now, but she has no idea how much time and energy I wasted on fearing vulgarity, on worrying about not being taken seriously by others, or being seen to be playing on my appearance.

I should really ring Liv, I think after Mum sends me yet another message. It's almost impossible to have a normal exchange of messages with both Mum and Dad; they have no understanding of the medium of text messaging and it stresses them out when things don't take the same form as a conversation would. *Goodbye*, Mum writes, seeking a conclusion. I know that she's waiting for me to say the same, but she's acting as if she were someone half her age and she needs to learn.

I don't call Liv, knowing that she will expect me to put into words what she's feeling so that she can then comfort me. That's how things go between us, and it works for the most part. Or it did, at least, until Simen and I started trying for a baby; since then I've found it difficult to talk to Liv about anything. At first, I said nothing about trying, not to her and not to anybody else, for that matter, because I imagined the moment I'd ultimately reveal to everyone that I was pregnant, two or three months along, taking Liv by surprise after having her nag at me for so many years about becoming an auntie. I want to be an auntie too, she's said; I've never really understood that desire when she already has children of her own. My own joy at being an aunt is first and foremost the access it gives me to children who are partly mine, and all without having any responsibility for them, not least because it allows me to be so much cooler and more relaxed than Liv, in Agnar's eyes, giving him permission to do things she'd never allow him to do, leaving her to deal with the consequences further down the line.

Liv has been one of the most vocal about me having children before it's too late; ever since I hit thirty, she's warned me about waiting too long. Now that it's turned out to be more difficult than I'd imagined, it feels impossible to talk to her about it. She has a political agenda, it's not just about me – she thinks the fact that so many people are waiting too long to start families is a development that is to the detriment of society. She's written a number of articles about it, interviewing desperate women in their forties who have prioritised *living a little*, as Liv puts it. It's what everyone says, Liv told me after writing one of her articles, they all wanted to live a little before they had children, but when I ask them what that means, none of them can really give a proper answer, it's all vague dreams of travelling and working and partying more than they have done already, but in reality it all comes down to a fear of responsibility, a fear of becoming an adult. It's a long time since she issued me with one of her warnings, but a few months after I met Simen, she asked me if I could imagine having children with him. At the time I was frustrated that it seemed to be the only measure by which she and my friends could assess things – do you want to have children with him, can you see him as a father? et cetera – and I dismissed her. It's too early to be thinking about that, I said, but just a few months later Simen started talking about it too, the fact that he wanted children, that he'd always imagined having a big family. My family thinks I'm late to the game, he explained, adding that his younger brother already has two. And for the first time I thought seriously about it, and it was no longer just an abstract notion about a thing that would happen sometime in the future.

I can't talk to Liv because she does nothing but talk about her own children, reminding me of everything I don't have. In spite of the fact she's a journalist, and regardless of how up-to-date she is on most topics, Agnar and Hedda remain her key reference points. Something they've said or done, or, more often than not, her concern for them, however incomprehensible it might seem to me. You don't know what it's like, Liv says whenever I bring it up, repeating the arguments used by every parent of young children when they come up against anyone without children: Just you wait until you have your own, then you'll feel differently about things.

I send Liv a text, wish them a good trip to the cabin down south, tell her that we're looking forward to coming towards the end of July, then end the message with *let's speak soon*, leaving the next move up to her.

◈

A few weeks later Simen announces that he doesn't want to go to the cabin after all. He's agreed to take on some consultancy work as part of a large public project on language which is due to launch in August, and his only free week is at the end of July.

'That was your decision,' I say to him when he uses that as his argument.

We're lying in our new bed in the evening, a week and a half before the planned trip to the cabin. We've been having sex practically without touching one another at all, entirely without passion and without romance. Neither of us can face the prospect of pretending that it's anything other than a purely technical act at this point, we say nothing, making no acknowledgements or assurances, sharing no laughter. We are silent and focused. Tomorrow it will be one week since we embarked on an entire year of attempts, and I remember that night in our old flat, the old bed, the fierce lust and delight that was released by the same desire that now kills those sensations.

'We've already spent more than a week on holiday with your family this year,' Simen says. 'And we all know how *that* turned out.'

I haven't even got the energy to feel insulted.

'It's cheap,' I say.

I can tell from the way he's breathing that he's angry. It's strange how two people who work in the field of communication can be so terrible at discussing something with one another, I think to myself. As if on cue, Simen braces himself.

'Seriously though, Ellen,' he says more gently. 'It's not that I've got anything against going to their cabin. I just think we need a holiday of our own, just the two of us, after everything that's happened, don't you?' he says in his most pedagogical tone.

'Everything that's happened' is provocatively imprecise, and I want to reply that having some time to ourselves had been my argument back in June when I'd first discovered that he'd agreed to work all through the summer without discussing it with me at all. His reply had been that we spent every evening and weekend together, which wasn't true for the most part because we were usually both working. But there was something so unsympathetic about the way he had said it that I hadn't dared to push it any further. It's strange for him not to understand that it's a setback having to adapt to his needs, even on the one week he has free; it's offensive that he has the audacity to suggest doing anything other than what we agreed on several weeks ago.

'We have a whole annex to ourselves, it's not like we have to spend every waking moment with Liv and Olaf,' I mutter half-heartedly, knowing that I've lost the argument and that I can't force him to come anyway, not after saying no to a weekend away with his brothers, sisters-in-law and their many thousands of babies at his family's cabin just a few weeks ago.

It's not that I don't want to go on holiday with Simen. I don't exactly feel set alight with desire at the prospect, not the way things are between us now, still silent and tense, but I get that it's probably a good idea, that it might help us both to relax and find our way back to something resembling life as it was little more than a year ago. It's more about my need for some time down at the cabin, my impulse to cling on to a tradition that hasn't really held much importance for me over the past decade. As children, Liv, Håkon and I spent at least two weeks of every summer at the cabin, right up until we were each old enough to decide where we wanted to go on holiday. Nowadays Liv has effectively taken over the cabin, and she and her family follow the same pattern – at least two weeks there every summer. It's been a gradual occupation, and it's taken place in correlation with Olaf's chopping down of more and more of the surrounding forest with each year that passes, extending the terrace, painting the annex, switching the upstairs windows on the main cabin, and so on and so forth. Mum and Dad have spent the past few years visiting Liv and Olaf there more than the other way around, something that Dad feels in two minds about, despite the fact that he was more keen than anyone that Liv should take more responsibility for the place – and he's childishly, silently competitive with Olaf when it comes to lawn mowers, chainsaws and tinkering with boat engines for much of the time that they spend there together. But still they go, each and every year, jointly upholding tradition. This year is the first that neither of them plan to visit, and I wonder how much contact Liv has had with them, if she's told them they can't, or if they actually find some relief in the idea of *not* going. Both, perhaps.

I've spent the entire summer longing to head south, eagerly antici-pating the unchanging nature of life at the cabin, the routines, patterns and sense of security bound up in my memories there.

'I just feel the need for a little bit of actual summer, a bit of sunshine,' Simen says now, ignoring what I just said about us not having to remain glued to Liv and Olaf throughout our stay. 'You can choose where,' he adds.

I picture Liv and I miss her all of a sudden, wonder why she hasn't called me, what she'll have to say about us not coming down. Maybe it's all the same to her, maybe she's had her fill of family get-togethers.

'OK. I'll message them in the morning to let them know we're not coming,' I say.

'What about Greece? Or Croatia, maybe?' Simen says, suddenly brimming with the excitement of a small child.

◈

I get my period on the flight home.

Maybe you should talk to your mum, Simen suggested on our last evening in Croatia. I'd told him that Mum had experienced difficul-ties for a number of years before having Håkon, maybe it's hereditary, I said. I placed a hand on my lower abdomen, where something had definitely started happening; I'd felt something connect, just as I had every month for the past year, unambiguous even when I no longer believed it. I don't ask Mum for advice, especially not now, I replied.

Anyway, Mum can't do anything to help with this, she never got any real answers as to why it was so hard for them to have children after they had me, I told him.

That's not quite true, but it's too messy to explain that Mum actually blames me. Simen would be shocked at some of the things we say and think in our family, and then he'd pity me, feel that it must be awful to live with that kind of blame, that it must fester away inside me and come between us. It doesn't, even though one night I dreamt that this was my punishment for ruining things for Mum simply by being born. I won't accept any criticism, I told Håkon, you're lucky to be so much younger. Well, it's thanks to you that I am who I am, he sometimes says when I praise him for something or other. Mum isn't joking when she says it's because of me, but always adds that it's not intended as a reproach, that it's just a fact: It *was* probably something to do with your difficult birth, she says. Well, thanks for making it through, I hope it was all worthwhile, I reply.

Although Simen and I have spent a whole week together on holiday, we haven't talked as much as I'd both hoped and feared that we might. The days have disappeared in a warm, holiday daze, and even though we've both no doubt thought about the fact we ought to clear the air, we've put it off, talking about different things entirely. We've stumbled our way back to everything we used to talk about before the Baby – no longer referred to as the Baby, no longer discussed in definite form, but now an infected boil of silence – and after a few tetchy evenings at the start of the holiday, we also found our way back to the flow of previous conversations, the energy of our discussions. It was on the final evening that we dared broach topics that concerned us, when the waiter asked if we wanted to try a particularly good local wine. Simen hesitated as they only served it by the bottle, but I egged him on, it's our last evening here, let your hair down, and before he could protest, I replied to the waiter: A bottle and a glass for him, please, and just a sparkling water for me, thank you. Simen's gratitude was over the top, are you sure you don't want a sip, he asked me when the wine arrived, and I shook my head and smiled, no, it's probably best I don't. Simen smiled back at me. It was like being in a bad film, and we both knew the other was playing a role, but Simen wanted to give something back, asking how I was feeling, if I'd had any new symptoms. I shook my head, nothing new, I said. I read recently that these kinds of problems can be hereditary, that if your mother or even your grandmother has had issues then the same problems can affect you, he said. At first, I was surprised to hear that Simen still read up on the subject, certain he'd given up all that because we had stopped talking about it. I told him about Mum. I'll see the doctor if things don't work out this time, I eventually conceded.

I've put off making an appointment all summer long as part of a suppressive protest, waiting for Simen to challenge me, something he hasn't done, but our conversation at the restaurant was enough to push me onwards, the fact that there was still some engagement there, some hope, perhaps.

After a trip to the loo somewhere over Austria, I sit back in my seat beside Simen, who's fast asleep, connect to the plane's Wi-Fi and book myself an appointment with my GP, gripping my phone so tightly that my fingers hurt by the time I'm done, scared in a way that's fresh and new, more scared than I've ever been.

◈

I have to wait just over three weeks for an appointment with the GP, and neither of us can be bothered trying in the meantime, not even when the ovulation test tells us the time is right. I'm only taking it so that I can be precise when the doctor asks me any questions, knowing that it's the kind of thing he'll quiz me about. I've done the rounds on various forums several times – it's getting an answer that's the aim now.

My doctor is much more understanding than I imagined he would be. I was certain he'd tell me a year isn't very long to have been trying, that many people try for much longer than that, that there's nothing to worry about for the time being. But he doesn't say anything like that. Yes, that doesn't sound quite right, he says after I regale him with a detailed account of events. I've had it committed to memory for so long now; I don't want to come across as hysterical, more mildly concerned, I want to appear to be the kind of person who's mostly coming to receive some helpful advice. I tell him about Simen, myself, Mum's issues with Håkon, about my cycles, any previous contraceptives, that I've got no known illnesses, I'm taking no medication, I've had no miscarriages, no abortions, but also that there's been no baby. I've done some googling, I tell him eventually, attempting a smile. My doctor doesn't return my smile, just nods. That doesn't sound quite right, he says, and it takes every ounce of concentration not to break down in tears then and there. He asks me a few follow-up questions about my lifestyle and my body. I find it's more difficult to answer his questions about my mental wellbeing than it is about my physical health, when previously the opposite has always been true.

I have a greater awareness of my body now than I've ever had before. I can feel every nerve and spasm, I've spent more than a year seeking out and focusing on every possible physical sensation. I've never thought much about all the many processes at work within me, things that crumple and rumble and tickle and ache and run and sting and itch and tremble; there's always something happening, nerves signalling things I've never previously picked up on. Now I find myself aware of the slightest change and the tiniest of signs. I've become conscious of my own body in a completely different way, a consciousness that extends far beyond aesthetics or vanity. I remember our teacher at primary school talking about the body as a machine: It's the most complicated machine in the world, he said, with hundreds of thousands of tiny parts that need to work on their own and together in order that the whole thing – that's *you* and *you* and *you*, he said, pointing at various members of the class – will work too.

'And what about your partner, do you know if he's been tested or has had any illnesses that might affect the quality of his sperm?' the doctor asks after writing up some notes on his computer.

'I don't think so, he's only thirty-five,' I reply.

I haven't asked Simen, so convinced have I been that this is about me. Besides, I'm sure he'd have said something if there was anything worth mentioning, he's the most honest person I know, and he'd never allow me to go around thinking that it was me who had a problem if it was more likely to be him.

'It's not always about age where men are concerned,' the doctor says. 'You know, men can reproduce throughout their lives, theoretically speaking.'

'Do you think age is a factor for me, that I might have left things too long?' I ask, my voice shaking. I've never experienced that before, but now my voice sounds like the one I put on to make a point to the politicians I voice coach, weak and erratic.

I've never felt old before now. Never been afraid of getting old, either – it's not like I've blocked out the fact I'm approaching forty, but I simply haven't thought of it as old, not in the same way I did when I was fifteen. Forty's the new twenty, nothing to dread, a colleague who turned forty last year told me, and I joked that at this rate she'd feel as if she were hitting middle age when she was seventy. That was before Mum and Dad demonstrated the reality of a comment made in jest, and I understood it was something that is constantly shifting, that nobody feels their age these days, at least not with traditional perceptions of what a forty or seventy-year-old ought to be.

Strange that evolution hasn't addressed this problem, I want to call and tell Liv on the way back from the doctor's – my body is just as prone to ageing as my great-great-great-grandmother's was when *she* was nearly forty, we're all on the same downward spiral at the end of the day. I imagine Liv's childlike, rippling laughter, the soft, comforting voice of a big sister telling me that things will be fine, that I needn't be afraid, that what the doctor said about age is just something he *has* to say to be on the safe side, that he can't know any more before we've had any tests done. Really, I want her to tell me that he doesn't sound like much of a doctor at all.

I remember how much I wanted to be like Liv when we were younger. To wear her clothes, to walk like she did, to flick my hair like her, to listen to the same music and like the same artists as her. I admired her handwriting, the way she blew on her nails after painting them, I wanted to have friends who looked like her friends, to fall in love the way she could fall in love. I wanted to experience the things she wrote about in her diary, the things I never felt for myself, things I've never really felt at all. Even so, I bagged my first boyfriend after reading Liv's diary, learning how I ought to feel and talk and think – and even though I grew so tired of him that I virtually flinched every time he touched me, I held out, because this was what Liv wrote and dreamt about. I never considered what Liv might have felt about it at the time, not until Mum and I discussed it many years later. Oh God, do you remember how jealous Liv was, Mum laughed, it was hard having two teenage daughters so close in age, remember that when you have children of your own.

◈

The air between the buildings is calm and still for a few lovely days in early October. Finally, a hint of summer, I say to Simen one morning as we sat on the balcony eating breakfast while the sun warmed our faces. I buy a new summer dress, tight-fitting over my stomach, click-clack home in a pair of Prada shoes with such narrow, high heels that there's not a pregnant woman around who could bear to even look at them, I sit on the balcony with friends until long into the night enjoying dry white wine and cheese and cured meats. The gynaecologist told me to carry on with life as normal, I tell Simen, defending myself before he attacks, which he doesn't, for what it's worth – he could have countered my statement by stating that nothing I'm doing *is* normal for me, that I'm going over the top, over-compensating, but instead he says nothing.

I've had blood taken for testing, and Simen is being tested for low sperm count, something he suggested himself after I returned from my first appointment with the doctor even before I had the chance to explain that we both ought to be tested. But I can't imagine there's anything wrong with me, he said, before reluctantly explaining that his high school girlfriend had fallen pregnant with his baby back in the day. She had an abortion, there was no talk of keeping the baby, we were only sixteen and halfway through breaking up anyway, he said. Why haven't you mentioned it before now? I asked. I don't know, it's not important, and I was scared of hurting you when we can't ... when we're still trying, he replied, an unbearably pitying look on his face. It's just a fact, you haven't done anything wrong, I said, and I felt the walls close in around us.

I spent the next few weeks feeling embarrassed about the fact that I'd hoped to lay the blame at his door, against all expectations for a man of his age. His test results were fine; so good, in fact, that he only just managed to refrain from showing off, the boastful comments on the tip of his tongue as he relayed them to me – as if it were a result that made him a worthy winner of some sort. If there's one thing I can't stand, it's people boasting about being graced with good genes, I told a friend that evening, it's like bragging about finding money on the ground, it's nothing but luck, when it comes down to it. The only people who fail to understand that are the less intelligent among us, I said, pouring us both more wine. Ellen, you and Simen aren't in competition, she said.

Even so, I feel all the more delighted when my own test also fails to highlight any issues and we remain on an equal footing, even though I know that can't be the case – there's a much greater chance that the problem lies with me, that this is my fault. I'm the one who needs to undergo further tests, be submitted to various alternatives, there are several things I can try, and all while Simen sits there with his sky-high sperm count, twiddling his thumbs, as I put it to my friend. I know that he doesn't think that way, of course, I'm projecting, but I feel like a machine with a fault so severe that it's unable to fulfil its intended function. And despite the fact that Simen, a machine functioning beyond all expectation, is still showing no sign of it, I sense that it won't be long before he loses interest and decides to scrap the contraption that is failing to deliver or to live up to his standards.

◆

I was sitting in the chair in the medical laboratory with a butterfly needle in my arm when I received a text message from Mum, who's in Sicily, wondering if anyone was at the house. Is it OK if I check my phone? I asked the nurse when it pinged in my handbag on the floor beside me. No, you need to sit still for now, he said in a resigned manner. I'd warned him in advance that my veins were difficult to locate, my parents have always been relieved to know I'd make such a bad junkie, I joked. He smiled indulgently at the patient who knew so much better than he did, a smile that had faded by the time he was midway through his fifth attempt to insert the needle, missing the vein hidden far below the surface of skin, and which had disappeared completely by the time he was forced to resort to using a child's needle inserted into my forearm instead. I wasn't able to check my phone until half an hour later, on my way out of the building, late for a meeting, nervous about the results of the test, and I registered only the fact that Mum had been wondering if someone was at the house, and that Liv had replied that it was her.

I remember the message now, several days later, on my way to see a colleague who's been admitted to Ullevål Hospital; she's hit the wall, they said at the office. I'm not quite sure what that means and I'm nervous about how she'll be; I'm bad at dealing with ill people. But she's not ill, they said, just burnt out. Several of them seemed to blame me, assuming perhaps that since I'm the person she reports to, a sort of manager – something I've never ever referred to myself as, and that I've made clear to others is a prehistoric term, as far as I'm concerned – I ought to have seen this coming. I haven't seen anything other than the fact she's been given more work to do as she's become better at her job. No, it's that typical good-girl syndrome, Kristin said with a knowing look, Kristin, who calls herself *my* manager. I couldn't help but feel annoyed, even though I knew I'd been far too short-tempered for the last six months, at least. Do you realise what an inflammatory expression that is? I asked her. The idea that when a woman works hard, she's suddenly suffering from a syndrome as soon as she feels tired? I feel sorry for Camilla if she's having a hard time, but wearing yourself out isn't part of being a 'good girl'. If she'd been good, she'd have adjusted her workload in line with her abilities, like the rest of us do. Nobody has worked her too hard, I say, but as I do I realise that I can't be sure about that, I can't recall who's done what over the past year, can't remember the projects we've been working on or the conversations we've had. Maybe I have left too much to the others to deal with, I think to myself now. I'd never thought I'd ever feel so indifferent about work, ambivalent towards the thing that had held a position of such utmost importance for so many years.

I recall Mum's message, and Mum herself, as I think about recent events. The way she and Dad have always talked about work, the fact that they've always plugged away at things and found happiness in their jobs. Conversations in the family have almost always centred on work, or another theme emerging from that topic. The value of hard work has been indisputable, even if it's been unspoken, and I haven't considered it in such concrete terms before now, when it's suddenly no longer the most important thing in my life.

I make up my mind to pop home to Tåsen on my way back.

◈

From a distance I can see the light in the kitchen window; Mum must be back from her holiday.

We haven't seen each another since we had lunch together at the end of August. I'd just been to see the doctor for the first time at that point, and I can't recall what we'd talked about or how I'd acted, I just remember sitting there with a burning desire to tell her everything, but knowing that I would only regret it if I did. It's strange the way she still clutches on to her role as a mother, even after all these years spent declaring that she's done with the tasks of motherhood now that her children are fully grown. A woman's work is never done, but never more so than a mother's, she occasionally remarks.

When I was in my mid-twenties, I wondered when I'd ever become independent from my parents, as they had clearly done long before they turned thirty. It was then that I realised I probably wouldn't grow up and drift away from them in the way I had previously believed would be the case, becoming intellectually superior to them, but that in reality it would happen bit by bit, like now: it's only in exceptional situations that I feel the same need to talk, to seek advice, as I once did. Things are the other way around nowadays, in fact; it's Mum who confides in me while I hold everything back from her. My life is my own, not simply a function within theirs. I wonder if Håkon and Liv experience things the same way, but I doubt it – they're still attached to Mum and Dad in a very different way. That might also have something to do with the fact that Mum and Dad have always been less attentive to me than to the others, relying on the fact that I can take care of myself – within my strict boundaries, that is.

I sit for a while in the car on the driveway. Remember the way Dad used to play with Liv and me when we were younger and he was getting us out of the car. He would crouch down, out of sight just beneath the windows, tricking us and jumping out somewhere completely different from where he'd ducked down – and I remember how boring it was when Liv got so big that she didn't want to play along any more, when she got grumpy and wouldn't even pretend to be scared when Dad jumped up at her window.

Mum comes into the hallway to find out who's letting themselves in, her expression so filled with hope that I feel guilty both about the fact that it's me and that I haven't come before now. We hug; she smells of Mum the way she always has, always does, and, I wonder if she only smells that way to me, and how I'll smell to my children – what will they think of when they smell that smell?

'I was just about to eat,' she says. 'There's enough for you too, if you'd like some?'

I nod. I'm filled with sadness as I enter the kitchen to find that she's set a single place for herself in her usual spot at the kitchen table, with candles and a glass of wine. And despite the fact that the chairs where

Håkon, Liv and I usually sit are empty, only Dad's place appears so. Mum doesn't seem to be thinking much about it, and it strikes me that she's been living like this for several months now. And it was her own choice, so I needn't pity her; she could have been sitting here with Dad all along if she'd wanted to.

As we eat, we chitchat about a manuscript she read while in Sicily, an old colleague has sent her the latest work by a new, young author, but Mum isn't sure about it. She thinks she's read with generosity, and there's a lot about it that's good, she says, but there's also an awful lot of navel-gazing among so many of these young authors, they're so self-absorbed, their interest is so often only in self-fulfilment and taking the limelight.

After dinner we sit in the living room together. It looks so empty and bare, but I can't quite put my finger on exactly what Dad has taken, what's missing from the picture.

'It's like a memory test,' I mumble to myself.

'What was that?' Mum asks.

'Nothing. It's strange being here without Dad,' I say.

'Yes. It is odd. I think so too,' she says.'

'Do you?'

'Yes, obviously it's unusual to find oneself living alone all of a sudden like this.'

'All of a sudden?' I repeat. 'I thought you'd been imagining this for a long time.'

'We have, we did, there's no need for sarcasm,' Mum replies.

Then she shrugs, as if shrugging off the entire conversation.

'But it's been an education, too,' she says. 'Take this, for instance, I've installed new skirting along the base of the veranda door, it doesn't get stuck any more – look,' she says, placing a hand on the floor. 'Flush.'

'That's nice,' I say, smiling, going along with the change in subject. 'It's a good thing you're so practical.'

Mum has been complaining about the door that would drag along the floorboards for years now, and I wonder why it took Dad moving out for her to do something about it, since she's always been good at woodwork. I don't ask, because the hammer left lying on the windowsill is a reminder that one day she won't be able to do such things, that she and Dad will both become much more reliant on assistance. It hasn't ever presented itself as a problem, but now it's become a more pressing matter with the two of them alone and ageing. And what if something serious were to happen to one of them? Any security in there being two of them around to help, or at least keep an eye on one another, is gone.

'Yes, it's nice to be able to be independent,' Mum says.

I make up my mind to drive over to see Dad as soon as I leave, feeling a pang of guilt for having come to see Mum first.

'Have you spoken to Liv?' Mum asks after we've sat in silence for a while, and I wonder if she'll ever ask me anything else.

Seventy-four per cent of all mothers have a favourite child, Simen told me one evening long ago when we still had long conversations about the type of parents we would be. And seventy per cent of all fathers, he continued. According to a survey? I asked in an exaggerated manner, referring to our habit of poking fun at newspapers that would print 'according to a survey' based on figures from the communications office that had been thrown together in the same garbled fashion as the stone soup in the folk story, as Simen always put it. Yes, according to a survey, Simen admitted. But this one I believe, he said. More independent children are naturally lavished with less attention, they take care of things by themselves and don't seek out the same caring instincts in their parents. Attention isn't the same as love, I reply. No, but it can be difficult to distinguish between the two, Simen says, for parents and children alike.

'No, I haven't spoken to her for a while,' I tell Mum. 'Have you?' I add.

'No, she never gets in touch,' Mum says.

'Do you ever get in touch with her?'

'I try, but you know how Liv can be, so closed off and distant.'

I've always felt that Mum does a good job of describing herself when she describes Liv, particularly when it comes to what she perceives to be Liv's weaknesses. At first, I saw it as a form of projection, seemingly almost intentional, a kind of admission of something through Liv, but in the past few years I've come to understand that it reveals nothing more than a lack of self-insight.

'Now that I've got all the time in the world to look after Agnar and Hedda, I hardly ever see them,' she continues. 'It's quite the paradox.'

'Come on, Mum, be honest. It's hardly a paradox that you and Dad are getting divorced and Liv wants to protect the children from that,' I say.

It's as if she and Dad have imagined they can continue to be grand-parents in the same way as they once were, that the function they perform for Agnar and Hedda and any potential future grandchil-dren will be the same. They don't seem to understand that sharing one another's company and home – and not least actually *being* at home – is crucial if they want to create the same feeling in their grandchildren that their own parents did in their children.

'It doesn't affect them! Sverre and I can cooperate when it comes to that, Liv knows that too, but there has to be something to cooperate *on*,' Mum says, and before I have a chance to say anything, her phone starts to ring.

Both Mum and Dad remain affected by the old-fashioned notion that it is both special and expensive to own a mobile phone, so much so that they feel duty-bound to answer, regardless of where and when it rings. It's as if they haven't quite understood the self-explanatory concept spelled out in the fact it's a *mobile* phone, that they have the option to ring back at a more convenient opportunity, even when the person concerned isn't *at home*.

Instead of ignoring the phone, which is ringing at maximum volume, Mum grabs it, though she's clearly reluctant to do so. She answers in her most professional tone of voice, and if it hadn't been for the fact that the speaker is so loud I can hear every word, I might have believed it was someone from the publishing house. I can hear a man's voice quite clearly; he says her name in a familiar, almost inquisitive tone, as if to ask what's going on, clearly not used to Mum answering the phone in such a detached manner.

'Ell— my daughter is here with me just now, can I call you back?' Mum asks, and I think this is the first time I've ever heard her postpone a conversation while solely in the company of family.

She hangs up without waiting for a response. All of a sudden, I feel glad that Håkon and Liv aren't here. She turns to me, smiles, and offers no explanation as to who has been on the phone, as she usually would: That was just Liv. That was just Anne. That was just my manager. That was just Granny. I remember the way Dad used to call Granny 'Just Granny', gently mocking Mum's habit of referring to her that way after she phoned.

Instead, Mum resumes our previous conversation as if we'd never been interrupted:

'I wish Liv would realise she's making things so much more difficult than they need to be. She's the architect of the change she so clearly fears,' Mum says.

LIV

I've been looking forward to autumn since our holiday at the cabin, but it never seems to come around. It's October, and the sun is getting its own back on the constant cloud cover that enveloped the country all summer long. That's an exaggeration, of course, I know it's been nice in the north, but that doesn't count. Summer didn't arrive on the east coast until the middle of September, and it feels all wrong to kick back and relax on the sofa when I get home from work, the sun and its warmth force me out into the garden. I spend the afternoons digging aimlessly in the flowerbeds, mostly to give myself something to do as I wait for the rain and cold to set in. It seems as if everyone is walking around feeling pleasantly surprised that summer has finally come, I tell Olaf. Even Ingrid, and she's a member of the Green Party, all she does is talk about how lovely it is to finally get a bit of a tan, I say one day when I get home from work and Olaf has just finished mowing the lawn, which is growing with demonstrative speed and unruliness. He laughs, but agrees that there's something uncomfortable about the abnormal nature of it all, as he puts it.

I'm embarrassingly unengaged where environmental issues are concerned. I sort my recycling out of a sense of obligation, but I don't believe it really helps in the slightest that a minority of Norwegian middle-class households scrupulously separate their food waste from their plastic in green or blue bags – or is it the other way around? – particularly not since travelling to Asia for a news story and wading through great heaps of rubbish piled up high in the streets of Kathmandu and New Delhi. I'd never say it aloud, and obviously I sort my waste, it's a given, every little helps, but this autumn it feels as if the weather is underscoring an all-encompassing, uncomfortable shift; everything is going wrong, nothing makes any difference.

I've been walking around all summer long with an unspoken sense that autumn will dawn, wielding its power to normalise, that the chaos that has reigned all spring and summer will be forced to yield to routine and fixed frameworks. But then the sun came out instead, the temperature of the water rose, and I was gradually overwhelmed by the sense that everything is disjointed and somehow out of reach.

◆

Olaf, the children and I spent more than three weeks of the summer holidays at the cabin in Lillesand. At first it seemed far too long, as if the summer would never end. It was just the four of us all summer, something we've never tried before, and it hit me towards the end of the holiday that we've never spent three weeks straight all alone, and that what makes us a unit in everyday life – Agnar, Hedda, Olaf and me – what makes us a family is entirely dependent on the gaze of others, their interference and input, ensuring we function normally, ensuring we function at all.

Ellen and Simen were supposed to come down for the third week but they jetted off to Croatia instead, hoping to find some summer, as Ellen put it in her text message to me two days before they had been intending to arrive. Up until that point they'd been our lifebuoys, the thing that was preventing my new-found desperation over the virtually airtight company of my own little family from revealing itself in some way other than through the long interval-training runs around the island.

Agnar wanted to do nothing but lounge around indoors and play computer games on Håkon's old Gameboy for the entire holiday. He was moody and grumpy and pimply, refused to use the cream I'd bought to help prevent the angry breakouts that had recently flared up on his face and back. It infuriated me. Use the cream in the morning and at night, I shouted at the end of the second week after receiving Ellen's message. It was a rainy morning and we were all indoors, all on top of one another in the cabin without anything to do, and though I had no idea where my wrath emerged from, his spots were suddenly intolerable to me. You're crazy, Agnar shouted back at me. You're the one who's crazy, *choosing* to look the way you do, I said, and swallowed the dawning realisation of what I'd actually just said to my insecure fourteen-year-old son. Olaf slammed the front door demonstrably, taking Hedda out to look for crabs along the sandy stretch of coastline, and I ran around the island as my conscience gnawed at me, promising to pull myself together, swearing I wouldn't ruin the holiday for the children; it's not their fault it's raining or that nobody else is coming to join us here. But I felt furious the following day when Hedda wanted to go out in her new trainers rather than her boots, and Olaf allowed her to so that she'd experience wet feet for herself and understand the discomfort that comes with it. Those shoes cost four hundred kroner, I shouted at Olaf, thumping the wall in front of Hedda and Agnar, breaking our rule not to argue in front of the children for what was probably the fiftieth time in the space of two weeks. I ran after Hedda, who was on her way out into the rain, picking her up and carrying her inside as she wailed and writhed in my arms, pulling off her shoes, and she ran out again in her stockinged feet. Is she uncomfortable enough for you now? I screamed at Olaf.

It wasn't until the very end of the holiday, when everyone knew there were only three or four days left, that the mood lifted. All of a sudden Agnar wanted to go out fishing, like he always used to do with Dad, Olaf brought me coffee in bed, and Hedda wasn't endlessly clingy and whiny. Luckily that's the kind of thing you remember about a holiday or an event, I said to Olaf on the way home in the car, the average of the best and most recent parts of the whole thing put together, I'd read it somewhere, couldn't remember where, until Olaf replied that he wasn't so sure if Kahneman's theories on memory could really be applied to a family holiday in Lillesand.

◈

I bump into Håkon quite by chance on the way home from work one day. I'd popped into the electronics store on Carl Berners plass to buy a new belt for the washing machine, which had broken after Olaf had stuffed too many bedsheets and towels into it the previous afternoon. He blamed me afterwards for leaving them in the machine for a whole week; they'd grown mildew, he said, which was the reason he'd had to wash them again to begin with. I wasn't sure that I agreed it was my fault when he was the one who had stuffed the damp, heavy sheets back in along with all of his exercise gear, but I told him I'd fix it. He looked almost disappointed when I didn't launch into further discussion about it, as we've discussed and quarrelled about almost everything over the past few weeks, months, even. I need my exercise gear for the competition on Wednesday, he said. You'd best call the engineer. It's half past eleven, Olaf, I'll call them in the morning. He won't be able to come out before Wednesday, and then it'll be too late, you know that as well as I do. It's your own fault for putting off doing your washing until you've nothing clean left to wear. I'm sorry, I do all of our laundry every single week, and on the one occasion that you do it, you leave it all in the machine and ruin it. What the hell do you want me to do about it now? I eventually shouted. I want you to get your act together.

The combination of exhaustion and anger is impossible, I'm trapped in this new pattern with Olaf every evening. Even though I do my best to avoid it, we always end up in the same place, just as we did yesterday. I had tried withdrawing from the situation and our discussion. Don't walk off in the middle of a conversation, Olaf said, you know how much I hate that, you don't need to get like that over a washing machine. The wilfulness, the unrecognisable self-righteousness, the situation brought a smile to my lips. I'll fix the machine, I said quietly, knowing it provoked him all the more to see me acting so calmly when he was so cross. I closed the door behind me quietly.

Fortunately, he didn't follow me as he might have done previously, and it took all my strength to pull the machine out into the middle of the room. I stood there for a moment feeling utterly perplexed before realising that there was a cover on the back of the machine; I found a screwdriver and carefully loosened all of the screws, popping them into a little bag as I'd learned from Dad when he'd shown Ellen and me how to change the tyres of a car, then lifted the cover. I'd imagined a chaotic mess of incomprehensible parts, but I was surprised by the simple logic: drive shaft, belt, a small motor and drum. The belt had split in two and I fished it out from the bottom of the machine, stuffing it in my dressing gown pocket and going to bed in the guest room, leaving the washing machine door gaping wide for Olaf to see when he went into the bathroom the following morning.

Håkon emerges from the greengrocer's just as I'm crossing at the roundabout. It strikes me that I've never bumped into him or Ellen by chance out and about before. He looks down at his phone then down Finnmarksgata, looking for the bus, maybe, and he doesn't see me until I touch his arm and say his name. I raise an arm, ready to give him a hug, but the motion halts somewhere between us, Håkon fails to meet me halfway. But he smiles.

'Hi,' he says. 'What are you doing here?'

'I've just picked up a belt for the washing machine. It was the only shop that had the right kind in stock,' I add, nodding at my bag.

His forehead is sweaty, his hair has grown a little long, he's shaved his beard and he looks younger than he did when I last saw him. I don't remember when that was, early August, maybe.

He nods, doesn't ask about the belt.

'What about you?' I ask.

'I was just getting some vegetables, I'm on my way over to a friend's for dinner.'

'A friend?' I repeat back at him, smiling. I know most of Håkon's friends, at least by name, and he tends to refer to people that way, regardless of who he's speaking to.

'A friend,' he repeats. 'What about you?'

'I just told you, I was buying a belt for the washing machine, Olaf broke it yesterday,' I tell him. I feel a brief stab of guilt, but it's absorbed by the heavy atmosphere that lingers between Håkon and me, the staccato conversation. 'It's ages since I saw you last,' I say, my tone inquisitive.

'It's ages since I saw you last too,' he replies with a low chuckle. 'No, but things have been busy since then.'

He turns his head, and I follow his gaze to see a red bus coming to a halt at the crossing by Helgesens gate.

'But things are well?' I ask with slightly less patience, emboldened by the sight of the approaching bus.

'Well?'

'Yes, are you well, is everything good with you? Have you spoken to Ellen, by the way?'

'There's a lot going on, like I said, but things are good,' he says, fiddling with his earlobe. 'How are things with Agnar?'

'Agnar spends most of his time these days feeling angry, it's pretty frustrating,' I reply.

'Aha,' Håkon says, 'maybe I should take him to the cinema or something one day.'

The bus approaches the roundabout and Håkon half turns away from me.

'It was good to see you,' I say, on the brink of welling up. 'Could you pop by one day, maybe? Or we could go out for a beer, invite Ellen along too?'

'Sure, of course, we'll do it, call me,' he says, pointing at the bus. 'But I need to run.'

I go to the greengrocer's too, plucking Turkish yoghurt and vegetables and spices from the shelves and placing them in my basket; I want to make tikka masala for Agnar, but I change my mind as I stand in the queue, it's too hot to be eating Indian food, and so I put everything back; I've spent what must be half an hour buying nothing at all. Olaf can make dinner. I make my way home and install the new belt in the machine, and it strikes me that it's been three months and seventeen days since I've felt the satisfaction I feel when I turn on the machine to find that it actually works.

◈

Uplifted by my triumph over the washing machine, I call Ellen. It goes straight through to answerphone and my courage gives way when I hear her voice. I don't leave a message, don't know what to say, don't remember why I'm ringing. The notion that I need a reason to call her is a new one. Previously it was an automatic thing, something I did at least three times a week without thinking, while making dinner, on my way back from the office or on my way to nursery. Now I can't even recall what we talked about, the idea of ringing her just to tell her about the washing machine or an argument I had with Olaf seems silly, somehow. I get the feeling she's making a point about something, I don't know what, but something aimed at me, and the thought leaves me despondent.

The house is quiet. I feel a momentary panic when it occurs to me that I've forgotten to collect Hedda, but then I remember she was due to go to a friend's house after nursery. I set the alarm on my phone to remind me to pick her up when the afternoon of kids' TV programmes comes to an end; I don't trust myself or my memory, I feel like I'm forgetting everything I need to do, everything I *am* doing. Agnar should have been home from school an hour ago; he hasn't messaged to say he's doing anything else, or he hasn't messaged me, at least, and I feel resigned to it, as though I can't be bothered to nag him any more. I've made half-hearted threats about consequences I know I've got no power to see through, and Agnar can read me like a book, so much so that he doesn't even go to the effort of objecting. A few days ago, he even told me he had made an agreement with Olaf that he could do as he liked as long as he made time for his homework and other obligations. I couldn't face the discussion with Olaf that I knew would unfold, a labyrinth of accusations.

I change into my exercise gear and then spend half an hour sitting on the bed and staring at the wall. I can't summon the motivation required to get up until I receive a message from Olaf telling me he's on his way home and will pick up some food en route.

Olaf and I bought the house in Sagene when Agnar was born. It was between the one we chose and another in Ekeberg, which was cheaper and larger, but Olaf felt it was more important to live close to Mum and Dad in Tåsen. Just imagine living in such easy walking distance, especially when the children are big enough to go there themselves. I agreed with him. I grew up with my grandparents' house as a second home, remember how liberating it was to walk there by myself after school, to be an only child for a day, no Ellen or screaming Håkon to steal the limelight. I feel like Grandma and Grandad were always at home, that it was always a good time for me to pop in – I can only remember one occasion when Grandma told me it wasn't convenient, when I called her one morning and asked if I could come around after school and stay for the night. My cousin had beaten me to it. Even though Grandma continued to dye her hair dark right up until three days before she died, thereby distinguishing herself from the grey-haired grandmothers in fairy tales, they were absolutely typical grandparents in every other way. Always at home, always all ears, and with a mantlepiece bustling with trolls and pixies and ornaments and drawings, an apparently random amalgamation of bits and pieces gifted by five grandchildren with varying degrees of talent. I never considered them independent individuals until I became an adult and had my own children; they simply fulfilled a function in my life. It was even difficult for me to comprehend them fulfilling that same role for Ellen until she spoke at Grandad's funeral and described my upbringing and escapes and childish grief as her own.

I wonder what Agnar and Hedda will think about their grandparents when they become adults, what they might come to represent in their eyes.

◈

I run to Mum and Dad's house. My legs don't just take me there of their own accord, I don't suddenly find myself standing in a meaningful location without realising quite how I got there, as I've read with irritation in so many novels. I make my way there with purpose, fully aware that Mum is in Sicily with a friend. She had sent a photograph of the horizon over the sea, which could have been anywhere, along with a poem by Tomas Tranströmer that I couldn't be bothered even to attempt to interpret. Mum often sends things like that, usually with a blatantly obvious message to be found when one reads between the lines. I'm clearly not as receptive to artistic overtures of this nature in the same way as Håkon and Ellen, who refer to the subtexts of poems she sends as if these things were obvious.

I haven't been home since we got back from Italy in April. I feel almost disappointingly detached as I open the gate and make my way up the driveway; I might as well have been here yesterday. I still carry keys to the house on my own keyring and I unlock the front door. The alarm goes off – Mum has clearly installed a new, more up-to-date system. I try keying in the old code, Grandma's birthday: 0405. *Code invalid*, the display flashes back. I try once more. *Code invalid*. Eventually the alarm starts, a piercing wail, and the noise awakens an intense and familiar sense of discomfort within me, a reminder of when I was young and my greatest fear involved setting it off. The sound of the alarm is amplified in such a way that any potential burglars become so stressed by the din, it paralyses them, in the same way elk are paralysed by car headlights. I assume the security company will call Mum so I try to beat them to it, pull her number up on my phone, breaking a rule I've set myself and which I've managed to stick to over the past seven weeks. She doesn't pick up, so instead I try ringing the number on a sticker beside the box by the front door, but as I key it in, the alarm stops. A message comes in, it's been sent to Håkon, Ellen and me and it's from Mum: *Is one of you at the house, reply quickly*. I reply with a *yes*, initially just to Mum, and after that to the group, exposing myself in every possible way. Mum simply writes: *OK, the new code is Håkon's birthday*. Neither Håkon nor Ellen respond.

All houses have a smell. The sunlight and warmth intensify the characteristic smell of the place, the smell of Mum and Dad, books, dust, coffee, detergent and woodwork. There is no doubting the fact that the rooms still smell of Dad, but perhaps it's the house that's imparted its smell to him and not the other way around, since he hasn't been here for several months now, at least as far as I know. He hasn't taken anything of any significance with him, as Mum also assured me on the phone just after he'd moved out. His chair is just across from Mum's at the little table, but the reading lamp that had once been placed beside it, the one he received as a sixtieth birthday gift from Olaf and me, has gone. I run a finger along the spines of the books on the shelves in a pattern, just as I've done since I was young, nothing amiss there. I go back into the hallway and see now that there's an empty space where Dad's slippers were once lined up beside Mum's; go into the kitchen, help myself to a a glass of water; it's hard to swallow. The house is so similar and yet so different, as if someone has simply shifted all of the furniture or walls or rugs a centimetre one way or the other.

I go upstairs, the fourth step creaking predictably beneath me. Mum and Dad's bedroom door is closed. I don't open it, don't know what it is that I don't want to see there. I go into the bathroom. Dad has retrieved all of his toiletries from his shelf. A hairbrush still sits on my shelf, the same one I've had since I was young, plus a few of the old pieces of jewellery I made with hemp cord and painted wooden beads that Mum hasn't had the heart to throw away – though perhaps she simply likes the fact that the house is still filled with our things, since some of Ellen and Håkon's old belongings are still here, too. I go into my room, where Agnar usually sleeps when he's here. Was here. The old poster of Madonna from the 'Who's That Girl' tour is hanging above the desk, but someone has taken down the poster of the Eurythmics that used to hang by the mirror – Annie Lennox stares at me intently from the desk where she now lies. I sit on the bed, rest my head against the wall behind me and listen to the silence from Ellen's room across the hall. I remember the way we'd both sit with our own stereo systems as close as it was possible for them to be through the uninsulated walls, first to drown out the sound of one another, and then to play music in synchronisation, when Ellen started copying all the music I liked. Three, two, one, go! I'd shout through the wall. Ellen was always slightly too slow when it came to pressing play, so I'd wait an extra moment before pressing the button on my own player – then Madonna, Ellen and I would sing 'Express Yourself' in sync, each in our own rooms.

◈

Dad is living in a rented flat in Torshov. As far as I know, only Olaf has been there so far, helping Dad carry a table there in June after Dad had done so much jogging on asphalt that the doctor had threatened to have him admitted to hospital against his will for reasons entirely unrelated to his knee if he didn't give it a rest. Olaf is the only one to have told me this story. The little that I've spoken to Dad, we've talked about Agnar and Hedda, and I've pulled myself together for their sake, but I didn't want Dad inviting them to his new flat. No, sorry, I told him the first and only time he asked, feeling a physical aversion towards the place rise up within me, it'll only upset them, I told him. He's taken them out for pizza a few times, and one Saturday they took the ferry out to the islands to go swimming.

I put off telling Agnar and Hedda about Mum and Dad for as long as possible. But one morning at the beginning of May, after Dad had sent me a Facebook message with an advert for a flat he'd seen online, I told Hedda on the way to nursery that Grandma and Grandad would each be living in their own houses from now on. She stopped and looked at me, then asked where Grandad was going to live. I can't say why she immediately assumed it would be Dad living elsewhere; perhaps she felt the way the rest of us seemed to, that Mum belonged in the house in a different way to Dad, that she and the house were one, that it was impossible to imagine the house in Tåsen without Mum being there. Olaf was annoyed that I'd told Hedda without informing him, this situation isn't just yours to deal with, he said, but he calmed down quickly afterwards, as he used to do, saying that he would at least like to be there when we told Agnar. That was much more difficult; it became more real when we asked Agnar to sit with Olaf and me at the kitchen table that evening. I felt mostly embarrassed in truth, a familiar embarrassment about my parents, the same I'd felt as a child when Mum was so much louder than the other mothers at playgroup, or when Dad came to collect us from friends' houses in his far-too-tight cycling shorts. I had such difficulty explaining to Agnar that his grandparents were getting divorced, it just seemed so unnatural. I had a feeling that the conversation would unfold in almost exactly the same way if it were Olaf and I who were getting divorced; we would assure him that we both loved him, just as I assured him that Grandma and Grandad obviously still did, that it was about other things. What other things? Agnar asked. He seemed afraid of the answer, that I might say one of them had met someone else. I don't think either of them has met anyone else, it's more that they've grown apart, I said, using Mum's words, the same words Ellen had laughed at and mocked so openly in Italy, and which Olaf had also tried to joke about in hindsight, with varying degrees of success. It wasn't funny in that moment, sitting opposite Agnar, and Agnar wasn't laughing either – he started to cry. I hadn't expected that. Almost half the parents in Agnar's class are divorced, which had led me to believe that it wouldn't be so difficult for him to get his head around the idea, that it wasn't such a foreign concept for him, but Agnar was heartbroken about the whole thing. He buried his face in his hands and sobbed, and I felt so guilty that it took everything I had not to burst into tears myself. Once he'd calmed down and was able to speak again, Olaf gently asked him what he felt was the worst part of it all, but Agnar couldn't tell him, it was just the whole thing. That, and the fact that nothing would ever be the same again.

◈

Agnar's reaction was much like my own. One of the worst parts about it was the change. I've always hated change, the complexity of it. I'm too dependent on being in control, as Olaf puts it. I need to be able to anticipate things, to plan for them after they come into practice, and even the slightest deviation knocks me completely off-balance.

The tradition and security found in routine had been shattered. We've had Sunday lunch at Mum and Dad's almost every Sunday at seven o'clock for as long as I can remember, for instance. Even on those Sundays when I haven't been able to make it, there's been a certain subconscious reassurance in knowing that the others have been sitting around the table as usual. *We'll still have dinners together, obviously*, Mum wrote in one message a few days after we returned from Italy, *but we need to take a break for the moment, just to see what shape things might take.*

You're taking it all too personally, Olaf told me one day in the summer, before a split really started to form between us. It's getting to you too much, you have a life, *we* have a life. Anyway, you've got me, I'm going to Liv my whole life long with you, isn't that right? he joked as he always did when he was trying to cheer me up. But the sense of catastrophe had hit me with full force, and it felt indisputably personal. Things are unravelling, just like the jumper Mum knitted me many moons ago, triggered by a hole low down at the back that grew and grew the more I tried to knot and fasten the loose bits of yarn. And even though I've done my best to think rationally, as Olaf has asked me to, I can find nothing to hold on to. Mum and Dad, independently of anything and anyone else, have represented such a fundamental source of security in my life, a safety net always there to catch me should I ever fall.

You're dependent on them because you've never tried being alone, Ellen said to me once after I'd argued with Olaf in our early days as a couple. We were sitting on the sofa in her old flat. I'd gone straight home to Mum and Dad's first to find they weren't home, only to then turn up at Ellen's door, shaking with fear that Olaf might accept a job offer in Germany. Ellen almost seemed disappointed when she realised I hadn't come to her first, and spent most of the time telling me that I couldn't go running back home with every little problem I had. This isn't a little problem, I said. Either way, Ellen replied, you need to be less dependent. You'd only been living away from home for about three minutes before you met Olaf, it's almost like you replaced Mum and Dad with him. You've got no inner sense of security, she said with an unbearable look of self-satisfaction, and I wrote off what she said as self-assertive, nothing more than a defence of her own way of living her life.

I've wondered lately if she's right, if the reason the divorce might be getting to me so much is that I don't have any independent sense of security, as Ellen still calls it. I am entirely anchored in those around me. But I've never wanted to be alone, to be independent, I've always considered it important to relate to others, to fit in, to be a part of something bigger, a community. Ellen's solitary existence never appealed to me, it always seemed fickle and indistinct, something I've been happy to escape. Whenever Ellen told me in my twenties that I was missing out, I thought she was referring to the parties, the flirtations, the freedom. It never struck me that I might have been missing out on something more fundamental, something that exists – or at least ought to exist – within me.

All studies indicate the middle child is most independent while the eldest is most intelligent, Håkon told me once many years ago out of the blue. He'd been reading up on the significance of the order of siblings. I think it was during dinner one Sunday, but I remember Ellen nodding with satisfaction across the table, at any rate. And all of the typical differences between the eldest, the middle child and the youngest are a result of the way parents treat their children differently, Håkon continued. Of course people treat their children differently, Mum said, children themselves are all different. The chicken or the egg, Håkon replied. Although I later found out that the results of the research were somewhat different from Håkon's cocksure assertions at dinner, I remain convinced that it's the fact that I'm the eldest that matters when it comes to the lack of independence Ellen is talking about, and which she claims to possess. No, it ought to be the opposite way around, Olaf said when I ran the theory past him, an eldest child himself. All of the world's most successful people are eldest siblings, he said, the leaders in their fields, the research makes that quite clear. But a good leader is dependent on others to do a good job, I replied. That's very female logic, Olaf replied, holding his hands up in the air as if Ellen might overhear what he'd said.

In any case, I've always taken more responsibility than Ellen and Håkon; it's easy for them to be independent and do as they like when I've paved the way for them. Mum and Dad have always expected much more of me than of them. They made it very clear, for instance, that I should go into education straight from sixth form, while Ellen travelled to the US to 'consider her options' just a few years later, all without any major objections from either of them – and Håkon started studying at least three different subjects that he gave up on after a few semesters, messing around and doing nothing for an eternity while still living at home.

It's beyond dispute that the eldest child is subjected to the most pressure, I said to Olaf. The situation is what you make of it in a lot of ways, he replied, and I ended the conversation there, just as certain as I always had been that it must play a role – that the lack of independence could be explained by a personality that Mum and Dad had created for me.

Now it makes no difference where the blame lies. It's a bloody nightmare regardless, any sense of security is gone, and I'm losing control of every part of my life. I can't seem to get a grip.

◈

After locking up Mum and Dad's house, I consider running to Ellen's. She recently bought a flat in St. Hanshaugen, but for the same reason that I can't simply pick up the phone and ring her, I can't just swing by. Ellen is the most confrontational of the lot of us, besides Mum, and she can't let anything go, she wants it all out in the open, we have to be able to talk about this, she says. The fact that she hasn't confronted me about the recent situation is worrying, the fact she hasn't called me to discuss Mum and Dad, hasn't turned up at my door to cry and question things, to curse, to mock. That's her role, and I don't dare undertake it myself. In one sense there has been something comforting in her absence; I've escaped the need to relate to the reality of the situation. But now too long has passed, and I'm starting to fear for our relationship, for our friendship and the close bond that I've always taken for granted. Even when my hatred for her peaked during my teenage years, the bond between us remained strong – we were sisters and would always have one another. I've never considered there to be any alternative.

I run home instead and let myself in. I can tell all my keys apart even in the dark, I know exactly which shape of key corresponds to which lock. When I was at primary school, I wore a house key on a piece of string around my neck, a responsibility that was never conferred on Ellen, and one which I've never granted to Agnar – out of consideration for him, myself and for the other parents. In the hallway I remove the key for the house in Tåsen from the keyring and place it inside a drawer.

'Hi,' Olaf says behind me, and I turn around.

He's leaning against the doorway into the kitchen, one leg crossed over the other. He looks as if he's been standing there for some time.

'Hi,' I reply.

'Been out for a run?' he asks.

'Yes, then I popped by the house in Tåsen,' I say so casually that I hope he reacts.

I feel a need to ascribe words to the experience of having walked through something that felt almost like a museum of my own childhood, an exhibition of all that's been lost. Or perhaps of what never existed in the first place, just scenes in a play about a family, my family.

'I thought your mum was on holiday?' Olaf replies, taking a bite of the piece of bread he's holding in one hand.

'She is. I just felt like popping in,' I say.

Olaf nods. He doesn't appear to be thinking about moving, but says nothing. I don't know what to say next. Ellen has always remarked on how glad she is to have language at her disposal, and I know what she means by that: I've always felt grateful to have grown up in a family that talks, and I've recreated that feeling in my own family – in spite of Olaf's limitations when it comes to putting his feelings into words, that is. I'm glad that Agnar and Hedda have both learned to express themselves when they feel upset, for example, rather than simply wailing or slamming doors. Olaf and I have also always argued in concrete terms, rather than enforcing demonstrative silences or playing games. Now I find myself unable to put into words the very thing that is splitting the earth beneath my feet, tearing up the foundations of everyone around me.

'So, how was it? Has Sverre taken all of the furniture with him?' Olaf eventually asks, smiling.

'No, there wasn't much missing. He's taken the lamp we gave him. Other than that, just a few bits and pieces. But that almost makes things worse,' I say, and I know that's true, that it really would have been better if Mum and Dad had more clearly emphasised the change, if they'd reacted in a way that would legitimise my own feelings.

'What do you mean?' Olaf asks. 'How can that be worse?'

'Because I want them to acknowledge the change!' I say with some volume, and Olaf jumps. 'They're the only ones acting as if nothing is any different, as if they're going to continue their lives just as they were before – only, by themselves from now on.'

And Mum and Dad seem genuinely surprised that their decision has seen consequences great and small rippling across the landscape between them like waves. In a conversation with Mum just a few days after we returned from Italy, she furrowed her brows when she realised I was crying. Are you really so upset by all of this, she asked, and when I nodded, she told me that I had to try to understand that this wasn't about me, or about any of *you children*, as she put it, before continuing somewhat paradoxically: We're all adults, each and every one of us. This is between Sverre and me, she said, and her words punctured and left deflated every desperate question I had and the need I felt to receive any kind of apology.

'But they might have a point, this doesn't necessarily need to be as disastrous as you're making it out to be,' Olaf says, and I feel speechless in the face of his lack of understanding, his lack of support. Who is he really, the man standing in the doorway of our shared home and shared life, the man snacking on a piece of bread, the one who's been my partner for almost twenty years now, yet who reveals at this crucial moment that he doesn't know me at all?

'Doesn't need to be as disastrous? Giving up on a forty-year marriage, on an entire family?'

'They're not giving up on their family,' Olaf says. 'Now you're overreacting.'

'They're giving up on everything that we were,' I say, and my voice cracks, a result of Olaf's cold lack of understanding and the realisation that has hit me full-force: 'With a shrug of their shoulders they're tearing down everything I've built my life on.'

Olaf falls silent, inhaling as if about to say something but instead letting the air out in one long sigh before turning around and heading back into the kitchen.

◆

A few days later I take Agnar to the doctor. His spots have become much worse, it can't be normal, I said to Olaf one evening, and as usual he responded by telling me he'd had spots at that age. Firstly, that doesn't sound right, I've seen plenty of photos of Olaf as a teenager – he looks like a slightly less well-proportioned version of a fairy-tale prince – and secondly, it's not a case of him having lots of spots, there's more to it than that, I said to Olaf. He can't sleep, it hurts him even just to lie there, it's not normal. I booked an appointment with the doctor mostly for my own benefit. To fix something.

The doctor asks Agnar if he wants me to come in, and Agnar looks at me.

'It's your decision,' I say, making a half-hearted attempt to look as if I mean it, not trusting for a second that Agnar will speak up well enough for himself.

'She can come in,' he tells the doctor, and I'm sure I fail completely to disguise my relief and pride.

Once she's examined his face, she asks him to remove his shirt. I'm surprised; I haven't seen his back and chest for a long time and his shoulders are broader, almost manly. He resembles Håkon, but most striking of all is the line that becomes visible when he removes his t-shirt, a line that reveals the fact that he can't have spent any time without a t-shirt on all summer, as well as the enflamed spots spreading from the nape of his neck and down his back, closely packed, like tiny, angry volcanoes. Poor Agnar, I picture him on the beach with his friends, in the showers at school – Olaf has forced him to shower in spite of the fact that Agnar has been on the verge of tears about it all, telling us nobody else did – and all of the looks from all of the girls, their gazes lingering on his forehead, around his mouth, looks that cause every tiny pimple on Agnar's open, honest face to sting angrily. I'm furious, my anger aimless to begin with, but thereafter directed at Olaf. I don't know why and can't face thinking much more about it.

The doctor asks Agnar about how things have been up until this point, how long he's had issues with his skin, his daily habits, diet, that kind of thing. I squeeze the arm of the chair to prevent myself from interrupting Agnar, who stumbles over his words and misunderstands her questions, turning every so often to look over at me. I nod encouragingly, smiling with my lips pressed tightly closed. I don't want to appear controlling and overprotective in front of the doctor, don't know why I'm so concerned about what she thinks of me and us, but I feel as if we have something to prove – and I let Agnar tell her about things himself. About the pimples that appeared around Christmas time, that worsened over the course of the spring, that then got better, he can't really remember everything, but March and April were OK, then everything got worse in July, he had a bump on his shoulder that he thought was cancer, but which turned out to be a totally sick spot, as he describes it, and over the course of the summer things only got worse and worse.

'Have your habits changed at all during this time?' the doctor asks him. 'Are you eating differently, for example, or have you started using a new type of soap or any other skin products?'

Agnar looks at me. I shake my head. He shakes his head.

'No new environments or anything else that might have caused you more stress than usual?'

Agnar looks away.

◆

At the end of October, the cold finally sets in. All of a sudden it is as if autumn is in a hurry to catch up with itself: the trees change colour, the leaves wither, and the branches become bare in the space of just a few weeks. At the beginning of November, we wake to frost coating our lawn and windscreen.

I felt certain I was waiting for autumn to come, waiting for normality to set in, but neither the darkness, the cold nor the frost do anything to banish the chaos. Olaf gets on my nerves more and more each day, and I know it's unfair; I can't decide if it's him who's changed or my feelings for him, but either way I'm seeing him in a new light.

Olaf and I met in our early twenties, and it's embarrassing, but neither of us remembers where we met for the first time. We just gradually became part of the same circle of friends. I noticed you, of course, Olaf remarked after the fact, but that's just something he says to be nice, I don't think he noticed me any more than I noticed him, not until I fell virtually head-over-heels in love with him practically overnight, and quite out of the blue. The worst and least predictable months of my life were to follow, brutal and out of control. I hate being in love, I told my friends, and they said yes, the best and worst feeling there is, and I thought no, actually, just the worst. And even though I felt that being in love seemed to light me up from within, making me all too obvious, almost as if I were standing there waving directly at him, it took a long time for Olaf to see the signs. You never said, he commented afterwards, how could I have known? It was three months before we got together, and that awful sense of freefall gradually morphed into the opposite, the fantastic feeling that I had solid ground beneath my feet.

We got married eleven years ago. We'd already had Agnar by that point, and our lives were so entwined, so mutually dependent, that Mum thought it superfluous for us to marry at all, at least any more formally than on paper. She and Dad laughed when I told them we were planning a church ceremony. Olaf would have been perfectly happy with a civil ceremony in City Hall with a party to follow, but I wanted that framework, as I put it at the time, the framework of church and priest. Now I'm uncertain why that was so important to me, but it seemed more real doing things that way, as if we were making a promise to one another, as if it were worth more if we made it under the gaze of a priest – even though neither Olaf nor I are the slightest bit religious. And I meant what I said with a passion: I promise to love and honour you, and I will be faithful to you until death do us part, and most likely far beyond that if you should die before me. It didn't seem difficult, there were no alternatives.

Even so, early on in the relationship we agreed on a few fundamental conditions that we've lived up to ever since, such as the fact that there could be no threats of leaving whenever we had an argument, no notion of walking out whenever things felt hopeless. I'd done that kind of thing previously, back when I was afraid that he would leave me, I'd beat him to it and threaten him with the idea that I couldn't take any more. We agreed that any threats to break things off would no longer be allowed to creep into our arguments, something we've both stuck to for the most part, and with that the notion itself has grown more obscure, not something to grasp at or console oneself with.

Nowadays that seems very naïve. The knowledge that there is always a way out has been writ large on the walls in my life, and most likely also those in Olaf's, since our arguments end increasingly quickly and increasingly more often with an unspoken, threatening undertone of *if not, then dot dot dot*.

The worst part is that the only person I have any desire to talk to about this new feeling is Mum. I want her to tell me about the importance of refusing to give up on something, just as she's done all through my life; in every phase, Mum has been the one to convey the significance of not giving up on something you've started, of making good choices and standing strong, whether through words or actions or a meaningful look. It's something I've passed on to my own children. We don't give up. We don't stop. We pull ourselves together and we stick at things.

Dad's car turns into our driveway late one afternoon. He called yesterday to ask if he could pick up Hedda early from nursery, maybe take her out to a café or somewhere else she might enjoy. I didn't have the heart to refuse him, and a quiet afternoon to myself was a tempting prospect. Agnar has gone to a friend's house for a gaming session, something he's obviously been permitted to do by Olaf in spite of the rules that computer gaming is a weekend activity, and Olaf is out at a meeting.

I stand at the kitchen worktop and watch Dad as he parks the car. He remains inside for a few moments, chatting to Hedda, laughing at something, I can just about make out Hedda's curls around the edges of the car seat that he and Mum bought when she was born.

He gets out, walks around the car and crouches down beside Hedda's door. She cranes her neck, looking for him. He can't bring himself to wait long enough for her to genuinely begin to wonder where he's disappeared to, and instead leaps up at her window all of a sudden. She jumps at first, then dissolves in such a fit of giggles that I'm sure she must have wet herself. I see her shouting, 'Again! Again!' as he opens the door and reaches in to unbuckle her, and he closes the door and crouches down once more, this time creeping around the car and surprising her on the other side. Hedda cries out with delight. Dad laughs, opens the door and lifts her up out of her seat, carrying her across the gravel driveway in one arm. Neither of them has spotted me, and I realise I'm standing there with a smile on my face. I shake my head, go into the living room and wait for them to let themselves in.

'Hello,' Dad calls from the hallway.

'Hello,' Hedda shouts.

I go out to meet them. I stop in the doorway, blocking the way into the living room and kitchen, but luckily Dad hasn't had a chance to take off his shoes. I try to keep my interactions with him and Mum as brief as possible, want to show them that I'm engaging with them for the sake of the children, but that I don't want them close to me. I want to show them that things have changed. We only ever talk about Agnar and Hedda or other practical matters. On those few occasions that one of them has tried initiating a conversation either about themselves or about the other – or about me, for that matter – I've shut it down. I feel too tentative to trust myself in a conversation of that nature, can't tell if it would coax out my anger, my sympathy or my grief, and I have no desire to expose any of those sides of myself.

'Hey there, Heddy,' I say, bending down to accept a hug from her. Her hair smells of coffee. 'Have you been to a café?'

She nods and runs into the living room.

'Aren't you going to say bye to Grandad?' I ask her.

'But he's coming in,' Hedda replies.

I don't look at Dad.

'No, Grandad's going home now. Come and say goodbye,' I say, looking only at Hedda, smiling, my arm outstretched towards her.

Fortunately, she doesn't throw a tantrum, returning to the hallway instead. Dad crouches down and wraps his arms around her, and she almost disappears in his embrace as he hugs her tight.

'Thank you for coming out with me, Hedda,' he says as she wriggles free.

She disappears off into the kitchen and I'm left standing there alone with Dad. I swallow. He looks old.

'Well, I should be off home, I've got some work to do,' he says, my conscience searing within me.

'Yes, I'm working on something too,' I lie.

'I'd be happy to take Hedda again one day next week,' he says. 'Or maybe Agnar, we could go out for pizza or something like that.'

'Maybe, I'll have to have a word with him and see if it's convenient,' I reply, unwilling to make any promises, reluctant to make any firm arrangements.

'I'm at the office on Monday and Tuesday, but I'm free other than that,' Dad says, and turns to leave, making his way down the front steps. 'It was nice to see you too,' he adds, smiling.

'Thanks for picking Hedda up today,' I say. 'Bye.'

◆

I spend a lot of time contemplating memories. I feel the need to call Håkon and Ellen at least three times a day, both of whom I still haven't spoken to about anything other than the utmost superficial matters, just to have my suspicions confirmed or denied in terms of how I remember things. In my mind's eye I scrutinise Mum and Dad's facial expressions, their gestures, their glances and turns of phrase, searching for signs of how unhappy they were, seeking out some sort of foreshadowing of things to come.

I find precisely what I'm looking for every single time. Memories are suddenly no longer tinged with a naïve ignorance and sense of trust, emerging instead with clearly defined contours. Christmases, summer holidays, Sunday dinners, conversations, debates – fresh details, expressions and intonations that I had never previously picked up on surface in my mind.

They've never been particularly affectionate with one another, Ellen said when she joined me in the kitchen after Dad's birthday meal in Italy, passing me a piece of kitchen roll. I wiped my nose and face, embarrassed at the fact I had broken down like a small child. What do you mean? I asked her. Just that, she said, I don't ever remember them being particularly affectionate with one another, only ever with us. That's not true, Ellen, I said. You ought to know better than anyone just how much love there was in their conversations, how much trust they share as partners in any discussion, plus the fact that they still *have* so much to discuss, the way they feel that there's something at stake when they speak their mind – and how much trust they share as a result of the fact that they continue to make demands of one another. Don't you see that? I asked, and my voice approached falsetto levels in the realisation that everything that was suddenly so clear to me was no longer relevant in the slightest. Or what about all the small things they remember to do for one another, all the practical things – Mum always leaving a little cup of warm milk out for Dad in the morning, Dad putting the radiator on in Mum's car before he leaves for work, the books she takes him, the sudoku he saves for her, all the love that exists in the routines and habits they've formed and continued over the years, I said. Ellen said nothing, looking down at the floor. She doesn't know, I suddenly thought to myself. She doesn't understand, she's never experienced it for herself. For her, gestures have to be grand and physical, declarations steeped in emotion. In the numerous brief relationships that she's had, she hasn't experienced anything other than the highest highs and the lowest lows, and my God, how I've envied her, resenting the endless passionate drama, but I've never reflected on what she might be missing, all of the meaningful things that lie somewhere in between.

◈

I don't know why the memory of one summer distinguishes itself so clearly from the memory of all the other summers that seamlessly glide together in my mind, the most fleeting of moments that prove impossible to date. It no doubt stems from the drama that arose when Ellen wanted to rescue the crabs from the giant pot over the open fire outside. I can clearly picture her coming around the corner just as Dad tipped the red bucket of crabs into the pot. The way she ran towards him to knock the bucket out of his hands, and his instinctive leap back out of the way, and Ellen, her small frame emboldened with a force that had anticipated the resistance of Dad's body unexpectedly coming up against the scorching pot, arms outstretched. The pot over-turned, and the half-dead crabs poured out with the water, the littlest ones too stunned to move while the largest scuttled off in every direc-tion, red and steaming.

I watched from the veranda bannister where I had perched myself; I always found it exciting and endlessly fascinating to see the crabs being cooked, and Dad promised that they didn't feel any pain, something I was content to believe since they tasted so delicious, but Ellen was less willing to accept this claim. You don't know that, she replied to Dad's overly simple explanation of the cabin activities she declared to be animal cruelty; she challenged him on the cooking of live shellfish, the use of the maggots that wriggled on the ends of hooks as bait, the

catching of fish that gasped in the bottom of the boat and the killing
of flies using sticky paper hanging in the cabin porch.

Ellen suffered a few superficial burns, but otherwise got away lightly.
I can remember running to fetch Mum while Dad checked her over,
but she was already on her way out after having watched the scene
unfold through the window. Lately I've also remembered the atmosphere that followed, the discussion that played out between Mum and
Dad after Ellen and I had turned in for the night in the room next
door to the living room, where they were still sitting at the dining table
with our uncle and aunt. I suddenly recall the entire conversation word
for word. It was pure instinct, Dad said about the way he had stepped
out of the way. Your instinct should have been to protect your daughter against thirty litres of boiling water, Mum said. Now you're being
unfair, Dad replied. But I'm forgetting that you're infallible, of course.
I think we ought to continue this conversation in the morning when
everyone has calmed down a bit, my uncle or aunt chipped in, the most
important thing is that everything was alright in the end. Dad replied
that he was very happy to have the conversation there and then, if that's
what Mum wanted, given that there was nothing *she* could be called to
account for. There was something unusual and unpleasant about the
way he said it, and that feeling returns to me now, my own uncomfortable realisation that something was concealed beneath it all, the way
Mum got up to leave without a word, and my uncle telling Dad that
he ought to go and get some rest too. I'll wait until she's gone to sleep,
Dad said. I can't remember anything from the following day, can't place
that summer on a timeline, but Ellen was about eleven at the time.

◆

I've obviously thought about Mum and Dad's relationship before,
since becoming an adult, but I haven't succeeded in shaking off my
childish outlook until now. I've recognised that they've had problems,
some that I can remember, others less well defined, but I've always seen
the way they've stuck together all through my life, their relationship a

fixed variable. How can I have continued to think that way as an adult, when I recognise all the phases that Olaf and I have already been through ourselves? Everything that has ever driven us onwards, every external force that has affected us, every internal shift, everything we've created, Agnar and Hedda – everything that has left its mark on us, events that have divided the past into episodes and taken us in new directions when viewed with hindsight, onwards, backwards, up and down. From a rational perspective, I've obviously acknowledged their marriage as something greater than and independent of the framework that it has provided for me, for Ellen and Håkon, and occasionally I've marvelled at their way with one another in daily life. On other occasions I've felt frustrated by it, but the power of this dawning realisation suggests that I've either chosen not to care, or that I've failed to penetrate even slightly below the surface.

Agnar asked a few days ago what we'd be doing at Christmas, who'd be celebrating where, unleashing a landslide of more or less coherent recollections of previous Christmases. I lingered on one from Christmas three years ago, when I had stepped into the living room at three o'clock in the morning to find Dad sitting alone in his armchair with a glass of wine in his hand, listening to music. I had forgotten how strained that Christmas had felt, the way nobody had really managed to get into the Christmas spirit, how conversations had faltered and any sense of sincerity had been sorely lacking. I had blamed Ellen, I can't even remember why, maybe she'd just broken up with a boyfriend and was being fractious or keeping herself to herself, as she was prone to, no desire to pull herself together for anyone else's sake. Now I look back on it, it's obvious that it all had much more to do with Mum and Dad – the details emerge more clearly to me now, the discussion they had in the kitchen about something trivial, a dish for the sauerkraut, and Dad's distant, almost resigned tone, as if he were holding the conversation on autopilot, paired with Mum's silent disdain during the meal when it became apparent that the sauerkraut had been tainted by the flavour of the casserole dish she hadn't wanted him to use in the first place. That had lasted for the remainder of the holiday; Håkon made no input whatsoever, Ellen was grumpy, and Olaf and I did our best to lift everyone's spirits for the children's sake. During the obligatory moments spent together, there was friction and unease, so inexplicable at the time. I remember it being the first time I'd ever felt glad when the daily routine kicked back into action once again in January.

Agnar's question about Christmas inspired me to send a message to Ellen and Håkon. *Fancy a beer?* I asked them, after drafting what must have been at least twenty different attempts in my notes app before deleting them all, one by one.

◈

Ellen, Håkon and I meet in a café in Tøyen one cold night in November. We woke that day to the news that Donald Trump had been elected as the new President of the United States, and that ought to make our reunion simpler, having something concrete to talk about, I think to myself on the bus. Days like this are good for seeking out difficult social situations; I picture all the meetings or dates or hospital visits where the topic of conversation is a given, something simple and extraneous, far removed from our own lives and anything that might otherwise prove difficult to discuss.

I'm running fifteen minutes late because Olaf was delayed in coming home from the gym; he gets home late more often now than he used to, usually without letting me know in advance. We sat and discussed the election after we were done, he said, throwing out his arms apologetically when he finally arrived home in his hat and cycle shorts. Good to see you've got your priorities straight, I said, pointing at Hedda, who was sitting at the top of the stairs and watching us through the banisters. I had been trying to get her to go to sleep for two hours; she'd come down to the living room what must have been ten times already and I'd gone back upstairs with her to sing and stroke her hair at least as many times. The last time I'd heard her footsteps on the floor, the door opening, her light tread on the first step, I'd called out to tell her that she wasn't allowed to come downstairs again. Go to bed,

Hedda, I said. No, she said, stubbornly sitting at the top of the stairs, not angry or upset, but simply determined. I've often felt curious about her decision-making processes, what accounts for the dramatically clear decisions she formulates in her young mind. Well, you'll just have to sit there, I eventually conceded, you can't come down here again tonight. And so Hedda sat there. I didn't feel the slightest hint of guilt about leaving Olaf to deal with the issue – quite the opposite, in fact.

Ellen and Håkon are each sitting with a beer when I arrive, discussing the election, as predicted. I hug them both in turn, missing them intensely the moment I smell them, and it takes a huge amount of effort not to burst into tears. It would have made the situation unbearable all round, though especially for Håkon, who's had a tendency to cry out of sympathy for anyone who happens to be upset ever since he was a boy, unable to stop himself, a fact he finds embarrassing to this day. I smile behind my scarf.

'Are you talking about the election?' I ask.

'Yes, and the fact that Håkon has finally got what he wanted all along,' Ellen says.

They both laugh.

'What do you mean?' I ask. 'Got what you wanted?'

'Trump as President,' Ellen says.

'Is that really how you feel?' I ask.

'Obviously not,' Håkon says. 'I feel the same way I've always felt about it.'

I try to remember how Håkon has always felt about it, but that chops and changes year in and year out, if not by the month, and I can't keep up.

'Which is...?' I enquire, smiling.

'Firstly, it's crazy that so many people should have any kind of opinion on the results of an election in another country, it's only because it's the US. Secondly, I couldn't give a shit about anyone who isn't Sanders. He was the only interesting candidate, and he was a symptom of something greater too, which is what they're now saying about Trump. But Hillary was still a better alternative,' he says.

I wonder if this is an opinion he's formed for himself; it resembles everything else I've read on the subject, and I nod even though I'm not sure I agree. My views are constantly shifting in line with whatever I read, whichever article most recently makes the best point. Håkon has refuted me on many an occasion, you said something totally different yesterday, he might say, you always agree with the last person you heard. Occasionally I've pointed out that his opinions also change every time we see one another, for the most part, but he always rattles off an endless list of arguments to explain the nuances in his opinions that I've failed to understand, before asserting that his opinions haven't *changed*, they've just adjusted to encompass new information.

'Why do you use Donald's surname and Clinton's first name?' Ellen asks.

Håkon laughs.

'Sorry. I should have learned my lesson after last time,' he says.

Last time, I think to myself. It hadn't struck me that Ellen and Håkon might have been in touch with one another without including me, and it scares me slightly. Given that neither of them has made any special effort to get in touch with me, I'd automatically assumed that it was communication between the *three* of us that had been left in tatters.

I sit and listen for any further indications that they've kept in touch beyond their effortless tone, their expressions and easy laughter, all a far cry from the awkward silence I'd expected to encounter. I'd believed that it would force us to engage in a conversation about us and everything that's happened, why we had distanced ourselves from one another almost as if on command.

I take advantage of a brief pause when a silence of the kind I'd anticipated finally arises. 'It's ages since I've seen you both,' I say after an hour of small talk, strikingly superficial considering our usual ease in one another's company.

Håkon takes a sip of his beer. Ellen looks at me, waiting for me to elaborate. I don't know how to continue, can't find the words to describe everything I've been thinking about over the past few months, the way everything has unravelled. Neither of them does anything to help me. I take a deep breath.

'What's actually happened here?' I ask, and my fear of losing them, losing my grip, losing everything, grabs hold of me, I feel the need to swallow.

Ellen's smile finally fades, the same smile she's worn since I arrived. She looks away and runs a hand through her hair, lets it rest by her ear, fiddles with her earring. Håkon seems uncomfortable, he looks down at his glass.

'What do you mean?' Ellen asks.

I don't know what *she* means. I'd expected that she would be more forthright about everything, as she always is, that she'd take over the conversation almost as soon as I'd initiated it, that she'd be confrontational or upset, that she'd play out all of the feelings pent up inside me, that she'd put the chaos into words. Had I not known her better, she would have appeared perfectly unmoved – though Ellen is never really unmoved, and it's that which exposes her. She's putting it on, and I feel emboldened.

'I just think it's strange that we have so little contact all of a sudden,' I say.

As usual I expect nothing from Håkon, and I become aware that it's Ellen I'm confronting in reality, Ellen who I blame, that Håkon is too young to understand or take responsibility for anything, but I check myself, look over at him, the thirty-year-old child with the heart condition. He deserves no more sympathy than the rest of us.

'Why are you keeping your distance?' I ask him.

'I'm not keeping my distance,' Håkon says. 'What are you on about? You're the one who never gets in touch any more.'

My desperation and anxiety manifest themselves in a flash of anger.

'Exactly!' I reply, my voice loud this time. 'See what happens when I stop getting in touch? Everything goes quiet. What does that tell you, Håkon? Hmm? You sit around waiting to hear from people, waiting to be asked to dinner, waiting for everyone to do everything for you.'

'Come on Liv, you need to calm down,' Ellen says.

'It's not a case of me calming down, it's a case of you two realising that what I'm saying is true!'

'What is it you want us to realise?' Ellen asks, looking genuinely curious.

'The fact that you've left me with all the responsibility, as usual. For everything. It shouldn't simply be a given that I take care of things, but I do anyway, even now, and you're sitting here as if nothing's happened,' I reply, when really I want to shout: Aren't you both as scared of losing me as I am of losing you?

'I don't think that anything goes without saying, and what you're saying isn't even true – I often get in touch,' Ellen says.

'You get in touch, sure, but you never take any *responsibility*, never, you never have, you're never the one to suggest that the three of us meet up, you've never been the one to invite us all to dinner – neither of you do – and now you're leaving it to me to take responsibility for this, too,' I cry, almost shouting now.

'Responsibility for what?' Håkon asks.

'For this entire situation. You just disappear and expect me to sort things out, without either of you having to figure out what's going on with Mum and Dad or get your head around the chaos they've created. The fact that they're destroying everything we are, everything we've ever been, trampling onwards without looking back. And nobody seems to want to acknowledge the fact that we've been living a lie, nobody seems concerned about it in the slightest,' I shout despairingly, aware that I'm waving my arms now and again, almost uncontrollably.

Both look dumbfounded, and there's a brief pause.

'We haven't been living a lie, Liv. Even though Mum and Dad have decided to get divorced, we're still us, we're still sitting here, the three of us,' Ellen says. 'And actually, I have a fair bit of contact with Mum and Dad, I do keep in touch with them, perhaps more than you do, as far as I hear,' Ellen says.

It appears everyone has had more contact with each another than I have with any of them. It becomes impossible for me to reply, the patterns are so unfamiliar, the roles reversed.

'Plus, this is a situation they've created for themselves,' Ellen replies. 'There's nothing you can do, Liv. Mum and Dad need to take responsibility for their own choices, and to be quite honest, Mum in particular seems confident about the divorce, she's moving on,' Ellen continues with a knowing look.

'What other choices has she made? How exactly is she moving on?' I ask, looking from Ellen to Håkon and back to Ellen again. I need to swallow.

'With this new chap ... what's his name again? Morten?' Ellen asks, looking at Håkon.

Håkon nods. The child within me comes up against my mature common sense, it triumphs, and I find myself almost unable to draw breath. How come Ellen and Håkon both know about this? Why has Mum chosen to tell them and not me?

'I'm sorry, God, I thought you knew,' Ellen says when she registers my reaction.

'They're not *together* together,' Håkon says, trying to smooth things over.

'They're just friends,' Ellen says laughing, imitating Grandma in an attempt to make light of the situation, to lift the mood, but neither Håkon nor I are laughing.

The wind has been knocked out of me. I realise that I've been certain that things would sort themselves out, that this was a crisis between them that would ultimately pass, that everything would blow over.

I think about Olaf, sitting at home, and I wonder if he's managed to put Hedda to bed. Then I picture Dad sitting alone in his flat. I can't seem to gather my thoughts.

◈

I sit in a bar down in Grünerløkka after bidding Håkon and Ellen farewell. I call Kjersti, a friend of mine who has just divorced her husband, one of only a few friends I've been in touch with over the past few weeks. I haven't told anyone else about the divorce, haven't been able to face the prospect of being confronted by my own fears or the cracks that have formed as a result, and anyway, I've been convinced that this was a temporary state of affairs.

I tell Kjersti that Mum has a new partner, even though Håkon explained after a while that Mum didn't view him that way at all, that actually she had her doubts after things had moved so quickly. I receive no sympathy from Kjersti, who asks *me* to stop being so egotistical, telling me I ought to feel happy for Mum, grow up, she says. I play along while silently writing off everything she says as her own way of justifying the decisions she's made.

I don't have any desire to go home, so I order myself another beer. I never got the chance to say anything else I'd planned to bring up with Ellen and Håkon. We're not the ones getting divorced, I'd imagined myself saying to them, we need to stick together. I'd pictured myself comforting them, reassuring them, putting things into perspective for them. But as it turned out, *they* were the ones to put things into perspective for *me*: I'm the one who's overreacting, and I've laboured under the misapprehension that both Håkon and Ellen must feel the same way, that we must have the same experience of the situation, that their foundation has been shattered just like my own, but it's just you, I think to myself, it's just you who was stupid enough to build your life on the illusion of something real, while Ellen and Håkon saw through them both long ago. I drink quickly to stifle my shame.

A man approaches me and asks if he can sit beside me at the bar. I gesture to the seat beside me, in spite of the fact that there are any number of free tables behind us. He orders a beer, checks his phone, asks how my day has been. I start laughing. He nods in agreement.

'Yep, it's absurd, the whole thing,' he says, picking up his phone, a newspaper article on the election glowing in my direction.

'What's absurd is how much we care about a US election,' I say, my mind filled with a comforting rush.

I repeat a few of Håkon's arguments, he disagrees. We sit and discuss things for a while, and it takes half an hour and another beer before I realise that I'm ingratiating myself, seeking out something in him.

I wonder if I ought to just let everything go to ruin, if I should give up too. But I have children, I tell him as we stand outside the bar, one hour and several beers later, sharing a cigarette. He tells me he's not been trying to pick me up, that he's actually happily married, but he's enjoyed our conversation, he says. I can't bring myself to even feel embarrassed about the misunderstanding, instead simply laughing and repeating his words back at him: happily married. He nods. I thank him for the cigarette, pull up the zip of my coat and walk all the way home before lying down on the sofa and falling asleep.

◈

Agnar wakes me, seemingly annoyed.

'Why are you lying here?' he asks.

My head is aching, my mouth is dry, the low November sun stings my eyes through the window while revealing a grey film of dust and dirt on the outside of the glass.

'What's the time?' I ask him.

'Almost ten,' Agnar says.

Olaf must have got up with Hedda without me having heard them. I wonder if Hedda is quieter when she's alone with Olaf, or if I've slept abnormally deeply here on the sofa, which is right next door to the kitchen.

My working hours are flexible, and though it's a rare occurrence, I do occasionally work from home in the mornings; I convince myself that this is the reason Olaf didn't wake me, an act of consideration rather than one of illustrative neglect.

'Why aren't you at school?' I ask Agnar.

'It's Thursday,' he replies brusquely, before turning to make his way into the kitchen.

'Oh yes, of course,' I say, and see that he's wearing his sports kit. 'How's training going?' I ask, feeling so sick that I have to suppress the impulse to throw up then and there, the end of my sentence disappearing with the effort required to do so, and Agnar's expression hardens.

'For fuck's sake,' he says, slamming the kitchen door behind him.

◈

For the first time in my life, I send a message to my manager telling a lie. I write that I'm at home with Hedda, who's unwell, sending it before I have a chance to reconsider, a cold fear creeping over me as I imagine all the possibilities – that someone might pass by the nursery and see her playing, healthy and happy in the sandpit just by the fence, or that they might bump into Olaf and Hedda on the way home. I consider picking her up, but remember that they're making Christmas cards today, something Hedda has been talking about and eagerly anticipating since yesterday.

I hear Agnar slam the front door as I step into the shower, and I stand on my tiptoes to catch a glimpse of him through the high window above the bathtub. I can just see him disappearing behind the hedge. He's fading away from me, I no longer have a sense of him the way I used to. I shiver under the cold jet of water as it hits my breasts and stomach, force myself to stand under it until it comes up to temperature. I should have gone after Agnar and spoken to him before he left. What's he thinking now, my little man? I don't know what I should have said to him, how to speak to him; nowadays he's too old for me to lie to but too young to understand. I don't know any in between.

A year ago, I found myself standing in his doorway and watching him sleep, and I reflected on the incredible fact that he was lying there dreaming dreams of his own. I pondered everything his growing body accommodated, his experience and knowledge, all independent of me, all beyond my control. I had simply created him, and there he was, so very much himself thirteen years later, with opinions and thoughts and secrets of his own. I grabbed Olaf as he walked past me, whispered to him, told him everything I was thinking. Olaf nodded, then said: And just think of everything he'll go through, think of everything he's yet to learn. Now I flinch at the thought of his teenage years, at the disappointments and emotions that will surge above and beyond all those that have come before, but at that point I had no concept of the fact

I might not understand him or find myself able talk to him; he was Agnar, my boy.

I step out of the shower after half an hour, dry my body and wrap a hand towel around my head like a turban. I brush my teeth and my tongue, which still smells and tastes bitter, tinged with alcohol and remorse after the previous night's activities. I rub my face with moisturiser, my skin feeling three sizes too small. I open the door into the hallway and find myself faced with Agnar on his way to his room. I stop.

'That was a short run,' I say.

He turns away, looking at the wall as he passes me by, and I realise that I'm naked, that Agnar is embarrassed at the sight of me. I'm almost moved to laughter, if it weren't for the fact that it only serves to underscore the new unfamiliarity that has arisen between us. He's grown up with a natural relationship to nudity, an unspoken aim for Olaf, who has a theory that it will allow Agnar and Hedda to enjoy a healthier relationship to their own bodies in the long, and short, terms. Now Agnar slips past me and into his room without looking at me, and without replying to my remark. I go to my room and climb under the duvet, which feels cool against my warm skin; the hangover ravages my body, my heart beats hard inside my chest, and my nerves prickle on the surface of my skin.

◈

I can't sleep. I fetch my computer and try to work; I need to write a long piece on our ageing population, which was hyped up as a worst-case scenario a few years ago, but which lost its sensational edge in the years that followed. A colleague and I have been to view a model flat with automated solutions designed to replace real-life home help. A relentlessly calm woman's voice is activated and speaks to you if you forget to turn off the hob, for instance, or if you step out of your front door in the middle of the night. *It's half past one in the morning. Are you sure you want to go out now, Berit?* the voice asked softly after our guide set the time and opened the door. He looked at us expectantly and said: This is the future, ladies. I was uncertain whether he meant *our* future or more generally. Oh God, my colleague said as we drove back to the office, I'm never getting old, at least not on my own.

I write a few emails to potential interview participants, with the subject line: *The senior citizen of today*. I wonder if it's too patronising. I picture Mum, but then I shake my head; they need to get used to being called elderly once they hit sixty-five. I remember Dad taking it as a personal insult when he automatically started receiving *60+* magazine in the post after he turned sixty, and I imagine he ran twice as far and twice as fast as usual the following morning.

I can't sustain my concentration for longer than half an hour, and it feels good to blame the previous day's events for once, even though I know that the past few months have seen me experiencing the same difficulties maintaining any sense of focus, and all while stone-cold sober. I close the lid of my laptop, lie there for a while listening to the sound of Agnar taking a shower, drying his hair, packing his bag, his characteristically arrhythmic sequence of footsteps as he runs down the stairs and makes his way into the kitchen – I've no idea if there's any food in the fridge, I hope that Olaf's stocked up – puts something in his bag, goes into the hallway, pulls on his shoes, slams the front door. He doesn't shout goodbye. It suddenly feels so crucial to call him back, hold him close, understand; I long to run after him, yet still I lie there.

◈

Several hours later, when I hear Olaf's bicycle on the gravel driveway and Hedda's earnest laughter – how can he make her laugh that way after a long day at nursery? – I get up. I quickly pull on a pair of leggings and an old checked shirt I find hidden at the bottom of the wardrobe, the only item of clothing I can find that doesn't look as if it will chafe uncomfortably against my skin. I run my hands through my hair, make the bed, leave the laptop open on the desk in the corner, open Word and place a notebook and pen beside it. I go down to see Olaf and Hedda, who've come into the kitchen where they now stand in their coats, each of them peeling a banana. There are two full carrier bags on the bench.

Olaf casts a glance in my direction, looks down at his banana, then looks back at me as if he's missed something. He looks at my shirt and smiles.

'I'd forgotten about that one,' he says.

I don't get it, and I look at him with puzzlement.

'My shirt,' he says.

I realise that it's Olaf's old shirt, the one I adopted when I was pregnant with Agnar. Back then, just like now, it was the only item of clothing that didn't pull or rub uncomfortably, draping loosely over my stomach instead, and I think I wore it every day for four months straight.

I smile and nod, starting to unpack the bags.

'Thanks for doing the shopping,' I say.

He doesn't respond. He doesn't ask about yesterday or why I slept on the sofa, but instead simply demolishes his entire banana in two bites to Hedda's great excitement, then leaves the kitchen.

'Did you have fun at nursery?' I ask Hedda.

She nods and runs out into the hallway, fetches her backpack and carefully pulls out at least ten folded pieces of paper. Some are covered in stickers and drawings, others feature only a half-finished pencil stroke, and for a moment I catch myself thinking that nursery should try restraining her creativity, just a little, but I stop the thought in its tracks.

'Gosh, they're lovely,' I say to Hedda. 'Are they Christmas cards?'

'Yes,' she replies, laying them all on the kitchen table. 'We have to send them in the post,' she adds.

'Oh really?' I reply, and feel annoyed once again, cursing the person whose useless, pedagogical benevolence led them to explain that Christmas cards ought to be sent in the post. 'Who should we send them to, do you think?' I ask her more gently, the image of the other children's enthusiastic parents in my mind.

'This one is for Daddy and you,' Hedda begins, pointing at one.

'Well, we probably don't need to post that one, then,' I say, relieved. 'You can leave that one in the post box at the end of the driveway.'

She doesn't understand what I mean, and I can't be bothered to explain.

'This one is for Agnar,' she says, pointing at the next one. 'And this one is for Grandma and Grandad,' she says.

It hits me that I still don't know Dad's address. Hedda has had someone at nursery write on the front of the card, *To Grandma and Grandad*, spelled out clearly in black marker pen. I feel like everyone employed in nurseries and schools has the same handwriting, the women at least, soft, round letters, perhaps it's part of their training. I pick up the card. I feel sad as I read the words, but I smile at Hedda, wondering if she's forgotten that they're living apart now, or if she's just too young to understand the concept. For a split second I imagine next year's card, Grandma's name and Morten's beside it. I feel as if I'm about to break down, then I remember Håkon and Ellen's condescension and pull myself together. I clear my throat.

'You know, Hedda, we could just give all of these cards to the people they're meant for, we don't need to post them. Don't you want to see how happy Auntie Ellen is to get your card?' I say, even though I know that Ellen will probably just point out Hedda's slapdash approach to her artwork. She thinks it does children good to grasp that merit comes as a result of effort, and that there's no value to be found in praising a Christmas card, for instance, if it's clear that Hedda's work has been sloppy.

Fortunately, Hedda nods.

'When can we give them the cards?' she asks.

I don't realise I'm thinking it before I speak:

'Maybe we should see if everyone wants to come over on Sunday?'

'Yes!' Hedda cries, smiling.

◈

'I feel bad,' I say to Olaf.

For the first time in a long while, we've come to bed at the same time. These past few weeks I've gone to bed on my own while Olaf has sat up doing something or other, or when he and Agnar have been in the middle of a film or a television series – either that, or I've waited until he's fallen asleep before joining him. After meeting up with Ellen and Håkon and my encounter with the man at the bar just yesterday, and following Agnar's coldness this morning, which was intended to make a very clear point to me, I lie down and shuffle closer to Olaf. He hesitates before turning to face me and putting his arm around me, over the duvet, but still, it's such a conciliatory act that it brings a tear to my eye.

'I think it's a good idea,' Olaf says. 'It's about time we normalised the whole situation.'

'Mum has a new partner,' I say, refusing to give any nuance to the situation in my explanation to Olaf, keen to gauge his reaction.

He falls silent.

'There's something I need to tell you,' he says after a short while, and I freeze up in the knowledge that he knew about it all along, that I'm the only one who's been frozen out of every conversation over the past six months, and all without knowing why.

'Did you know about it too?' I ask him eventually, as Olaf lies there in silence.

'What? No, no,' he says, chuckling. 'How could I have known?'

I shrug my shoulders under the duvet, fill my lungs with air. I haven't drawn breath for what must be about a minute now, and I realise then that that's not the worst thing that Olaf could have to say to me. The worst thing is what's yet to come. I tense up as Olaf clears his throat, and I feel his body working up to something.

ELLEN

Simen has stuck some of my misspelled notes upon the fridge. I still have to read them two or three times to spot what's wrong with them, but it's always amusing once I do.

Early on in our relationship, Simen found it strange that I'd chosen a career which had so much to do with language given the fact that I was dyslexic. Not that strange, really, I replied, I've always been more interested in language and communication than anyone else I know, precisely *because* I'm dyslexic. The feeling that there is a system I can't prise open and force my way inside remains with me to this day, just as I remember it from my days at primary school. Endless lines of unbreakable code, inscrutable until I devised my own method that didn't involve reading word by word, but instead saw me guessing entire sentences simply by picking out a few familiar words. It was surprisingly successful for a surprisingly long time, when I think back on it, but then again, that probably tells you a lot more about the level of reading books they used back then, I tell Simen. I can't remember feeling any shame about my inability to read, not like others with dyslexia have described; for a long time, I believed that I *could* read. It was only at secondary school, when my dyslexia was discovered by one of my Norwegian teachers, that I realised that I'd never actually *read* anything at all. It was to become one of my life's greatest challenges, altering an internalised system I'd trained myself to master, a system that seemed to work, in spite of everything. I put every effort into convincing myself that a method that slowed me down and often caused me to make *more* mistakes than before was the right and proper way of doing things, a method in which the pointy bits of every letter seemed to poke the wrong way up and down and all over the place, endlessly tripping me up in my attempts to make things work.

Even so, my clashes with the letters of the alphabet only resulted in making me all the more preoccupied with language. The knowledge that I'd never master the written word in the same way as my peers drove my interest and obsession, and I became fascinated with the other side of things, the effect words and letters could have on people, the power they wielded. That's something the two of us have in common, at the very least, a firm belief in the power of words, Mum says, having never accepted any criticism for the fact that neither she nor Dad discovered my dyslexia early on. Quite the contrary, in fact – both had objected when my teacher had contacted them to discuss an issue she believed them to be aware of. She's a fluent reader, Dad assured her, better than her older sister, Mum said. But when they accompanied me to a session with a speech and language therapist, where one test made it impossible for me to *cheat* – which was how the speech and language therapist referred to the method I'd relied on up until that point – they saw with their own eyes that I wasn't, in fact, intuitively capable of reading simple words like *play* and *walk* and *window* without issue.

No one else in the family is dyslexic, Mum explained to the speech and language therapist, eventually recognising that even if this didn't represent a problem, it certainly presented a *challenge* – Dad was ahead of his time in that respect, refusing even back in the 1980s to refer to something as a *problem*, preferring to label things a *challenge*. He has certain challenges to overcome, he would say about our cousin with multiple disabilities, a young man who had to wait until his adult years to gain access to places that had previously been the domain of those who could climb stairs – it was as if Dad felt his paralysis and illness should be viewed as a struggle to overcome. Håkon, Liv and I have always poked fun at this habit of his, they've got certain challenges to overcome, we would say about awful situations that cropped up in conversation, until it became something we said in all seriousness about everything from natural catastrophes and epidemics to celebrities' various psychological disorders.

I've never managed to get my head around the trend for describing genuine problems as challenges, almost as if it were intended as a vague gesture of goodwill to the person in question; I'd much rather my doctor tell me I have a *problem* if I'm simply not able to fall pregnant, for instance, rather than hearing it described as something I should challenge to no avail.

Either way, and taking both sides of the family into consideration, I was the only one as far back as anyone could remember who was to experience the challenges presented by dyslexia. I don't think about it all that much these days, it's just a part of who I am, and in spite of everything, it's much easier to live with since the introduction of computers and mobile phones with autocorrect.

◈

Some of the handwritten notes on the fridge had been written when I wasn't concentrating, when I've been in a rush on my way out the door. Mostly they're about things that need to be bought or collected, remembered or fixed.

Don't forget hopsital! one says. It's a new one, just three weeks old, and was intended to remind Simen to meet me at the hospital. An extra ultrasound examination I'd had a few weeks ago at a private clinic, just to be on the safe side, had revealed that I *might* have a small deformity of the womb. Half of me was relieved to finally receive the tiniest hint of an answer, while the other half immediately wondered if I needed to share this information with Simen. I couldn't keep it to myself for longer than four awful hours and eventually told him over dinner. I felt sure I could see the relief in his face, no doubt because it confirmed what we both already knew, that the blame lay with me, and he became extra generous and considerate with the information I shared. Of course I'll come with you, Simen said when I told him I was due for an examination known as hysterosalpingography. But can you spell it? he asked me, and I laughed for the first time that day.

◈

They couldn't find anything conclusive. But occasionally the examination itself, the contrast agent we use, it encourages things to open
up and helps in its own way, the doctor said, you just have to keep
trying. Simen looked disheartened, and I knew there were few things
on earth less appealing than the prospect of continuing to try. I don't
see Simen's body as anything other than mechanical these days, I have
to close my eyes and concentrate in order to recall how attractive I
find him, his long, lean biceps, his broad shoulders, his neck, his large
hands. His slightly crooked nose, his heavy brows. His gaze upon me.
The latter has all but disappeared these days, he no longer looks at me
the way he once did, and the grudge he holds against my body is all too
unmistakeable.

November has come around, and we haven't been trying, we
haven't even talked about it. Plus, there's been the American election, and I've been busy trying to explain the rhetorical strategies
used by each of the candidates to journalists working in newspapers,
radio and television. Håkon doesn't think it takes a master's degree
in rhetoric to see through Hillary or Trump. You're talking about
speech-making as if it's some kind of trick, something to be exposed,
I said. That's a naive take on things, I wouldn't have expected quite
such an oversimplification from you. Anyway, it's very revealing the
way you use the surname of the male candidate and the forename of
the female one, I added. I wouldn't have expected such a cheap shot
from *you*, Håkon replied.

I rang Håkon for the first time in a long while after visiting Mum
and overhearing a phone call with a softly spoken man. My first impulse
was to call Liv, but for some reason it felt simpler to call Håkon, less
intimate somehow. Have you spoken to Mum lately? I asked him. Nah,
well, a little, he replied. Did you know she has a partner? I asked him.
What, Morten, you mean? he replied. How do you know his name?
Have you met him? I asked, surprised at Håkon's awareness of the situation. No, of course not, Mum just mentioned him a few days ago,
Håkon said. I couldn't think of one good reason why Mum should tell
Håkon about a new partner while hiding the situation from me. Does

Liv know too? I asked him. I'm not sure, but I assume so, Håkon said, she always knows everything, he added, and actually it is typical of her to confide in both Liv and Håkon before ever telling me anything. But what's the deal with it? I asked. They're just friends, Håkon said. *Friends*, what, like Grandma's 'friends'? Grandma always referred to our boyfriends and girlfriends as friends – Olaf remained Liv's friend until long after they were married. I don't know, Håkon said. I don't think they've really defined it yet, as such, he said.

He explained that Mum and Morten had met in Sicily, and that they'd kept in touch after that. That was basically all he knew about it, he said. I let it go, couldn't work out if his approach to things was as casual as he made it appear, or if he was actually upset. My irritation took aim elsewhere, shifting instead to Dad and Mum, who were always so keen to protect Håkon against any evil in the world, but who, as a result of their close bond with him and his dependence on them, burdened him with more than they ever did Liv and me.

Have you spoken to Liv lately? I asked him instead. No, I haven't heard from her, he said. Have you? No, I said, she's probably just busy with work and the kids and everything else. Yes, that must be it, Håkon said. Although Håkon is much better at making small talk than I am, and generally finds it easy to talk to anyone at any time about anything, a silence arose between us. Eventually he told me he had to go, and I replied that we'd talk again soon, without quite believing it, but it was an automatic response, and he agreed before ending the call.

As if she'd been listening in on the entire thing, Liv sent a message to us both the following day, asking if we'd like to meet up for a drink.

◈

We met up in Tøyen a few days ago, the most convenient location for Håkon, naturally. He's bought a flat in Kampen. Even though he lives closest and ought to have been the first to turn up, I arrived ten minutes before him. Liv messaged to tell us that she was running late, apologising so profusely that I didn't have the heart to let the frustration I might otherwise feel take control – I've never understood how certain people can constantly be running late for things. People like my siblings, for instance. There's nothing cool about turning up late, I've told Håkon in the past. I suspect he thinks that's the case, that he thinks by refusing to worry about five minutes here or there, or to think about *time* at all, he's somehow displaying strength of character. It's just plain rude, I tell him, showing such unwillingness to take other people's time or prior arrangements seriously just exposes a person's own insecurities, I say. I think the word 'rude' is the greatest insult anyone in our family could give or receive. It was introduced by Mum and Dad as something awful from an early age, something to be feared, a trait considered equal to being vulgar or brash. On several occasions over the past few days, I've wanted to call Mum and tell her how brash her behaviour is, how incredibly *vulgar* it is to meet a man on holiday in the Mediterranean when you've only just separated from your husband, and in your seventies, no less.

Håkon walked into the café in Tøyen at ten past seven. It's ten past seven, I told him as he hung his jacket over the back of his chair. Liv's not here either, he said apologetically. No, but at least she got in touch to tell us she'd be late, I said. Sorry, Håkon said. Can I get you a beer? Something to help you bear the burden of your pain and suffering? Yes, a toast on the occasion of Clinton's wake, I said, knowing that Håkon would launch into the same discussion we've had several times over the past year. Talking to my siblings is one of my favourite things to do – the combination of everything that goes without saying and all those things that still surprise, the similarities and vast differences in the ways we think and express ourselves. Though they're capable of surprising me with fresh arguments, I find that I can almost always predict the direction they're headed in and tend to recognise the build-up.

I hadn't predicted any of the accusations that Liv launched at Håkon and me when she did finally arrive twenty minutes later.

Liv and I have always argued, and right up until we were teenagers, we even engaged in physical fights. I remember how Liv used to grip on to the fridge with one hand to gain more leverage for the punches or shoves she'd aim at me, while I pulled her hair or dug my nails into her forearm, scratching and nipping her. But very few of those fights left their mark on us, as far as I can remember; they've never been significant. Rather, they've been part of our process of socialisation, and have given us something to laugh about with hindsight; the after-effects don't run deep within our psyches. In those few arguments I do remember, something else played a part, like that one summer at the cabin when Liv said that Mum and Dad were getting divorced and it was all my fault – I spent the entire autumn walking around with a unpleasant lump in my stomach, looking for signs that it might be true. There was an undeniably horrible atmosphere that summer and autumn, and it's all your fault, Liv said. I was convinced that what she was saying was true, that it was all a result of my difficult behaviour during the summer.

Now I realise it had nothing to do with me or with the hormones that made my mind and body so unrecognisable to me at the time. Nothing to do with the fact that I felt angrier and more upset than ever before, that I hated my body and marched along the beach bundled up in enormous hoodies, that Mum and Dad both left me feeling permanently enraged. In my eyes they were stupid and unfair, and I constantly challenged everything they did, making awful, sly digs at Mum at every possible opportunity, rejecting any attempt she made to get close to me. The situation culminated in me knocking over an entire pan of crabs one evening towards the end of the summer as part of an ongoing argument I'd been having with Dad, who had refused to let me visit a friend in the neighbouring cabin because our uncle and aunt were coming to visit.

Whenever there was any sign of an argument brewing between Mum and Dad in the autumn that followed, Liv would look at me as if it were my fault. I still remember how horrible it felt to have her blame me, both because I feared that she might be right, but also because I've always wanted to impress Liv, to make her proud of me, even to this day.

They should have separated, I think to myself now. There's something deeply disturbing in Dad's repetition that things haven't been right between them for years, if they ever had been right at all, in fact – the idea that they've gone along with things for so long while wishing for something different all this time.

◈

The doorbell goes the day after I meet up with Liv and Håkon. I'm lying in bed, my white pillow case flecked with eye make-up. I've called the office to tell them I'll be working from home, as I often do, and that I'm not quite feeling myself – it's true to a certain extent. The conversation between Håkon, Liv and me has left me feeling sick, and my head is aching after the argument I had with Simen before he left first thing.

As I'd been lying beside him this morning, before either of us had properly woken up, he had pushed me away in a fleeting moment of pure instinct. We were both half-asleep at the time, and I'd placed a hand on his chest without thinking, my body driven by a vague desire for intimacy and some sense of belonging, no doubt triggered by the confrontation with Liv and Håkon the previous evening. Simen had woken up with a start, pushing me away with a shout. He'd seemed taken aback after the fact, embarrassed perhaps, I can't be sure, but either way he was quick to get up out of bed. You could at least have asked me first, he muttered crossly, looking for something to wear for the day ahead. What, ask if I can touch you? I replied. Simen said nothing, making his way into the bathroom and turning on the shower. Later, I heard the front door close from where I lay in the bedroom; I think it might be the first time he's ever left without saying goodbye.

◈

I get up reluctantly when I hear the doorbell, pull on my dressing gown. I shouldn't have slept naked, I should have worn pyjamas or a t-shirt so Simen would have known there was a secure line of defence separating us; he's probably been trying to get away ever since I dived into bed last night, naked, drunk and seemingly without a care in the world.

Only salesmen and TV licence people call at your door without warning, and I always go out onto the balcony to check who's waiting downstairs before letting anyone in. I lean over the railing and look down. Dad is standing there in his exercise gear, jogging on the spot four floors below me, his thick, grey hair like a lion's mane under his hat. It's cold; quick, small puffs of frosty air reveal the fact that he's out of breath. I stand looking down on him for just a little longer than I should; he tips his head back and looks up, doesn't know which floor I live on, he's never been here before. I jump back, don't think he catches sight of me, then run back inside and feign surprise at hearing his voice on the entryphone.

I hurry into the bathroom and wipe away the make-up that's become smeared beneath my puffy eyes, pulling on some jogging bottoms and Simen's hoodie. I only just make it to the door as Dad makes his way around the last turn in the stairwell and comes into view just below me. He's quick on his feet in spite of his sore knee. He must be in much better shape than me, I hate exercise. Both Liv and Håkon have inherited his impulse to move, to exercise – Liv goes as far as to describe herself as being dependent on it, she feels like she experiences genuine withdrawal symptoms if she doesn't manage to fit a run into her schedule. I'm more like Mum when it comes to that kind of thing, we're more laid-back, the two of us, she's often said to me, when we've been on holiday or away together and the other three have gone off for a run or some other physical activity. Often, she and I have settled into our armchairs or cosied up on the sofa, enjoying a beer and some crisps, a bar of chocolate or some other unhealthy treat, and I still can't imagine anything nicer than those short, special, somehow secret hours spent with her.

'Well, you get a bit of exercise for free here,' Dad says, nodding at the stairs before removing his hat and giving me a hug.

'Well, yes and no,' I say, smiling and pointing at the lift door behind him.

He laughs.

'Have you been out for a run?' I ask, letting him past me and into the hallway.

'Yes, I was just out and thought I'd see if you were at home, plus, I haven't seen your flat yet,' he says.

'No, things have been busy lately,' I reply, my conscience and sense of self-righteousness busy doing battle with one another. 'Do you want a coffee? Tea?'

'I'd love a tea,' Dad replies, removing his shoes.

I make my way into the kitchen and leave Dad to have a look around the flat on his own, listen to him opening bathroom cabinets and bedroom cupboards, letting himself out onto the balcony, hearing knocking sounds as he taps on walls and pipes and goodness knows what else. I can't help but smile, pleased that he still checks these things, happy to know he's looking out for me. Simen would probably see it as a disparaging move on Dad's part, the way he goes around doing his thing like this, and I'm glad he's not at home to see it. It's as if the atmosphere in the flat changes with Dad here, the place feels warmer, smaller.

'A lovely place you've got here, Ellen,' Dad says as he comes into the kitchen.

'Yes, we're happy here,' I say, pouring the boiling water into the teapot and placing it in front of Dad on the small kitchen table before digging out two cups.

'The layout here is almost the same as in mine, though my place is quite a bit smaller,' he says, measuring the size of the kitchen in his mind's eye using the skirting board as a guide.

Dad is taller and broader than the average person, and my mind has a tendency to exaggerate these features. He's always represented something strong and safe and stable in my eyes. Now, as I picture him in his little flat, he suddenly seems small, weak, sad.

'So, how's it going living on your own?' I ask him, as if he were a student who's just moved away from home.

'Fine, thanks, still a little unusual. And a little empty, I have to admit,' Dad replies. I ought to have been to visit him.

'You could always call off the divorce,' I say, smiling even though I mean it, but also in an attempt to check whether he's heard about Morten or not.

'That's not just up to me,' he says.

'And if it were up to you, would you be moving back?' I ask him.

'No, that would be too easy. I still think this is for the best,' Dad replies, and I'm not sure if he means it or if it's his pride that's causing him to say it, or a sense of shame, or perhaps a combination of all these things and more.

I pour us both a cup of tea, the same tea he and Mum have always bought, and the only tea that Liv, Håkon and I drink.

'I think you're being silly,' I tell him.

'Your mother and I are two relatively well-informed people who have reached this decision together. As I said, there's too little left to be drawn from our marriage,' and once again I have the desire to point out the strangeness in thinking that anyone should draw anything but children and grandchildren from a marriage at their age, but I hold back, can't face the discussion that would ensue.

'What size is the flat?' Dad asks, changing the subject in a neutral tone.

'I think it's about seventy-five square metres, including the balcony,' I say.

He nods, smiling.

'Have you spoken to Håkon?' he asks after a short pause.

'Yes, I actually met up with him and Liv yesterday. We had a beer in Tøyen.'

'Did you now?' Dad replies, looking almost relieved.

I don't have the heart to tell him about the conversation I had with Håkon and Liv, how awful it was, how upset Liv is, and how clearly Håkon seems to be demonstrating how unaffected he is by things. I can't bring myself to describe how we sat there, around the table, all three of us so distant, with Liv almost hostile in our presence. You do nothing, she shouted at me, you're completely irresponsible. You always leave me to deal with everything, turning up whenever you feel like it, enjoying the benefits of everything that falls within the category of family life as and when it suits you. And now here you are, leaving me to take responsibility for this, too.'

I thought she knew about Mum's new partner, I wasn't trying to make a point, I told Håkon after Liv had left. And I think I believed that she knew, but I don't know for certain; perhaps in the moment I mentioned it to Liv I wanted to hurt both her and Mum – to exact revenge for the accusations that had rained down upon me, for the injustice of being held responsible for Mum and Dad's decision. All the same, I didn't feel even the faintest hint of schadenfreude when I saw how crushed Liv was.

We've been living a lie, Liv said several times that evening, the same notion expressed in numerous different ways. Håkon was silent. It's not a lie, I tried to tell her, they might be divorcing now but it *was* real, I said, I couldn't understand what she was getting at. But today I feel myself coming around to understanding her point of view, beginning to see how the whole thing draws a veil of insincerity over every memory and experience and belief I have relating to family life, with Mum and Dad clearly able to brush off forty years of marriage, to abandon so easily the union that created us. That is, at least, how I think Liv perceives things, although I can't read her the same way I once could.

Personally, I've never felt that there's anything heroic in the act of remaining in dead-end or miserable relationships, regardless of the reasons for feeling that way – if people have children, those children will be better off with happy parents, I've always felt – and it seems helpless and rather pathetic not to break free from such a relationship. Nowadays I chop and change between standing for what I've always believed and leaning in the other direction, particularly in light of Liv's reaction – surely if they managed to hold out together for so long, they might as well keep it up for the remainder.

I want to confront Dad, to tell him about the conflict between Liv, Håkon and me, to force him to take some responsibility and to tidy up the mess he and Mum have left for us. Even so, I can't bring myself to feel angry.

It feels so safe to have him sitting here in my kitchen, I can't do anything other than cling to that feeling. He just needs to be here, to be Dad; we can pretend nothing's amiss for a short while, or at the very least pretend that I have *one* family I can pin my hopes on, trust in, rely on. I'm so tired. I'm so small.

'What are you going to do with the extra room?' Dad asks, clearly not thinking about anything other than the fact it's an empty room, not sensing what the room might be missing, ten square metres teeming with fragments of unspoken hopes and expectations.

Oh, Dad.

◈

I'm lying in bed when Simen gets home, unconcerned that it might seem like I'm trying to make a point one way or another. I haven't checked my emails or phone all day; it's the first time in as long as I can remember that I've set them to one side for so long. Liv believes I'm genuinely afflicted by Internet Addiction, and it's true that I experience physical and mental symptoms if I don't have access to the net for a few hours at a time. From a rational standpoint, I'm aware that I'm probably not missing out on anything important, and as a rule it's not crucial for me to check my emails or Facebook messages every half-hour. But it's like losing a limb, if I'm being honest, as I explained to Simen in Croatia one day when I'd managed to leave my phone behind at the hotel. It's a sense of being disconnected from the world, of being on the outside, I said. And I don't find that enjoyable in the slightest, I continued. No, but it's enjoyable for me, Simen said. He's designated at least two hours a day as mobile-free, often longer over the weekends, and he believes that it's only during those hours that he feels connected to the real world. You're just old, I tell him, that's an old-fashioned notion, the idea that the internet and the possibilities it brings aren't part of the real world.

It's just as real as that tree is, I said, pointing to a tree trunk beside the pathway one afternoon as we walked around the lake at Sognsvann – for the simple reason that Simen grows restless sitting at home without being able to use his computer, his mobile, his Netflix account and everything else that's hooked up to the internet. Simen thinks I'm wrong, that I'm the old-fashioned one – wait and see, he says, you're part of a generation for whom the internet is so new that we're all amateurs really. Everybody who grows up with it today will relate to it completely differently in the future, even a teenager nowadays has a better grasp of it than you do, a more natural relationship compared with our forced ways of using and understanding what it has to offer. I couldn't be bothered to point out the forced nature of Simen's self-imposed, clearly taxing quarantines.

The first thing I tend to do in the morning, while still lying in bed, is to check emails, news and social media on my mobile. I haven't given it a single thought today, I've simply lain there in silence without moving, barely able to formulate a single coherent thought since Dad left. I wrap my duvet around me, hear Simen making himself a coffee while on the phone to his brother. They speak to each other much more formally than I do with my siblings – they're so polite. The kind of confrontation that erupted between Håkon, Liv and me yesterday would seem absurd to them. My entire family situation would seem absurd to Simen's well-ordered family, and even though I've thought before that it must be awfully dull living in a family where so much goes unsaid, never having an honest conversation, never engaging in a real confrontation, I do wish now that my own family might occasionally have said a little *less*, kept more to themselves, been less concerned with what's authentic and 'real', values that now seem self-centred and pretentious.

I check my phone for the first time today as I listen in on Simen's conversation. I open up Facebook and an ad for a private fertility clinic pops up on my newsfeed out of the blue. I hear a rushing in my ears and feel pressure building in my chest before closing the app and putting my phone away again. I hear Simen confirm that we're still coming on

Sunday before he ends the call. I can't recall us being invited anywhere on Sunday, but then Simen's *we* might be a different *we* than the two of us, him and me. I close my eyes and pretend to be sleeping when I hear his footsteps approaching the bedroom. I hear him pause in the doorway, try to imagine what he looks like, but I can't do it, can't envisage his features, I don't know him. It strikes me how distant we are, and how strongly I'm clutching on to something I can no longer justify. He and I are no longer *we*, but instead two separate parts, unable to work together.

He knocks gently at the open door. I open my eyes.

'Are you sleeping?' he asks.

He's changed into the grey jogging bottoms that I'd pulled on earlier today, along with a white t-shirt. The curly hair I've always hoped our child would inherit sticks out from beneath a red cap. Suddenly he looks like a small child. I shake my head, sit up in bed. He sits on the edge of the bed and I pull my legs up to make room for him. I don't know if he interprets it as a rejection or something more positive, but he sighs. He looks down at the floor, then up again at me.

I hope he's going to break up with me, inwardly I pray that he's about to tell me that he can't do this any more, that he's leaving me.

'I'm sorry,' he says. 'I was pathetic this morning, I don't even know what happened, I just had this sudden sense of claustrophobia, like some kind of attack.'

I look at him. Don't know what to say.

'It's a destructive pattern. I can't live like this, we can't carry on this way,' he adds, and now it's on its way, I brace myself for it, squeezing my eyes shut.

Simen starts laughing.

'What are you doing?' he asks me.

'Bracing myself,' I reply without opening my eyes.

I feel his hand on my cheek. He strokes my hair, my bare arm, not the loaded gesture I had expected, but friendly, almost resigned, then takes my hand, squeezing it hard.

'Bracing yourself for something I'm about to do?' he says, and I can hear from his tone that he's still smiling.

'Yes,' I say.

'Well, so you should,' he says aloud after a short pause, then climbs on top of me, his every gesture exaggerated, pulling me close in a great big hug, pinching my side, kissing my forehead, and it's so lovely just to be close to him without any lingering expectation that I laugh and cry in turn. I actively ignore the fact that this conversation hasn't gone anywhere, that everything remains suspended in the air between us like a cluster of barrage balloons.

◆

Simen and I met at a party held by a mutual acquaintance. I knew who he was – and I always mention it when I tell anyone the story of our meeting; I don't know why it's so important for me to point it out, it just seems so trite to say that you met at a party. I'm convinced that it's an opinion I've inherited from Mum and Dad. They've always told us that they met at university rather than at the party it turned out had actually formed the backdrop of their first encounter.

I've been captivated by that story for as long as I can remember. Even though it's not all that exciting in itself, there's something mystical and faraway about the idea of the two of them in their younger days, the lives they had before me and Liv and Håkon. Plus, it's virtually natural law that offspring take an interest in how their parents met; that meeting is the starting point of one's entire existence, I explain to Simen, who has never asked his parents how they met, telling me he's either never been told, or that he must have forgotten. That would be a first, I said, you could never forget something so significant.

Mum and Dad usually say they met at a student debate. Dad tells us that Mum put her hand up and posed several critical questions, and that he was drawn to her engagement and strong opinions. Mum thinks his memory of events is less than perfect, that she was only curious and asked one prudent question, as far as she can recall – she and Dad tend to have rather different views on how politically active they were during their student days, but maybe they were engaged to different degrees, I've suggested, though neither of them has wanted to hear it. Either way, for a long time the approved version of events claimed that they had met at this debate, right up until one day we discovered that it had actually been at a party a few weeks later where they'd spoken for the first time. It made a deep impression on me as a fourteen or fifteen-year-old to discover that their starting point, and therefore also my own, had been so different to the story I had initially been told.

I've always taken it for granted that they've been reliable, that they are essentially our witnesses, and it's never occurred to me until now that there are numerous things they might have embellished over time, kept hidden or quite simply lied about. Even though I've always thought they were different, and though I've never quite understood their marriage – and never thought too much about it, for that matter – I've taken it completely for granted that *they* found meaning within it, that they've had something I've never seen or understood, something I couldn't quite grasp, but which obviously existed beneath the surface. I've thought that I just lack the experience required to understand it, as Liv tends to say.

When they first told us about the divorce in Italy, it was one of the first things to occur to me, the fact that they'd never been particularly affectionate with one another, not like Simen and I are – were – but Liv corrected me, unable to curb her anger. You wouldn't understand how much love there is in everything they do for one another, everything they are to one another, she said. But she and Olaf have a pretty dull, uneventful relationship; she's simply copied Mum and Dad's marriage, leaving her no choice but to dispute my point.

When I next check my phone, just to see what time it is, Liv has sent me a message. I regret checking, turn the phone over without reading the message, I just want to stay where I am – Simen and I have been lying in bed for a while, minutes or hours, I can't be sure, just holding one another, talking about the things we used to fill our days with, small anecdotes about our bosses or colleagues, rumours, possibilities. But time sprang back into action when I saw the message from Liv and I can't leave it any longer than a few minutes before opening it.

'Liv's wondering if we want to go over for dinner this Sunday,' I say to Simen. 'It's a group message to everyone, Mum and Dad too.'

'Has the day of reckoning arrived?' Simen asks.

'No, I think it's more a case of reconciliation,' I say, but don't feel in any way certain that what I'm saying is true.

'We were supposed to be going over to Magnus's on Sunday,' Simen says. 'But there's no harm in us doing our own things. You can go to your family and I can go to mine.'

I remember it now; his brother had invited us for dinner more than three weeks ago. I want to respond to Simen in the way I would have done before: Look what happens when people do things your family's way, planning in minute detail way too far in advance; things end up being forgotten about. And Simen would have said: Look what happens when you never plan anything, like in your family, then it clashes with everything that's already been planned.

'I know it's a long time since we spent any time with your family, and I do want to see them soon,' I say. 'But what with Liv asking, I feel like it'd be hard to say no. Especially after yesterday,' I add, realising that I haven't told Simen about what happened, and neither does he ask me to elaborate.

'That's OK. I think you should go to Liv's,' he says. 'It might be good for us to have some input from elsewhere.'

◆

Even though I force myself to arrive five minutes late, naturally I'm still the first to turn up. Why is it that the rest of the family are such incompetent timekeepers when I'm so punctual? There's been a fault in our make-up somewhere along the line.

You do know that you're adopted? Liv said when we were young. She claimed she could prove it by asking Mum and Dad to place their arms across their chest in the shape of a cross. Do it in whatever way feels most natural, Liv said one day as we were standing in the kitchen making dinner, and Liv had brought me all the way downstairs to show me the secret test in action. Look, both of them, and then me, she said, crossing her skinny arms, we do it the same way, with our right arm over our left. You try, she said. I remember deliberating trying to place the same arm on top as they had done, but it just didn't work, it felt all wrong, and my arms did the opposite of their own accord. Mum and Dad laughed, not realising Liv had told me beforehand that it was an adoption test. Well, well, well, I'm starting to wonder where you came from, Ellen, Dad teased. That would be telling, Mum said, elbowing Dad in the ribs.

I hadn't ever thought about how happy they were at that point in time until now, the way they teased one another so effortlessly; the memory of just how awful it was to see it confirmed that I was adopted had cast a shadow over their faces and the atmosphere and the looks they exchanged.

I ring Liv and Olaf's doorbell for once, rather than walking around the house and looking in through the veranda doors before either making my way in or knocking at the window if it's locked. It's Liv who comes to the door; she's wearing make-up and looks better than she did just under a week ago, despite the fact that she looks even thinner now than before – she's wearing slim-fitting black trousers and a wide-sleeved, low-cut blouse that I could never get away with wearing without looking cheap and rotund. Liv looks fashionable, almost coolly distant, and I hug her quickly to break the invisible barrier between us created by everything left unsaid since I last saw her. She gives me a quick squeeze then makes her way towards the kitchen, telling me she's left something in the oven and I should join the others in the living room.

Agnar is sitting in front of the television in the living room with his back to me, and I place an ice-cold hand on the back of his neck. He jumps and turns around, smiling when he realises it's me. There's a momentary pause. A distance has grown between us too, made more obvious by the fact that Agnar looks completely different now – he must have grown ten centimetres over the summer and autumn, he's had a haircut, his shoulders and jaw look broader.

He gets up and I hug him.

'Have you been eating magic beans lately, or is it just your extremely good genes to blame for all this?' I ask him as I let go and realise that he's just as tall as I am.

'Must be genetic,' Olaf says from behind me, and I turn around.

'Hmm, you seem to have shrunk since I last saw you,' I tell him, smiling.

Olaf laughs. I wonder if I should hug him too, but he maintains a safe distance, his arms crossed over his chest, also with his right arm over his left; after several years working in the field of communications, this no longer calls to mind adoption, as it once did, but instead hints at a person's need to defend themselves.

'Is everyone coming?' I ask him.

'I think so, yes. But no Simen?' he says.

I shake my head, wonder what sort of *input* Simen is receiving at his brother's just now, if he's holding his three-month-old nephew, making eye contact with him, if he's stroking a hand over his soft little head, lulling him to sleep and feeling the weight of a tiny person in his arms, the weight of what's missing from his own life.

'No, he'd already arranged to go for dinner at his brother's house,' I tell him. 'Is Håkon coming alone too?'

Olaf nods. I don't know why I asked about Håkon. Perhaps I wanted to underline the fact that there's something not quite right with him, either, never having a partner, not beyond his odd connections with strange women who, much like Grandma, he never refers to as girlfriends – they're only ever *friends*. But that's where the similarity between Håkon and Grandma's way of looking at things ends; I think Håkon and Grandma, if she were still with us, would have very different ideas about the kinds of things that friends get up to together.

Do you think Håkon is gay? I once asked Mum a few years ago. She didn't need any time to reflect, she'd clearly wondered the same herself. No, she replied quickly, I just think he's a little immature. Håkon was twenty-five at the time. OK, but he might be immature in the sense that he doesn't dare come out of the closet, I suggested. What closet? Mum asked, I think Håkon is well aware that none of us would raise an eyebrow if that's how things were, she continued. We're not his entire world, Mum, I said, smiling at her. We're not far off it, she replied, looking as if she hoped that might be true.

My theory about Håkon was rooted in stereotypical views. Liv and I had discussed it a few years beforehand, the fact that he was so sensitive and quick to take other people's feelings to heart, vain and concerned about how we and he looked. Plus, he preferred sleeping in a nightie rather than his Superman pyjamas when he was young, Liv reminded me. Have you considered the fact that he grew up with two rather over-bearing sisters? Mum asked. That what he says and how he feels has been influenced by two women he's spent his life trying to keep up with? Håkon hasn't tried to keep up with Liv and me, I replied, he's always done his own thing, thought his own thoughts and made his own decisions. If anything, he's constantly countering the arguments we make. And what does that tell you? Mum asked me. I know she was getting at the fact that Håkon felt he could square up to us in a debate. Mum considers it a compliment to live in unspoken disagreement with someone, she feels that finding an adversary worthy of engaging in discussion with is a compliment in its own right. You've got no patience for engaging in discussion with anyone who's opinion doesn't matter to you, Mum often says. I don't doubt that Håkon thinks the opinions that Liv and I hold are of some importance, but I'm also fairly certain that he feels he grew apart from us both a long time ago, and that any sense of appreciation he has for us lies in the fact that we're family.

Why don't you just ask him? Mum said at the end of our conversation, it's hardly an offensive question, she added. Ask him yourself, it's not like it matters, I retorted. In spite of the almost entirely sincere political correctness we were both so keen to demonstrate, neither of us ever did ask Håkon. And a few weeks later he appeared with a new 'friend' in tow, which Mum called specially to tell me all about – since it was of so little consequence, after all.

Even so, Håkon doesn't come to see Liv on his own, he comes with Dad. Both Liv and I watch from the kitchen window as they pull up in Dad's car, but neither of us comments on it. I wonder if Liv finds it as surprising as I do. How much do Håkon and Dad actually see of one another? And then I also start to wonder how much contact Liv and Dad have – if the chance visit earlier in the week was actually the result of a pang of guilty conscience after calling on Håkon and Liv in this way.

◆

I've always bragged about the relationship between Liv, Håkon and me. I've never felt the same jealousy I'd heard friends or partners talk about, constantly locked in bitter, petty competition with their siblings. I've always hoped that Håkon and Liv would do well in life, better than me, if I'm honest, and there's nothing self-sacrificing or altruistic about that, quite the opposite, in fact: I see us as one and the same entity, so intertwined that if one of us enjoys success, it reflects well on the other two. It's also liberating when things go well for them, a cause for great relief; I no longer need to worry about them – on the other hand, an almost physical discomfort weighs down upon me when either of them is struggling with something, exposing the disadvantage of such a close bond.

Even though I've never been jealous, I've always felt that Mum and Dad have shown the other two a different degree of attention to that which they've shown me. I don't think they love Liv or Håkon more than they love me, but in some sense my siblings represent something more important than I do. Liv is the eldest, and the eldest child is, of course, an event unto themselves by virtue of being the firstborn, the one who changed two parents' entire existence, the child who represents the shift from life as a couple to that of a family unit. Håkon is the youngest, and the youngest in any family is the one who completes the unit, who puts a full stop neatly in place and makes things whole, the one who benefits from all the trying and failing with any previous children, the one who positively gleams in virtue of always being the smallest, and in this case, the deeply longed-for third child. Add a heart condition and an overdeveloped emotional intelligence into the mix and you are left with a recipe for something approaching a child prodigy.

My role in family life is less well established, in my own mind, yes, but also for Mum and Dad. I'm difficult to place, like a filler between the other two. This might be underlined by the fact that it took so long for Mum to fall pregnant with Håkon; she spent long episodes of the first eight years of my life waiting for him to appear. There was an unspoken conviction that they were waiting for someone. When he finally arrived, he took up so much room with his special needs and his extra special behaviour, as I've explained it to Simen. It sounds like jealousy to me, Simen said. But it isn't. I'm not jealous. It can hurt sometimes, but it doesn't take the form of anger or bitterness against either Håkon or Liv, it's more like a painful sense of certainty that flares up from time to time in arguments or other situations, particularly in Mum's company, a learned recognition that I go unseen, an awareness that Liv and Håkon are more important than I am, and through the years it's become a self-fulfilling prophecy, as was demonstrated in the article on favourite children that Simen once referred to – I've made myself more independent, sought less validation and credit, and in doing so, I've also received less than the other two.

Standing here in the kitchen with Liv now, watching Håkon and Dad outside the window, that feeling gains new ground. The feeling that has haunted me more and more often and in very different ways over this past year, a sense of genuine jealousy, the feeling that I want what Liv and Håkon have: attention, consideration, sympathy, comfort – I want to be recognised as being just as important, perhaps even more so.

◆

Mum arrives last. I haven't spoken to her since that evening I spent at hers a few weeks ago. This is the first time we've all been together since Italy. I don't know how much contact Mum and Dad have had with each other, how much he knows, but he's quick to embrace her in his usual way, as if it's entirely normal now for them to greet one another in this distanced manner. It's hard to wrap my head around and I look at Liv and Håkon to see if they're reacting to what's happening, but Liv is standing with her back to them stirring the contents of a pan while Håkon is in the middle of a conversation with Agnar. It's as if nothing has happened, everything going on at this moment in time could easily have unfolded in precisely the same way a year ago, five years ago, and I don't know if we're good at pretending or if the change is simply less tangible in practice than it is in theory.

'Hedda has something she'd like to give you,' Liv says, coming through into the living room from the kitchen, rubbing her hands against her thighs, looking around at everyone, her eyes lingering on me. 'Something she's really been looking forward to handing out, just so you all know.'

I summon all of my effort to raise a smile.

'Hedda,' Liv calls upstairs.

Hedda comes downstairs in a blue Disney *Frozen* dress, then hands out folded pieces of paper on which someone has written our names. On my piece, Hedda has drawn a long, red line with a curl at one end. Inside the folded sheet are two more squiggles in the middle of the page, one blue and one black, and a Merry Christmas sticker. Mum and Dad have been given a card together, and they seem to be attempting to outdo one another in describing to Hedda just how fantastic her squiggles are, guessing them to be Father Christmas or a reindeer or perhaps a Christmas tree? Hedda smiles and shakes her head.

'It's a stone,' she says contentedly.

'A stone!' Mum and Dad cry in chorus, both equally animated.

All of a sudden, a silence falls and they look anywhere but at one another, almost embarrassed by their shared outburst – for a short moment perhaps they are reminded of everything they still share, of all the years together, the experiences and memories accumulated within their bodies, which no doubt reveal themselves several times a day in just the same way without them thinking much about it or perhaps even realising.

'And is this a stone, too?' I ask Hedda, crouching down in front of her with my Christmas card to fill the silence that has suddenly descended upon us, pointing at the blue squiggle inside the card.

Hedda shakes her head and giggles hesitantly, still too young to sense disappointment or to feel at all offended when no one can make out what she's drawn, simply contented with her pencil strokes, which make no attempt to imitate reality, and which have now evolved into some kind of guessing game. She's still wary of me, uncertain about approaching me; she remains watchful, acting differently to the way she does around others in the family.

'I think it looks a little bit like Daddy,' I remark without looking at Olaf, holding Hedda's gaze. 'This is his head, and this big circle is his tummy,' I say, pointing at the biggest squiggle.

Hedda breaks into laughter, safer in the knowledge that I'm joking around with her, getting closer to her, and I feel her breath on my face as she laughs. I want to hold her tiny body close to mine, to feel her arms around my neck.

'Time to eat,' Liv says.

◈

'This is lovely, Liv,' Mum says as we eat the venison stew Liv has made. 'Have you added something to it?'

Something means something other than what's in Mum's recipe, which she inherited from her own mother.

'I added star anise to the stock,' Liv replies, and Mum nods approvingly. 'It's just as nice without it, really, it was just something a friend recommended I try,' Liv adds quickly, apologetically.

'I think it might even be better with,' I say, looking at Mum and smiling.

'Yes, as I said, it's very tasty,' she replies.

'Delicious,' Dad says, chipping in, preventing the conversation from becoming any more loaded. 'And lovely butter from Kviteseid, I see,' he says, slathering a piece of cracker bread with it.

'Watch yourself with that butter, Sverre,' Mum says, and I watch as she immediately realises that she's spoken out of habit. Her expression is the same as when they spoke in unison before, and she laughs disarmingly. 'I imagine you still have slightly high blood pressure?'

Dad looks momentarily annoyed, impatience flashing across his face, ready to say something until he smothers the desire with his next thought, turning to face Agnar instead.

'Caught any good Pokémon lately?' he asks.

'I don't do that any more, got bored,' Agnar replies.

Dad looks deflated and I feel for him, he seems so alone.

Liv looks down at her plate. Håkon looks out of the window. Olaf glances at Liv every so often. I wonder if everyone around the table feels the way I do, as if someone has to shatter this smooth surface; I can't imagine anyone other than Olaf and Hedda failing to pick up on the atmosphere.

'Well, I've got some news, as it happens,' Dad says. 'I'm going to be retiring in January.'

I hope it was Dad's decision, that he hasn't done it for Mum's sake, in an attempt to save their marriage while she's busy moving on.

'Congratulations,' Olaf replies, inquisitive. 'What's next on the cards for you?'

No confrontation. Anticlimax! I texted Simen under the table during dessert. I'm not going to say anything if nobody else does, I had told him before leaving. But what are you hoping they might say? Simen asked. I fell silent. I don't know what I want them to say, I just want someone to put something into words, to poke holes in this supposed normality that I feel like I've found myself stuck in. It needs to be talked about, I concluded, there's so much left unsaid, it's always there, under the surface, and that's not how we are, I continued with vaguely ulterior motives. He nodded without taking the hint; it's probably best if someone else starts that conversation, you don't always have to be the one to take responsibility for things. Plus, if you don't say any-thing, someone else will have to. He was wrong about that, though, none of the others appeared to feel compelled to make anything other than the most matter-of-course additions to the conversation. Any sign of conflict was quashed before it was fully articulated. If they weren't my own family, I would have regarded the unspoken coop-eration with great fascination, the way in which everyone played their own part in taking responsibility either for protecting or smoothing things over for someone else, who would do the same thing in turn during the next loaded silence, and so it went on – everyone has been saved and has saved someone else, it's equal, and nobody could possibly feel that they've been walked all over or treated unfairly.

Neither Mum nor Dad want to be the first to leave, thereby giving the other the opportunity to spend some time alone with the children and grandchildren. Perhaps I'm the only one to notice it, but the atmos-phere between them is different now than it was when they announced their divorce. I don't know what they agreed, what they hoped might happen or what the cooperation Mum had boasted about them being so capable of actually involved, other than the fact that they might be able to look after Agnar and Hedda together now and then.

Eventually Håkon breaks things up, he has somewhere he needs to be, he says. In the past we would have fired a barrage of questions at him about who he was off to meet, but nobody dares tease him now, the atmosphere is so tense that it wouldn't bear up under the pressure of any slip-ups such as Håkon's frustration in the face of any questions, not even mock frustration. He looks at Dad, who's also standing up and bidding farewell to everyone, clearly preparing to drive Håkon wherever it is he's going. Mum looks relieved, says she also has to go home and get to bed. Liv and I both look at the clock at the same time, it's nine o'clock.

◆

'Do you think she's off out to meet him now?' Liv asks.

We're sitting on the steps that lead out into the garden at the back of the house, each wrapped in a blanket. We've brought the remainder of the bottle of wine out with us and we share a cigarette. Liv sits with her left hand to her ear, rubbing a finger around and down towards her earlobe, just as Dad does when he's reading or doing his sudoku, holding the cigarette in her free hand. It's been more than a year since I last had a cigarette and I feel immediately dizzy. Liv pulls out an ash tray from behind a flower pot, the contents of which suggest she's smoked her way through at least fifty cigarettes in recent days, the ends still orange and fresh. I don't mention it. This is a delicate situation in itself, Liv and I on the steps together, sitting just as we have done what must surely be a thousand times before, yet it feels entirely new and crucial all the same.

'Perhaps,' I say, glancing at her to gauge her reaction, trying to work out if she's just as upset, but if so, she pulls herself together, seemingly calm. 'Isn't it a little odd that she only told Håkon about this Morten chap? I wonder if she expected him to tell us so she wouldn't have to, or if she was actually trying to shield us from it,' I continue.

Liv takes a long drag on the cigarette. She nods.

'Olaf has met someone too,' she says all of a sudden.

I'm caught completely off-guard. It can't be possible, it would never have occurred to me. I've always considered their relationship to be static, unchanging, just like Mum and Dad's, in fact – constant in a calm and safe and, quite honestly, very boring way. I turn to look up at the window, as if to check that Olaf is quite himself, and see him washing a saucepan at the kitchen sink. I feel a sudden urge to run inside, grab him by the throat and drown him in the sink.

'What do you mean?' I ask.

'Well, not *met*, not like that,' Liv begins. 'He's in love with another woman, someone from work,' she continues, then starts to laugh. 'Well, I think it's a woman, at least, I haven't actually asked.'

'But what happened?'

'Nothing's happened,' Liv says. 'He's just fallen in love.'

'So, nothing's happened between them?' I ask.

'No. Nothing other than the fact that I can clearly imagine the way he behaves around her.'

I can't imagine Olaf behaving in a way that demonstrates anything other than calm enchantment with Liv, and it's almost embarrassing to picture him as miserably lovestruck.

'Is she in love with him?' I ask.

'No, I don't know. Neither does he, for that matter, he hasn't spoken to her about it.'

'So, he's just told you he's in love with one of his colleagues?'

Liv nods, then takes a few large swigs of wine. How stupid is it possible to be? I think to myself about Olaf. And egotistical. And clichéd.

'But,' I begin, then pause, feeling the need to weigh up my words to ensure that Liv can't write off my question as a mark of my lack of experience and shy away once again from showing this level of confidence and trust in me, an experience that makes me so happy, in spite of everything. 'Why?'

'Why what?' Liv asks.

'Why did he tell you if there's nothing more to it than that?'

'Probably because he wants to be honest,' Liv replies. 'Or perhaps to provoke a reaction. To threaten me, maybe.'

'Why would he want to threaten you?'

'To make me pull myself together, to show me the consequences of my actions.'

'What actions?'

I no longer care if Liv thinks me childish and inexperienced, it's probably true, anyway, I just want to understand what's going on, I don't know what's happened between Liv and Olaf and I'm scared by how little I know, how different and unpredictable everything is, the fact that Liv hasn't called me to tell me about this, that she's relaying it to me now in such a controlled, filtered fashion, pulling herself together for my benefit.

'The way I've been acting,' she says. 'I haven't been functioning properly for the past six months, I feel like everything's falling apart, myself and my marriage included, even though it's actually Mum and

Dad's marriage that's gone to pot. I don't know why I'm so affected when you and Håkon are so untouched by it, I've been so childish, so childish, it's just...'

She stops. Shrugs. Takes a puff of her third cigarette.

◈

You're not childish, Liv, it's me who's been self-centred. That's what I should have said, I think to myself now, on my way to work a few days later. I couldn't bring myself to say much more at the time, and we had sat there in silence for a short while before I'd asked if she wanted me to beat him up for her, at which point she laughed and said, but he hasn't done anything wrong, Ellen, things aren't that black and white. She brushed cigarette ash off the step beside her, mulled over something that she chose not to share with me after I'd killed the conversation with my stupid attempt at a joke, and then she smiled at me as she stood up. It's too cold to sit outside, you'll end up with cystitis, she said. Come on, let's go in and see if Olaf has any more wine for us.

I had another glass of wine at the kitchen table with Olaf and Liv, feeling upset when I saw his arm draped over the back of her chair, the apparent normality of the situation. On one hand I wanted to cry out to him to pack up his things and go to hell, and on the other hand I wanted to implore him to stay with her. I'm still torn: my instinct to protect her made me want to scratch his eyes out, to defend Liv against every disloyal thought to have crossed his mind, yet the self-centred part of me couldn't bear the idea of a break-up, the changes and all of the turmoil it would bring.

Christmas is fast approaching; Oslo is dark and without a hint of snow to speak of, the glittering imitation stars and Christmas bells hanging over Karl Johans gate appear misplaced. Anything resembling Christmas spirit is long gone now, my friends complain, referring to the childlike sense of anticipation and joy that only ever emerge in momentary flickers of nostalgia. The only natural continuation of any so-called *Christmas spirit* comes in the attempt to recreate the same feeling in one's own children. Over the past few years, celebrating Christmas as an adult without children has been a void that I've filled with work and few thoughts of the festive season beyond the family traditions that I've come to take for granted.

I'd have given a lot this year to sink into the same stable pattern of events that once inspired a restless longing to escape, the predictability of everything being done in the same way, year after year. I was actually supposed to celebrate Christmas with Simen and his family this year, but after Mum sent a message yesterday hijacking Christmas Eve, writing that it would be held at hers, I told Simen that it would be impossible to leave the others in the lurch this year of all years. *We're having Christmas Eve at mine this year*, she wrote. I sent a message to Liv to see if she knew if Dad would be coming too, happy to have an excuse to get in touch with her, continuing our cautious return to normality. She still hasn't replied, and perhaps it was inconsiderate of me to message her when she probably has enough on her plate. Simen almost seemed relieved to hear that I'd have to spend this year with Mum, and for the second time in three days he said it wouldn't be a disaster for us to do our own things. I couldn't tell him that wasn't what I'd meant, that actually I'd meant that he and I should both go to Mum's together. But we're not a family, there's no reason to pretend, Simen's relieved body language seemed to tell me, and I couldn't muster the energy to object.

A politician is sitting outside the office, waiting. I've no recollection of having arranged a meeting today. I check the calendar on my phone and there's nothing in today's square other than a large, red *P*. In November last year I signed up to a fertility calendar that would inform me where I was in my cycle. I haven't made a note of any meeting; I can't even remember what it might be about. Rikke, who I employed last year, comes to my rescue. She's twenty-six years old with two master's degrees, and had applied for numerous positions before ending up with us.

'So, you're ready for a debate, I take it?' she says to the politician.

'Well, we'll see about that,' he replies, and I remember then that we're going to be coaching him and devising a strategy for a television debate.

I let Rikke take charge.

'The most important thing is that you feel in control, don't let anyone else take the lead. You need to own the situation, not the other way around,' Rikke says.

❖

In the middle of December, Mum is admitted to hospital with chest pains. Liv called me in the middle of a presentation I was holding at the university; I always leave my phone in front of me on the lectern so I can check the time as I go. I still hadn't heard back from her about Christmas, and I thought that might be what she was calling about, so I turned the phone over to hide the screen and finished my presentation. When I called her back, she was on her way to Ullevål Hospital. She didn't know anything other than the fact that Mum had been taken there in an ambulance, that's what Dad had told her. How did Dad know? I asked. I don't know, Ellen, but that's hardly the most important thing now, Liv said, and it was only then that it hit me that something might be seriously wrong.

Both she and Dad are in good shape, they're fit and strong, and it would never occur to me to question their cognitive abilities – as Simen once put it long ago, they've become amplified versions of themselves, their inward and outward mannerisms have intensified, and both have become more self-centred, I think, though Liv disagrees – she thinks that I consider them more self-centred just because I'm an adult and therefore naturally receive less attention myself, something that would suggest that it's actually *me* who's become more self-centred, or at the very least, self-important. Not one of their other functions has failed them, besides Dad's bad knee and Mum's occasionally stiff shoulder. When our own grandparents were the age Mum and Dad are now, they were old; I remember them as hunched over, primed for an elderly existence. Almost all of Mum and Dad's friends are as fit and well as they are. At a get-together in Tåsen a few years ago, they discussed retirement as a fresh start, filled with opportunities. I've always regarded that phenomenon as a defence mechanism, for the most part, a denial of the fact that they're growing old and approaching death – but when I think about Mum and Dad in concrete terms, I have to acknowledge that I might actually be the one with old-fashioned ideas of what a retiree ought to be.

I take a taxi up to Ullevål. I feel increasingly certain that it must be something serious given how quickly it's come on. It might be a major heart attack, or a blood clot, maybe. Acute leukaemia? My guilty conscience intensifies in line with my concern, I've been so angry at her, so condemnatory, just because she's made a decision I don't support. The taxi creeps onwards in rush-hour traffic, it's too far to the nearest tram or metro stop, and I'm wearing heels too high to walk in the slippery slush underfoot. I lean back against the headrest, doing my best to relax, letting my gaze follow the people walking along the pavement outside the car window. My thoughts merge together, muddled. I'm surprised to realise that my greatest fear when it comes to the notion of Mum's death is the realisation that she would never meet my children.

I spend almost every hour of the day thinking about the fact that I'll probably never have children of my own. I'm convinced of that fact now, and it makes me feel genuinely despondent, angry and afraid – even so, the thought that I'll have children is so deep-seated and natural that it is the first and most powerful to occur to me in a crisis. The thought of my unborn children. I wonder if that thought is biological, if I'll still feel that way when I'm fifty years old.

◈

I stay behind at the hospital after the others have left. Everyone has been in, Håkon and Liv and Dad and me. We stood around Mum's bed; she was upset and afraid, embarrassed and tired. The pains in her chest were probably the result of an anxiety attack, the doctor had said, she'd been admitted because they couldn't rule out a heart attack in A&E. She had been reading at home when all of a sudden she'd had difficulty breathing, and had felt stabbing pains in her chest. Rather than calling for an ambulance, she'd called Dad, who had called an ambulance himself and had dropped everything he was juggling at the time, as he put it without giving any further details, making it to Tåsen at the same time as the ambulance.

Dad, for his part, seemed in better spirits than he had in a long time, even though he tried to hide it when we were in the hospital, no doubt a combination of relief that nothing more serious was wrong with Mum – I can only imagine the thoughts that had run through his mind on his way to the hospital – and reluctant happiness to finally see some indication that their separation had made an impression on her, as it had on him.

I read aloud to Mum from the newspaper. She's being kept in over-night, something she is happy to go along with, and I didn't have the heart to leave her alone when the others eventually went their separate ways. She looked so old all of a sudden, tiny and frail in her sickbed, afraid. She hasn't offered any explanation to anyone, other than to say there's been a lot going on lately, and more than anything she seemed keen to get rid of us when it became clear that her condition wasn't life-threatening, almost on the verge of tears with embarrassment. As usual, Håkon was the first to pick up on her signals; he knew it was the best thing we could do, to leave her in peace. We said bye to Mum and left, all of us – but I turned back before we reached the exit, telling Liv, Håkon and Dad that I'd left my phone in Mum's room. I made my way to the shop and bought a newspaper, a bottle of sparkling water and a chocolate bar, her usual picks for any car journey lasting longer than an hour, then returned to her room. She'd been crying, or perhaps still was when I arrived, but she smiled when she saw me. She dabbed at her tears with her sleeve. I took off my winter boots, sat down in the chair beside her and rested my feet on the bed. Have a listen to this, I said, then read her a book review for a novel written by a foreign writer I know she likes.

She's been prescribed sedatives, and by the time I've skim-read the newspaper, making the occasional comment to Mum, she's drifted off. I wait for a while, until I'm certain that she's not going to wake up again, and then I tuck the sheets around her, cocooning her, as Liv and I used to call it when we were little. Mummy, cocoon us, we'd say, meaning that we wanted her to tuck the duvet tight around us, as if we were in a little pupa of our own. She looks like a little child; I stroke her forehead gently, it's damp and warm.

I sit on a bench outside the hospital after leaving Mum. I don't want to go home to Simen, and it strikes me that I haven't even called him to tell him what's going on, where I am. In truth I feel lighter, my head and my body weightless in a way they haven't been in a long time, I've been freed from the repetitive pattern of thinking about myself and Simen and our childless future for a few hours now, absorbed by what's been going on, entirely preoccupied with it, and it leads me to a sort of liberating realisation, a recognition of just how self-centred I've been – it's like discovering all over again that there are other people in the world with problems. I picture Dad's face when he caught sight of us in the hospital corridor earlier today, his obvious relief at more than just the fact that Mum wasn't seriously ill, and Mum's shame at the same thing, at having exposed a fear she'd done her best to conceal. Of course she's afraid, I think to myself, and of course he's concerned about her, concerned that she's been affected the way she has. It's not that the child in me is happy to see it confirmed that they care for one another, I'm not holding out any hope for anything on that count, but I'm filled with sympathy for the two of them. I try to imagine Simen and me in thirty years' time. I've always thought there would be too much going on in our lives, too much to talk about, too much to engage ourselves in, so much so that we wouldn't ever become a mere habit for one another. Now I picture us sitting at the breakfast table in silence, only ever repeating ourselves if we do happen to say anything at all. That would be a bigger loss for me than if he were to drop down dead in the middle of a conversation, I think to myself now, losing our connection and one another in that way.

For the first time I don't feel angry, bitter or upset about the divorce for my own sake, but I'm sad for Mum and Dad's loss, and it's a melancholy experience, witnessing the ambivalence they feel, the sorrow of leaving one another and the simultaneous – and stronger – desire for something else, something more.

◆

The entire festive season disappears in a hormonal merry-go-round. I'm furious, quick to laugh, despondent and filled with such affection that I don't know what to do with myself. The hormones I'm taking every day to manipulate my dysfunctional body play havoc with my every cell and brainwave, there is no in-between. I am aware of it and yet it remains beyond my command, I've lost control. Even so, it's liberating, in a way, simply letting go.

State healthcare entitles you to three attempts, the doctor told Simen and me around Christmas time. We were sitting in his office, both of us together, and Simen was silent as the doctor explained the process of assisted fertilisation. I could sense his aversion, and it all seemed equally absurd to me, sitting here and listening as someone explained what ought to be the perfectly natural, private process of creating our own child in purely mechanical terms. There is no longer any sense of hope, our child is to be conceived in a plastic cup in a laboratory. I've googled it, pulled up images, the exact opposite to warm bodies in a warm bed filled with a warm sense of hope: face masks, plastic gloves and syringes. At the same time, this is our eleventh hour, we just have to go for it, I said to Simen afterwards, my statement almost taking the form of a question. Simen nodded. I suppose you're right, he replied, before checking himself, of course we have to do it, he said. It's worse for you, what with all the side effects. Well, you're the one who has to put up with them, I replied.

But he doesn't put up with them. Or with me. He walks out on me at least four times a day, and I can't keep a single thought to myself. You've lost hope, I scream at his back, why are you even bothering with all of this? Nobody's forcing you to put up with me, can't you just go out and find someone who can give you what you want? Simen never says anything, nor does he respond to the declarations of love that immediately come tumbling out of my mouth in the wake of my accusations, when my mood lifts and my line of thought shifts in a matter of seconds, when I tell him how patient he is, that I can see how hard this is for him, that I'd never get through this without him. You're everything to me, I say, you're really, truly everything, you have to believe me. I suspect that the problem isn't that Simen doesn't believe me; quite the opposite, he's all too aware that over the past year he's all that I have left to cling to, there is no longer any alternative, and knowing that makes him stressed and restless. I can't leave her now, I can imagine him telling his friends, what kind of bastard would that make me? And while I try to flatter him into staying, to impress him, I also play the only card I have: I play on his sympathy and his conscience. Because Simen is a nice guy, he's sincere, and leaving me now because I can't have children would turn him into the kind of man he has no desire to become, the kind he doesn't wish to own up to being – the kind he could never bear for others to see him as.

❖

I send a message to the whole family telling them I'm not well. I stay at home during all the usual family get-togethers that Mum and Dad both carry on with as one unit, at his brother's or her sister's, at home in Tåsen; they even spend New Year with a couple they're friends with. It's a quasi-divorce, I commented to Simen on Christmas Day, the insightful sympathy I'd felt for them while sitting outside Ullevål Hospital that day now challenged by their conduct, as well as my own mood swings – and I become disproportionately infuriated at the seemingly normal state of affairs. I long for some sense of revolt beyond the confines of my own body, somewhere to aim my explosive emotional outbursts. Perhaps they regret things, perhaps they've realised they want to be together after all now that it's Christmas, Simen suggested. No, it's the opposite, they want to be divorced while clinging on to tradition, I remarked. Some kind of asexual *friends with benefits* arrangement, Simen said.

We always have a buffet on Christmas Eve, a kind of compromise between Mum and Dad, who were brought up on ribs and cod respectively at Christmas time. The dishes on offer have always been the same, and are always laid out in the same way – during one of the first years Olaf joined the family, Mum spent a whole hour trying to work out where to place a dish containing sausages he'd well-meaningly brought along – and each is served with respect to taste, aesthetics and tradition. Mum puts a lot of work into this meal and places a great deal of pride in it, beginning preparations long before Christmas, making her own brawn and pate, fermenting fish – which, in spite of the fact Mum's only connection to Telemark is a summer cabin, must be baked in a wood oven following a traditional recipe from the region – curing trout and boiling ox tongue. When I was young, the smell of fermented *rakfisk*, which Dad would bring up from the cellar and place on the kitchen worktop, was synonymous with Christmas mornings. Now it's coming home, opening the front door and being enveloped by the same smell, overwhelmed by it, that awakens the child-like Christmas spirit within me.

This year I caught the unmistakeable scent of roasting pork as I stepped into the yard, and I hoped against hope that it was coming from one of the neighbour's houses right up until the moment I opened the front door. Look, Mum said, pointing at the ribs in the oven as I stepped into the kitchen, the crackling should puff up and become crisp, if everything goes to plan. She'd had her hair re-styled, her cheeks were red and her eyes shone. I thought it might be nice to try something new this year, Mum said casually, and as we both crouched in front of the oven and waited to observe the puffing-up of the pork crackling, I didn't have the heart to do anything other than play along with enthusiasm.

These breaches of tradition have been the only kind of change or disturbance on Mum and Dad's part this Christmas. Tiny but noticeable indications from each of them, all designed to spell out to us that things *are* different, that this is a new situation and a new era. I sway between acknowledging and challenging this as my hopes of one day having my own family rise and fall.

◈

I'm not lying when I say I'm not well; I've got a headache and I feel sick, I'm so hot and sweaty that I open all the windows in the flat, it's never cold enough for my liking, at least not with Simen following me around and closing each of them without a word, and I fill the bathtub with cold water and lie there. It's worth it, I think to myself as I lie in the cold water, which stings my burning skin like the pricking of a thousand needles. I try to convince myself that the powerful side effects I'm experiencing are also a sign that my body is responding, that something is working, and that, therefore, there might be a greater chance that our attempts will be successful.

Simen accepted an invitation on our behalf what must be six months ago now to celebrate New Year's Eve at his elder brother's cabin in Hallingdal. I don't dare not go; I need to show my face around his family, show them that I'm still here, still important, I need to bond with them and let them bond with me. It's only two nights, I think to myself as I sit in the car on the way there with my head hanging out of the window like a dog. Simen is in a good mood, he's wrapped up in his winter coat as I get some air; he laughs at me, occasionally resting his right hand on my thigh, just like he used to do in our early days together.

Simen's mother is the opposite of Mum. She's tall and slim, with dark hair and dark make-up around her brown eyes, and her neck and wrists and fingers are always adorned with expensive pieces of jewellery. I like her, she reminds me of Simen in a lot of ways, but she's more difficult to bond with. There's always a certain cool distance in everything she says and does, but that could also be due to the fact I haven't become properly acquainted with her yet, I haven't come to know them: I don't know his dad or his brothers particularly well either, but now, for the first time, I understand the importance of getting to know them – it's something of a revelation for me to appreciate the tactical side of investing in one's in-laws, as all of my boyfriends have insisted on doing with my own family.

Simen's brother, Magnus, has two children, and they're expecting their third in March. I greet his wife Synne gushingly. You look amazing, I tell her, gazing at her large stomach in her tight dress; she's standing in the hallway to meet us upon our arrival, her hands clasped under her bump as if she were holding on to it, cradling it or protecting it. She must be pushing forty.

'When are you due, again?' I ask as she follows me upstairs to the room Simen and I will be sleeping in, even though I know, of course, that her due date is 14 March; every due date I hear sears itself into my consciousness.

'March,' she replies with a smile. 'You can use this bathroom,' she says, pointing at a door and looking at me, and I can feel pearls of sweat gathering at my temples.

'And it's a boy, isn't it?' I say. I don't even know why I'm pretending not to know that they're expecting a girl, why I'm making myself appear indifferent, my plan coming in was the very opposite.

'No, actually, they tell us it's going to be a little princess,' she says.

It always used to vex me when people used such terms to refer to their unborn babies, prince or princess, sweetpea, it always seemed so put on, but when Synne says it now it sounds soft and lovely, tender and assured. I find myself on the verge of tears, managing to blurt out a few words of thanks before closing the door behind me and letting my tears fall. Simen follows me upstairs, he doesn't twig that I'm crying – or perhaps he does, but he's stopped reacting given that it's as unremarkable as me coughing these days – and he puts down our cases, whistling as he does so.

'What an amazing place,' he says.

I can't see what's so amazing about it, myself, other than the fact that it's enormous and everything looks as if it's part of the backdrop for a photoshoot in an interior design magazine, with sheepskin rugs and brown leather everywhere, the kind of standing lamps you see in glossy magazines with warm slate tiles underfoot in the hallway, imitation timber walls and dimmed lights. Then again, the view from the kitchen window is dominated by a large, yellow digger, which is busy making way for an identical cabin to be constructed just fifty metres away. In other words, it all lacks taste. I don't say that, of course, nodding instead as I dry my tears.

'Lovely,' I say, plucking up the courage to hug him.

He embraces me for a few seconds, his body unfamiliar against my own, his neck, his smell. I start crying again and he chuckles when he feels my tears tickling at the neck of his wool jumper. He frees himself from my embrace and looks at me.

'It's not *that* lovely,' he says, smiling and giving me a friendly nudge. 'Shall we head back down to the others?'

◈

I've dreaded seeing Simen with Magnus's one-year-old son more than anything else, and it is just as painful as I've anticipated when Simen picks him up and lifts him high in the air, arms straight, smiling at him. The natural way he holds him afterwards, balancing him on one hip as he talks to his mum. Simen's face when the baby is eventually placed in my lap and when I move him to the end of my knee, all too aware of Simen's expression – can't have the little one too close to me, can't bear to smell his baby smell. Even so, I feel I have something to prove, but before I have a chance to pull him any closer, he bursts into tears and scans the room frantically for his mother, just a few metres away, indignant at having been dragged away from the soft, natural embrace of his Uncle Simen and placed in the arms of someone who must feel like a cold, mechanical robot.

'I think someone wants their Mummy,' I say to Synne without looking at the baby's forlorn expression, and I do my best to laugh.

'Yes, he gets very impatient when he's hungry, he's a little too accustomed to getting his own way,' Synne replies with a smile, looking like any other attentive mother doing her best to erase any notion that the fault might lie with the other person; a habitual, natural reaction to alleviate any concern on the part of the awkward, childless person who may well have been responsible for the child's tears.

He stops crying as soon as he feels Synne's body against his own, and I wonder what that must feel like, to have that effect on someone, to be so important, so crucial, so naturally connected. To be the only thing that helps, the only thing that matters.

Neither Simen's dad, his mum, Magnus nor Synne mention the fact we don't have children, or that we ought to start trying before too long, or ask if we plan on having any, or comment on the fact that time is marching on, and so on and so forth, they don't even get as far as hinting at it. That, in itself, is more alarming than if they had probed or joked about the situation, because the absolute silence on the subject testifies to the fact that they've either discussed it prior to our arrival, making their own assumptions and agreeing not to bring it up – for whatever reason – or that they've taken it for granted that it won't be me providing them with the next grandchild or cousin to join the family. I do my best to suppress the worst, most paranoid thought to enter my mind, the fact that Simen might have informed them about what's been going on, that he might have explained the problem – me – and asked them not to say anything.

Last year, at New Year, as Simen and I had dinner with a pair of friends in New York, we summed up our year. It's surreal to think only twelve months have passed since then, surreal to think that an entire decade hasn't gone by since that point. The change in Simen and me is so striking, so tangible I can describe it: it is an abyss of detachment, of bloody disappointments; the image of what our future would look like, of what our relationship would look like; the transformation between us, everything that's come to a standstill, everything we choose not to talk about, all the desire that has disappeared, an alienation of body and mind. That would be how I would sum up our year, everything piled up there in the abyss, but I can't bring myself to fish any of it out, I keep any thoughts of past and future at bay, focusing only on existing in the here and now, eating turkey, talking about the subjects of inter-est to Simen's family: Norwegian education policy, the rise in property prices, what Brexit means for us in Norway. I get by better that I'd expected I might – it would have been an enjoyable occasion, had it not been for the sheepskin-lined oak cradle positioned in the corner of the room, a constant reminder.

Simen and I toast at midnight, kissing dutifully as the fireworks above us vanish in the misty sky, Happy New Year. Happy New Year, I don't know if Simen even dares to hope for such a thing, if he still has it in him, or if the only thing he longs for now is to get away, hoping deep inside that our attempts will prove unsuccessful. But within me I feel a tiny glimmer of hormonal hope flare up with the contrived transition from one year to the next.

◈

I *have* been pregnant, is all I can think on the third occasion that I find myself lying there, staring up at the ceiling in the hospital, while the same nurse, dressed head-to-toe in green, makes one final attempt to encourage a tiny, fused mass of Simen and me to acknowledge that my womb might be a suitable place for life to begin.

It's been five months, one failed attempt and one miscarriage since New Year's Eve.

My God, is it true? Simen blurted when I showed him the positive test a month after our second implantation. How can you be so calm about it? How can you be so calm? he shouted, not sure what to do with himself, walking out onto the balcony, coming back inside, shit, he said, wrapping his arms around me, hugging me, kissing me. Then he sat at the dining table, looking almost resigned, leaning over and resting his head on his forearm. Shit, he repeated.

I wrapped my arms around him from behind, leaned over him, my stomach touching his back. It was closer than we'd been for a year. It's not that I feel calm about it, I said to the back of his head, it's just so surreal, I can't believe it. But it's there, isn't it? he seemed to ask, sitting upright and pointing at the three tests I'd laid out on the table. Each one of them showed a clear blue line. Three tests can't be wrong, surely? he asked. No, they can't, I said, without mentioning the fact that two more with the same result were lying in the bathroom bin. I need to pee, I told Simen, I'd drunk so much water over the course of the day that I could still feel the pressure of it on my lower abdomen – but finally, no longer convinced that I was kidding myself, I was able to believe that it might have something to do with the little life in the process of commencing within me. When I returned from the bathroom, Simen was still sitting at the table. It's just… he began, then looked at me, stopped himself. He fell silent, reached out for me. I'd given up, he said, and was forced to swallow a sob. Honestly, I had, Ellen, he said, I took his hand and he squeezed it. Is that awful of me? I shook my head, of course not, I told him, I get it.

The following night I was awoken by cramps, and still half-asleep I imagined myself to be giving birth, and I pushed with all my might to bring a plump, healthy baby into the world, while in reality, my body rejected an embryo with a tiny heart that had only just started beating.

◆

'Is someone coming to pick you up?' the nurse asks me when she's finished.

I feel as if I've been laid out here a hundred times before, that this has become routine. The only difference on this occasion is that Simen isn't here with me. Just go to your meeting, I told him a few days ago, it's the same old same old, I said. Sure, but it feels weird not to be there at the point of conception, unnatural somehow, Simen replied. Everything about this process is unnatural, and anyway, it's not *conception*, I said, unable to stop myself from raising my voice. You know that, conception has already occurred, it's just a case of insertion, I continued. He raised his hands defensively. OK, as long as you feel alright about going by yourself, he said, before waiting to hear my response, quickly adding: Are you sure? I'm sure, I told him, and I meant it, because in spite of everything it was better going alone than feeling I was dragging Simen along to something he couldn't face, drawing him down into something that was my problem, and mine alone. My challenge to face.

'Yes,' I lie to the nurse. 'My husband is coming to pick me up.'

I squint in the May sunshine outside the hospital as I wait for my Uber to arrive, vaguely recalling years gone by, the first foray into a beer garden on Schous plass with my girlfriends around this time of year, the vast ocean of time and priorities that was once at my feet.

When I get home, I lie with my head at the foot of the bed, my legs resting up on the headboard. I know it's nonsense, but it can't hurt, nothing can hurt, nothing except beginning to hope again.

◈

He's left all of his things behind. Even the tiny cactus he's had since he first moved away from home sits firmly in its spot on the kitchen windowsill. I press two fingers against the tiny, white spikes, there's disappointingly little resistance, it doesn't hurt one bit. Pain is all relative, of course, I've come to understand that over the past few months.

It's not over, Simen said, that's not what I'm saying. I just need a little space, I can't breathe. Is that a metaphor? I reply, quiet, numb. It's not, actually, last night I woke up to find myself hyperventilating, he replied. He hadn't, I'd been awake all night myself, just as I had every other night these past few weeks. And the solution is to walk out? I ask him. It's not a *solution*, he cried, don't oversimplify things. I'm doing this for both of us. No, you're not, you're not doing this for me, you're doing this *to* me, I said, my arms by my sides, I no longer had anything to lose. What do you want from me? Do you want us to carry on like this, nagging at one another until we eventually end up like your parents? he said. Better that, I thought to myself, better to have three children and a family, something to look back on, at the very least.

◈

I realise that I'm not wearing anything. I'm standing naked at the kitchen window, poking at a cactus, and I start to laugh as I look out at the building across from ours, then even more so at the fact I'm standing naked at the window and laughing at a cactus. I look up at the clock on the wall above the kitchen worktop; it's five past seven, I need to be at the office in an hour. I take a shower, watching as clumps of my hair disappear down the plughole as I rinse out the shampoo. The only result of the hormone treatment has been to make me bald, I imagine myself saying to Simen as we sit in the kitchen drinking wine, and he laughs the way he always does when he feels sorry for me but sees humour in the situation all the same – you might not have ended up with a child, but you do get to bring a bald girlfriend home, that's something to consider, I picture myself saying.

I don't know how long I spend in the shower, but my hands and feet are soft and wrinkled like those of a newborn baby when I emerge. I wrap my hair in a towel and dot face cream over my forehead and cheeks before massaging it into my skin, it targets and reduces fine lines, the jar claims. Over the past year I've developed vast endless wrinkles around my eyes. I fill them with primer, then tint the lilac rings with a yellow-toned concealer before applying a thick layer of *diamond glow* foundation over my entire face, *star-reflecting* powder, highlighter on my cheekbones, the bridge of my nose, my eyebrows, applying eyeliner to both eyes, mascara to my lashes, *volumising* lip gloss. I dry my hair, scrape it back in a tight ponytail, pull on my jeans, shirt and blazer, then check my reflection in the mirror. Isn't it strange being with someone whose appearance is so transformed in the space of an hour in the bathroom in the morning? I asked Simen once as he sat on the lid of the toilet, watching me doing my make-up. Your appearance doesn't change, you just become a different version of yourself – I sometimes wish it was OK for men to use make-up, I could go for a dramatic look one day if I felt like it, he replied, laughing. You're well on your way to having your own hipster beard, though, that's pretty dramatic, I said, pulling at his trim facial hair.

I pull on my boots and jacket, run down the stairs and make it as far as the front door before remembering that I've been signed off on sick leave.

Extremely reluctantly, as I said to the doctor, unwilling that it should be the case. I was informed by my manager that I should see someone after she claimed I'd had some sort of breakdown at the salad bar in the canteen. It's not a breakdown, I told her as I sat in her office afterwards, it's just a physical symptom. It felt that way, too, and still does whenever my diaphragm contracts without warning, forcing me to gasp for air, my nerves sending signals to my tear ducts, which have gone into overdrive producing no end of excess moisture these days, my back hunching over protectively, my knees giving way beneath me. Don't underestimate the weight of what you've been through, the doctor said, before prescribing me Valium. I'll take the prescription, but I'm not going to use them, I told the doctor. I've always looked upon the idea of relying on unnecessary medication as a form of defeat, that feeling having only increased following the failed course of hormone therapy. I think I've got cancer, I said, genuinely hoping that to be the case.

I feel dizzy and sick as I make my way back upstairs to my flat. I suddenly can't remember what I was on my way out to do, can't recall what day it is or how long it's been since Simen left; I seem to remember doing the exact same thing yesterday, and the day before that. I sit in bed with my MacBook on my lap, aimlessly surfing the net. I've turned off the autofill setting that used to lead me down a rabbit hole of baby forums and endless threads of tips and tricks and hope and despair.

'Loneliness is the new epidemic', one headline states. One in three young people feels lonely. Young people, as in nineteen years old, with everything ahead of them, a vast ocean of time and opportunity at their feet. I scroll down the page, feeling the desire to dole out some advice to Mina, seventeen, who's copied a page from her diary and sent it in to the section of the news site aimed at teenagers, framing it as an opinion piece – hi Mina, I'm a thirty-eight-year-old girl, no, sorry, woman, and my seventy-year-old parents decided to get divorced last year, which shattered the frameworks that had obviously provided every prerequisite for intimacy and trust and sincerity in our family, and now we've grown distant and almost become strangers. Moreover, my boyfriend has just left me because I can't have children, I'll never know what it's like to have a child of my own, I've lost touch with my friends amid my desperate and, yes, rather self-obsessed attempts to procreate, but trust me, Mina, the world is your oyster.

◈

The world is overpopulated, Håkon remarked during one conversation at Christmas, when Mum told us our cousin was expecting her sixth baby. Having children is pure egoism, he added. Of course it is, Liv replied, what else could it possibly be? But it's biological, she said. Anyone who wants a child in this day and age should just adopt. It's a win-win situation, Håkon replied. He almost always falls back on biology in any argument he makes, but over the past year his reasoning has lacked any kind of logic and coherence, and he no longer seems quite as certain as he once did.

The only time Simen and I ever discussed adoption was the day that we found out I was actually pregnant, when we were able to discuss it without considering that it might become a reality for us. I can't imagine having a child I can't see myself in, a child who can't see themselves in me, Simen said. I can't imagine looking at them and not being able to recognise something of myself there, no glimpses of familiar features or personality traits. I think so much of what's important between parents and children is to do with what we see of ourselves in them, without us even realising it, don't you agree? It's instinctive. You and your mum, for instance, he said, you're virtually one and the same person. Sure, in terms of our appearance, I replied, but our personalities are very different. I think familiarity can be shaped, to a certain extent, I said, I think we attribute a lot to biology that's really got more to do with our environment. You've no idea just how like your mum you really are, even in your mannerisms, Simen replied. That put an end to our conversation, but either way, Simen had made his point, and if I were being entirely honest with myself, it was a disturbing thought to find oneself responsible for an unknown child born of a stranger.

That was then. Since the failure of our last state-financed insemination attempt, I've been open to everything I had ever previously rejected. The thought of adopting suddenly wasn't as remote as it once had been, it seemed more and more obvious, a win-win situation, I concluded in one long, desperate monologue to Simen who, for his part, was completely closed-off, exhausted. I can't face talking about this now, Ellen, darling, can't we just let it go, I'm so tired. I couldn't let it go, I was desperate, I put forward any number of possible solutions, and beneath each of them lay the fear of what I knew was coming, don't give up hope, Simen, please, don't give up on me.

I close the lid of my laptop. I don't know what to do with myself, no space is small enough for me, no space large enough, nowhere cool enough, nowhere quiet enough, nowhere loud enough; I have no one.

I have no one.

It's the only new thought to enter my mind in the course of an unknown number of hours or days spent in bed. I'm dehydrated, I think to myself as I receive a message from Simen. *I hope you're OK*, he writes, *I know you'll get through this, you're strong*, he writes in an unmistakeably conclusive tone. I feel nothing, numb, but my body contracts, my muscles working together, one, two, three, NOW, time to take hold. I break the seal on the Valium and take three.

◈

Håkon's voice on the entryphone.

'What the hell's going on, Ellen?' he says as he makes his way up through the stairwell, before he even catches sight of me. 'I've tried calling you at least fifty times, I've been ringing your doorbell all day.'

I can't remember hearing the phone, or any ringing at the doorbell for that matter, I can only remember Simen's message. He marches straight into the hallway before looking at me, furious with fear and relief, and I can tell from his reaction that I don't look normal. Somewhere deep down in my consciousness I recall agreeing that he could come by to borrow the car for the day.

'My God, what's happened to you?' he asks, grabbing me by the shoulders. I realise I'm still wearing my blazer.

'Simen's gone,' I tell him.

'Since when?'

'I don't know.'

I try lifting my arms, but I don't have the energy.

'When did you last eat something?'

'I don't know.'

'Or have anything to drink?'

'I don't know. I'm not thirsty.'

Håkon pulls me into the kitchen, places a large glass of red squash down in front of me. There's a whistling in my ears.

'Drink,' Håkon says, sitting down beside me before getting up once again, making his way into the empty room, speaking to somebody. I can only hear snippets, not sure, no, there must be more to it, yeah, sure, don't think so, great, I'll stay here, of course.

◈

Mum's voice in the hallway.

'But she hasn't said anything else?'

I've remained where he seated me at the kitchen table, sipping at my squash while Håkon has been boiling eggs, defrosting rolls and chit-chatting about all sorts, the weather and a friend of his who's getting married soon, no doubt bound to be having children before too long. I've managed a few mouthfuls of egg and feel myself slowly beginning to think more clearly with the help of the sugar and protein.

'Hello, my love,' Mum says, making her way into the kitchen, and I hear the door closing as Håkon takes his leave.

She sits in Simen's place, takes my hand which is resting at the corner of the table top, squeezes it. I can't look at her.

She takes me home to Tåsen, the familiar smell in the hallway finally releasing the tears that have been held at bay somewhere beneath all of the wrinkles I've developed since Simen left. Mum runs me a bath, makes tea. In the wardrobe in my room I find some jogging bottoms and a hoodie that still fits. As I open the wardrobe door, I remember

Liv shouting whenever the round wardrobe doorknob hit the wall adjoining her room. One day, the knob was simply gone, and although it was obvious who was responsible, Liv denied having unscrewed it and disposed of it. The absence of Liv, of everyone, or everything, of something, tugs at me, inviting thoughts that have lain beneath the surface as if sedated until this moment.

I sit in Dad's chair, his blanket draped across my lap. The wool fibres prickle at my legs through my jogging bottoms, the blanket itching just as it did when I was a child and Dad would cocoon me inside it whenever I was unwell and had to stay home from school. Mum sits beside me in her own chair. She rocks back and forth.

'I realise that things feel hopeless just now, Ellen,' Mum says.

I don't know what to say; I'm torn between wanting to uphold the embargo, to be sure she still feels the consequences, and the need to confide in someone, to benefit from some understanding and consolation – it takes no more than a few seconds of weighing things up before I come undone.

'No,' I sob. 'You don't ... you haven't...'

'But of course, Ellen, my love, I understand, of course I do,' Mum says after a brief pause.

I can't say a thing. I lean over, burying my face in my hands.

Mum comes around the table, crouches beside me, just like she used to when I was young and I'd hurt myself and she would comfort me, blowing gently on wherever it was sore, stroking me, hushing me softly, you'll be alright, it's going to be alright, my little love.

HÅKON

'You're doing it again!'

It takes a moment before I realise what she's talking about, then I pull my hand away from my ear.

'Seriously, your ear's going to fall off one of these days,' Anna adds.

'You're the one who says you're attracted to distinctive features, something you claim that I lack, surely you of all people can't possibly object?' I ask her, smiling, but still her remark lurks beneath the surface, stinging just as much as it has done these past few days.

'Oh God, are you still hung up on that? I've taken it back!' she replies.

'No, you haven't,' I tell her, and it's true, she hasn't, but I really shouldn't drag it out any more, this isn't keeping things carefree and easy.

Anyway, it's Dad's birthday, the first he's set to celebrate without Mum – today marks two years exactly since they announced their divorce – and I shouldn't say anything that might make Anna regret agreeing to come with me, I need her there, want her there, everywhere, all the time.

'It doesn't matter, I'm only joking,' I add hastily.

'I've explained what I meant by it anyway,' Anna says. 'You're very attractive, but you don't have any particular highlights, not as far as your appearance is concerned. Your personality is where your distinctive features are to be found – that's much more of a compliment!'

I don't believe her, but I'm flattered all the same, I just want her to keep talking to me, just want her to keep talking about me, it's intoxicating that her brain should formulate thoughts about me at all, that it might be filled with me, and that her voice should convey those thoughts. I pull her close, long to hold her tight, so unfamiliar, so incompatible, so new, so hopeless.

◈

I don't believe in monogamy, it goes against the laws of nature, I said to Karsten once as we left Blindern campus after an undergraduate lecture. We were about eighteen years old at the time, which was when I'd properly started to encounter and object to the structures that had made me increasingly surprised and furious with each passing day. Everybody conformed to a system to which they gave no thought, one that perhaps they weren't even aware existed. They believed that the world simply was the way it was, they didn't realise how submissive we were, subjected to religious notions and old-fashioned beliefs – systems that suppressed the biological nature of human beings in an attempt to control us.

I can laugh at myself when I look back on it now, I can see how extreme I was, how much I failed to grasp – and how hard-line I was all the same. But my views were rooted in a genuine desperation over the idea that I could never be free, that there would always be something – even in the unavoidably *learned* fragment of my consciousness – that would limit development in every area of my life. At times it weighed heavily upon me, so contrived that I could hardly stand it.

You just want to sleep with as many girls as you can, I remember Karsten replying with a laugh, failing to realise the gravity of what I was saying. It's more than just a sexual thing, that's way down the list, I said, genuinely on the verge of tears, these are the rules we abide by all our lives without ever questioning them, we just take it for granted that it's how we're supposed to live, that it might even be the *best* way to live. But just think of the alternatives, think of everything we've never tried. Think of all of the structures and rules and norms shaped by religion, do you realise how absurd that is? And more important than that, think of all of the choices you make every single day, things you aren't even aware are choices. Now you've been reading too much Sartre, Karsten said, humans need systems to situate themselves within. That's biological too, and I'm glad someone's created a framework for me to live within, at any rate, he said.

Even though I've had several life-changing realisations over the past twenty years as far as human nature and intelligence are concerned – as well as about the degree of freedom we have to begin with – I've always been of the belief that the twosomeness we consider a model in large parts of the world is simply a way to institutionalise emotion and love. It's a manifestation of oppression and control, and, until now, I've refused to enter into monogamous relationships. This was something that generally – and particularly during my studies – sparked unforeseen interest in several of the girls I met. It probably stemmed from the typically attractive nature of a man you can't have paired with the sincerity of my conviction. The fact that I truly believed in the free individual, in existentialism, and as an extension of that, naturally became a feminist – you don't *become* a feminist, Ellen said, that would mean someone would have to *become* an anti-feminist. I read up on de Beauvoir, quoted her in discussions; the very principle of marriage is obscene, I would often say, for instance, it transforms what ought to be spontaneous affection into a question of rights and obligations. I used de Beauvoir's relationship with Sartre as an example whenever I needed to explain what I meant, it's not that a person doesn't *want* to relate to another, I said, but it's about the *way* in which they relate to them: freely, with enjoyment, intellectually. It shouldn't be systematic and subordinate.

You can't just say it, you have to mean it, I told Karsten, who grew increasingly jealous as the girls came and went. You have to accept the fact that she's free too, that she's also sleeping with other people, it goes both ways. And the point isn't to sleep with other people just because you *can*, the point is freedom, independence.

For my own part, I've never had a problem with my girlfriends meeting other people. Now I wonder if this was more a case of me having a greater intensity of feeling for the cause than I ever did for these girls: I've been more in love with the concept than I have with them, the execution of the project, the feeling of being freer than those around me.

I viewed my sisters with scepticism, happy that I neither had to nor ever would end up living the way they did. Liv and Olaf, like an unalterable unit, a shared, irreversible life sentence. Ellen's eternal search for Mr Right, the one to give his all and be everything for her. You both know that you have a choice, you can choose differently, I once said when the three of us had met up for a beer and the two of them had done nothing but complain about Olaf in one case and a distinct lack of any Olaf in another. They dismissed me, just as they tend to dismiss most things they don't want to hear, or that they can't face taking seriously, all while continuing to explain that I'm too young to understand.

◈

You show just how spoiled you are, thinking the way you do, only an extremely sheltered, secure person could possibly allow themselves to act and live and think the way you've done! Ellen shouted at me when things ended between her and Simen last year, and I tried once again to formulate something absolute in order to salvage my own convictions.

We were sitting at Mum's house, where Ellen had been staying since the break-up a few weeks earlier. We'd had a lot to drink, and Ellen was initially aggressive, confrontational: And what about you, she said, why don't you get yourself a girlfriend? It's not something I'm aiming for, I replied. Mum thinks you're gay, Ellen said, staring at me. I couldn't help but laugh as I imagined the conversation between Mum and Ellen, no doubt Liv had been there too. I've said it before, I want to live as free a life as possible, I want to make my own decisions, I said.

I don't know why Mum and Liv and Ellen could never accept it, I'd been over it with them so many times. It was as if it weren't enough, as if they accepted my opinions as some sort of surface explanation, but that there must be something going on at a deeper level, something I wasn't telling them. But don't you want children? Ellen asked me, then looked away as she started to cry. Yes, maybe, but it makes no difference, I said. She grew all the angrier: So you don't want to be with the mother of your child, then? You'll have to define *be with*, I replied, I'm not all that sure if mother, father and child living in deadlock is the best model for society either, I continued. Ellen initially looked hopeful, then unsympathetic, then furious once again, and we started to argue – I pleaded my case without listening, impassioned by my own theories and Ellen's resistance, as well as the fact that for once she wanted to discuss these things with me. I didn't realise just how angry she was before she shouted at me about the position I was speaking from, how spoiled I was to be able to think and live in such a way. She didn't know the effect her words had on me, of course, I didn't appreciate it myself – I'd only just begun to sense an undefined change and a greater uncertainty.

I was drunk and snapped back with something almost unthinkably thoughtless about Simen and the biological instinct a man has to sow his seed, regardless of the circumstances – but especially when he hasn't yet produced offspring.

My God, to think I said those words to Ellen, it's so awful that it still turns my stomach when I think about it and I want to bang my head against a wall. The only explanation is my almost clinical approach to Mum and Dad's divorce, the way I very quickly decided that it was simply a manifestation of what I'd known all along: that marriage isn't natural, living with another person, relating to that one same person sexually and emotionally for more than thirty years, it goes against the laws of nature. I saw the divorce as nothing but a confirmation of this. In this day and age, when the majority of people are no longer confined by their religious views, when we're healthier and live longer, the natural consequence is that more people choose to divorce.

So, how do you explain the reactionary wave of young people donning enormous meringue dresses and getting married in celebrations that go on for three days or more? Mum asked one day as we sat and discussed this subject in the kitchen in Tåsen the autumn after Dad had moved out. It's just fear, I replied. They can't stand the freedom or the choices that come with that. They retreat to what they perceive to be safe, and with that, they destroy equal opportunity for everyone – it's not just anti-feminist, it's two steps back for every modern and liberated individual out there. I really believe that the women – and men – who are choosing to return to the gender roles of the past, following this hair-raising trend by emulating the description of the kind of family you might find in some home economics textbook from the fifties, apron-clad and showing off their baking, they're spitting on the entire fight for independence. *That's* spoiled – choosing to ignore the freedom that someone else has fought for, I continued. Oh, Håkon, is anyone out there *truly* free? Mum asked, sighing heavily as she loaded the teacups into the dishwasher.

I remember how intensely I argued that break-ups, divorce and open relationships were all entirely natural – a necessary part of the advancement of society – going around and looking at people with an expression on my face that constantly seemed to ask them what I'd said to instigate their reaction, as if Mum and Dad's divorce was a universal symbol for the rest of the world, too.

I think it was the first time in my life that I had so actively suppressed my own emotions.

◈

Håkon was born without a filter, Mum often said when I was young, smiling as if it were a compliment. It's no doubt turned out to be something of a self-fulfilling prophecy for us both – even very normal reactions have been attributed to my sensitive nature. I'm sure that no one would react at all if I were a girl, I once commented to a female friend who was equally fascinated by how *sensitive* I was. And by 'sensitive', she, Mum, my teachers and coaches all meant that I was affected more deeply than anyone else, that everything got under my skin that little bit more. I would cry over old people and disabled people and animals and insects; *highly empathetic*, as my primary school report phrased it. That makes it sound like a positive thing, and it was a long time before I grasped the condescending aspect of the fact that I always pitied others. It's no longer possible to describe it as a trait, or as a *part* of my personality, since being naturally sensitive to opinions, feelings and other people has become a kind of quasi-diagnosis with which everyone seems keen to adorn themselves: I'm so sensitive.

There's something feminine and enigmatic about the whole thing, and given that I've also inherited Mum's long eyelashes and full lips, my sensitive nature is something I spent long episodes of my childhood and adolescence trying to suppress. I probably put on more of a tough exterior than all the other boys in the class put together, without anyone ever realising just how much it went against my natural instincts. It's also made itself apparent in many of my political expressions over the years – fifteen years ago I was ahead of the curve, living just like every modern-day blog-writing, animal-loving advocate chooses to live now: I didn't eat meat, in fact I was virtually vegan after all the thinking I had done about the poor animals, I didn't wear leather boots or Canada Goose coats. The only difference is that it was embarrassing back then to live the way I did, I lied to people, telling them the fur on my coat was real, picking the ham and cheese out of my obligatory lunchtime baguette and smuggling it away inside a napkin, and so on.

I feel a great many things, and I feel them keenly, I've told myself as an adult. That doesn't have to be a negative thing; just think of all the exhilarating delights I've experienced that more neutral, balanced people miss out on, the enthusiasm, the glimpses of pure and explosive joy, the tiny connections in the human experience, the deepened understanding, the thousands of signals I pick up on without even thinking about it – I've realised that you're pretty much psychic, Anna said most recently just a few days ago – and that's a gift, I tell myself, as if in an attempt to convince thirteen-year-old me who harboured such shame over this part of himself, hating himself and his sisters for bestowing him with such a weak, feminine personality. Even so, it's nothing short of a curse to be so attentive to change, so exposed to it; I can sense the slightest tiny side effect of any medicine I might take, for example, and four days after a night out on the town, I can still feel myself trembling like a leaf in the wind. And not least, I'm haunted by an extreme intolerance to the sounds other people make.

Look at this, it's got a name, Liv wrote in a Facebook message a few years ago, sending a link to a page on misophonia. *The nearer and dearer the relation, the more intense the reaction*, she wrote, adding a heart-eyes emoji. Liv was referring to my near-phobia of what Ellen calls human noises – Håkon can't bear human noises, she explained to her high-school boyfriend over the dinner table. And it's true, the sound of bodily functions such as the smacking of lips and the drawing of breath and the whistling of air escaping a person's nostrils can drive me to the point of desperation – I grow so irritated and angry that I become incapable of focusing on anything else. It's particularly true if the source of these sounds is someone in the family, or anyone else close to me. When I was younger, I was prone to explosive outbursts at the dinner table when one of the others was guilty of making one of any number of unavoidable sounds associated with the natural process of food in contact with teeth and spit and tongue. The moist sounds that came from the back of Liv's jaw were the worst of all, and I dreaded her coming home for dinner every night. It was so unbearable that I wanted to punch her and tear my own hair out, and even though my place at the table was far away from hers, mealtimes often ended with me screaming at her. You're not the only person in the world, you know, Mum would often say after such mealtimes, you need to learn to put up with other people. Just imagine what it'll be like when you get yourself a girlfriend!

Most of my girlfriends have had to learn to put up with me, as it happens – either by taking this into account and eating more quietly, or by accepting the fact that we simply don't eat together. Even so, as an adult I've learned to control my irritation, though it's highly uncomfortable for me, and I don't reveal my aversion unless it becomes absolutely necessary. After all, it says a lot about you that you can't bear to tolerate other people's bodies, as an angry ex-girlfriend once put it.

In spite of my mind being the slightly imbalanced apparatus it has turned out to be, and in spite of the fact that every sound and abnormality and death and war and natural catastrophe and break-up – other than my own, that is – and argument with my parents and any number of other mini crises hit me square in the chest with full force, I quite quickly mustered a purely rational reaction to Mum and Dad's news that they were getting divorced.

◈

The morning sun shines through the window and falls on Anna's right arm and shoulder. I'm a typical Type B personality, she told me the first time she stayed the night here, and I thought she was dead the next morning when I couldn't rouse her before eleven. She's fallen asleep again now with her arms outstretched like a young child; she always looks like that when she's sleeping, as if sleep has overpowered her and she's drifted off mid-sentence or on her way somewhere.

I glance at the digital alarm clock on the bedside table. It's quarter past nine on Sunday 15 April 2018. This year, Dad has invited us to celebrate his birthday at the flat he bought recently, which is just an estate agent's stone's throw from Liv and Olaf in Sagene, closer to the grandchildren, as he put it. It's also around a kilometre from the flat Mum's bought in Tåsen. I look back at Anna, at her curls, her brown skin. She's lying on her back with her mouth wide open; imagine sleeping like that, so exposed and defenceless. I can only ever fall asleep lying on my stomach with my right arm under my chest, and I wake at the slightest movement or sound. Anna can drift off into a deep sleep wherever and whenever she likes.

She'll like Ellen, I think to myself. And Liv, as long as she loosens up, they'll both like each other. I pick up my phone to send Liv a message, I want to make sure that she understands the significance of Anna joining us, the importance of her having a nice time, but I don't know how to get that across in words. Liv will see right through me and my desperation. *Looking forward to seeing you both this evening, girls*, I write in a message, sending it to both Ellen and Liv, knowing at the very least that I've laid good foundations. When I was young, I always referred to them as the girls, one entity, and it's become a kind of nickname that Mum, Dad and I all use. Have you seen the girls? Dad often asks.

When I was seven, Liv was seventeen and Ellen was fifteen, and their lives seemed so mysterious to me: their arguments with Mum and Dad, the slamming of doors, chewing gum and perms, the scent of perfume and nail polish emanating from their bedrooms, Madonna and soft, coded knocks on walls, beyond my grasp, indecipherable. The reverence I felt when I was permitted to enter one of their rooms, to sit on their beds and watch Liv doing her homework, or when Ellen was granted permission to practise putting mascara and lipstick on me. I just need to know what it smells like *on*, she said, spraying both sides of my neck with perfume. There, go out and come back in again, she said, pushing me out into the hallway and closing the door.

There's still something about them that feels beyond my grasp, something about the bond they share. From my mid-twenties and right up until Mum and Dad's divorce, I felt that our relationship was gradually settling, and that I was becoming a more balanced and natural member of our little party, that we were three adults, all equally connected to one another. Since the divorce, it's become clearer that Ellen and Liv have a special bond that I don't share with either of them, that it's the two of them plus me.

It first hit me that evening in Italy when I found them in the kitchen after dinner and Mum and Dad's announcement. Ellen was standing there with her face buried in her hands, and Liv was reassuring her, arms wrapped around her, stroking her hair and murmuring to her. I stood in the doorway and observed them, their bond, feeling disconnected somehow, almost like an outsider. Håkon, Liv said when she caught sight of me, come here, come on, she said, giving a wry smile and beckoning with the arm that was no longer embracing Ellen. I chuckled softly. No, it's OK, I said, and headed to bed.

While Liv and Ellen both kept a demonstrative distance after we returned from Italy, like a united front, I sought Mum and Dad out equally. On the day that Dad was due to move out, I helped him carry his things to his car, finding myself hit with such a wave of emotion over the whole process that it was as if he'd cleared the entire house of fixtures and fittings. He roamed around aimlessly, seemingly unsure of how to bid farewell to both Mum and the house. Mum, for her part, sat at her desk in the living room in silence with her back to Dad and me as we walked back and forth behind her. Only the flame-red, hectic flush at the nape of her neck exposed her. Everything that had been so simple and straightforward up until this point, the way they talked about what had happened, the planning, their absolute agreement when it came to the separation, it all dissolved in a bewildered farewell.

Looking forward to seeing you too and excited to meet your new 'friend', Liv replied on behalf of the two of them, and I smile and lie back down next to Anna, taking care not to wake her, warmed to the bone by the sun at my back and Anna against my stomach.

◈

Dad's flat is spacious and bright. He's arranged the living room almost exactly the same way as the old living room at home in Tåsen, with one chair in the corner, the large writing desk pushed up against the wall and the bookshelf on the opposite side of the room. Everything he picked up when he and Mum sold the house has been positioned just as it used to be.

Anna touches the small of my back as we step into the living room, helping to subdue the pain of seeing the familiar furniture in its new environment. Liv is standing in the kitchen preparing food when we arrive, and she comes into the living room at the sound of our voices, casting a quick, appraising glance in Anna's direction in a way only she can before smiling and greeting us both, pulling me in for a hug. I'm strangely nervous; it's an irritating, troubling experience, and I pull myself together, freeing myself from Anna's grip and entrusting her to Liv. I make my way over to Olaf, who's reading a newspaper in Dad's brown armchair. It still manages to look naked without Mum's corresponding chair to the right of the small table. Olaf gets up and gives me a hug.

'It's been a while,' he says. 'But I see now that there's a reason for that,' he continues, nodding in Anna's direction.

'No, no, she's just a friend,' I reply. 'It's nothing serious.'

'Of course,' Olaf says, laughing.

Olaf is the only one in the family who's ever shown a genuine interest in discussing my theories with me, who's listened with curiosity and scepticism and taken me seriously, rather than writing them off as justification for my actions or a way of excusing my choices. But it's a little bit like what Liv says about sorting the recycling, he's said, one person making a little bit of effort now and then doesn't make much difference if the goal is to change the world. I'm not trying to change the world, Olaf, my goal is to think for myself rather than letting others dictate how I live my life, I've told him. In contrast to Liv, Ellen and most other people I've ever discussed this with, he didn't view this as an indirect criticism. By the same token, I wasn't able to write off his objections as jealousy; an open relationship is the very last thing Olaf would wish for, so concerned is he with stability and security. His loyalty to Liv knows no bounds.

◈

During the autumn after Mum and Dad's divorce came through, Olaf would often pop in to see me on his way to or from the gym or work, despite the fact that I don't live that close to either his office or the gym. Initially there seemed to be no reason for his visits, he just wanted to say hello, as he put it, or would use the excuse that he hoped to borrow a book or ask me to help him with some editing software that he used to have a handle on but could no longer quite remember how to use. Olaf, I said on the third occasion he turned up unannounced and perched himself restlessly on the edge of the kitchen worktop, what's going on? Nothing's going on, he said, then started to cry, laughing at himself through his tears, yet unable to stop them. Clearly not, I replied, smiling, as unsure as ever how to offer any comfort, yet overcome with sympathy all the same.

Sympathy is useless when you simultaneously don't feel in a position to offer any good advice, or when your uncertainty at the right thing to do hinders the natural development of things, as was the case with Olaf – my natural impulse was to comfort him physically, to put an arm around him and hug him. I grew up in a family of huggers, we

hug when we're happy, when we're sad, when offering our congratulations or comforting one another in more difficult times, we hug when
we're bidding one another farewell and often when we're saying hello,
and always, always, always when we're saying sorry. At primary school
I wouldn't think twice before hugging anyone who needed a little reassurance, if anyone had ever fallen over and hurt themselves, or if they'd
been teased by someone else or if I was simply making up with a friend
I'd quarrelled with. It wasn't until much too late, at high school in a
new class with new friends around me, that I realised it wasn't normal
for people to go around hugging each other all the time. I remember
one breaktime, one of my new friends was sitting with his face buried
in his hands after he'd failed a test, and I'd put an arm around him to
comfort him. Even now I can feel the deep, searing shame I'd felt when
he'd pushed me away. What the hell are you doing? he'd exclaimed,
wrenching himself from my grasp.

It's nothing really, Olaf said as he sat on my kitchen worktop crying,
taking deep breaths in and out and in again. Or, nothing final, anyway,
but I think Liv is going to leave me, he said, looking so desperate that
I felt on the verge of bursting into tears myself. Don't be daft, Olaf,
of course she's not going to leave you, you two are solid as a rock, I
said, but feeling ambivalent about the obligation to partake in any
conversation that would charge me with defending and promoting a
monogamous lifestyle. You can't always be so extreme, Dad said to me
once, a long time ago now, it's one thing to be convinced yourself, but
you can't judge others for their decisions and priorities.

We're not solid, Olaf said in my kitchen, not any more, things have
changed. I can't get through to her, I think she's depressed to be quite
honest with you, but that's not what scares me the most, it's the way
she seems to loathe me, as if everything is my fault, Olaf continued.
What's your fault? I asked. All this stuff with your parents has left
her crushed, you know that, don't you? Olaf replied. I didn't know
that, I'd only gained a sense of the vaguest contours of Liv's reaction
to things when I'd bumped into her by chance on Carl Berners plass
and hadn't felt able to stomach engaging with the desperation in her

eyes. I'd maintained a distance from both Liv and Ellen, escaping any reminder of family relationships or challenges to my own take on Mum and Dad's separation.

Olaf continued to pop round for a chat at regular intervals throughout the autumn. Things aren't getting any better, he said, and it's making me irrational. I do the stupidest things, he told me one evening in early December. I'd met up with Liv and Ellen just a few days beforehand for the first time in a long while, and I'd seen Olaf's description of the new Liv in practice. She trembled with anger and fear and despair. I couldn't say anything, so completely blindsided was I by the sight of her falling apart in such a way. We're siblings, she said. We have to stick together. But Liv, none of us are going anywhere, I said. We're here, this has nothing to do with us. It has *everything* to do with us when you both insist on leaving everything to me, when you let me down in this way, she said loudly. I didn't know what she was talking about, what we'd supposedly left to her; she was the one who had pulled away from us, and in truth I was the one who'd been in contact with Mum and Dad on an almost daily basis, I was the one who had talked to them and listened to them.

She got up to leave after Ellen mentioned that mum had a new partner. It was impossible to continue our conversation after that; Liv looked as if someone had died. She said goodbye and was halfway out of the café when she turned around and walked back to us. She gripped the back of the chair she'd been sitting in just a few moments earlier and stared at me. This is all wrong, Liv said loudly, her gaze unfaltering. Don't you see? No, I don't really, I replied, not understanding anything. Well that's hardly surprising, you've never been in a proper relationship after all, neither of you have. You don't appreciate the value of sticking together, of not giving up when you've made a *promise*, Liv said. What's the point in marrying someone, committing to them, if you can just break that promise later on? she added. I bit my tongue to prevent myself from agreeing with what was obviously a rhetorical question. I said nothing. No, but there you have it, Liv said, in their hypocrisy they've taught us the importance of sticking together, isn't that what we've always been told? Hm? she stated loudly, forging ahead with her monologue without waiting to hear anything Ellen or I might have to say. We don't stop until we've seen things through, how many times have we heard some variation or another of the same thing from Mum and Dad? But they've thrown in the towel, right on the home stretch – given up on everything they've stood for, taught, created. It's wrong, it's a betrayal of us, the ones who've taken them at their word, listened to them, tried to actually live by the values they've imprinted upon us. She was tearing up by the time she reached the last part, her voice cracking, then she wiped her nose on her coat sleeve and looked at us both, shaking her head before making her way out. We sat there in silence; I don't think either of us had seen Liv act in such a way before now. We should go after her, Ellen said eventually, but neither of us got up.

I saw Liv a few days later, over at hers for Sunday dinner. I'd prepared an apology. I wanted to tell her that I understood where she was coming from, which I did, in spite of my robust standpoint on the divorce. She was right that Mum and Dad had always taught us to see things through, to keep at things, not to change tack. You have to stand up for what you say, has been one of Dad's mantras in life.

But the fact that Mum and Dad are choosing to break their own rules needn't affect our point of origin or relationship, I wanted to tell her. Either way, you've got us, we'll stick together, our relationship is strong and true – regardless of what's going on around us. Even though my sympathy for Liv was almost overwhelming – my stomach churned for days after we met in Tøyen – there was also a part of me that was pleased to be able to assume the role I did in relation to her. Comforting and secure. Liv has always been the one to take control of challenging or chaotic situations before anyone has a chance to think or react to anything. She's consoled Ellen and me and come to our rescue all through our lives, and I can't even count how many times she might have gone to the door of the biggest boy in my class to reclaim the Pogs he'd cheated me out of, or positioned herself as a physical shield between Ellen and a gaggle of girls she'd found herself clashing with at school – in spite of the fact that Liv has always been more afraid and much more cautious a person than Ellen. She's been unafraid and uncompromising in her attempt to protect us, her family. Whenever she's needed someone to support her in adulthood, she's always turned to Ellen. I was pleased to have the chance to give something back, to be the one to offer security and support, a kind of older brother.

Nonetheless, I never got the chance to say everything I'd mulled over and prepared, because the mood at her house that Sunday was very different than I had imagined it might be, as if the conversation, the confrontation, the desperation within her, had never existed. She overcompensated for things, of course, but all the same, it became impossible to pick up on something that she had clearly decided to make out had never occurred.

◆

What kind of stupid things? I asked Olaf when he told me about his irrational actions a week after our Sunday dinner. All of a sudden, my guard was up, my fists clenched inside the pockets of my jogging bottoms, instinctively ready to protect Liv in the most primitive way. It's mortifying, really, I can't even bring myself to say it, he replied. Come on, now you *have* to tell me, I said, doing my best to smile. Olaf fell silent. Don't think I'm OK with the idea of you betraying Liv, I told him when he remained silent. And you've misunderstood me if you think I'm in favour of infidelity, quite the contrary, actually – if a person has been stupid enough to commit to getting married then they should keep that promise or end things properly, I continued, standing up without thinking, ready for a fight.

Come on, hit me with it, I said. It's not what you think, Olaf said, I haven't been unfaithful. No? I replied. I just felt so desperate after feeling so taken for granted, like she no longer appreciates anything we have or ever did have, you don't know what it's like to feel so invisible yet so despised at the same time – I've only ever been visible when there's been something she's wanted to blame me for, Olaf said slowly. Sure, I've heard this before, but what have you *done*? I asked him impatiently. I lied about having fallen in love with someone else, Olaf eventually muttered, and I've never seen anyone look as physically uncomfortable as Olaf when he spoke those words on my sofa, he shrank several sizes, wringing his hands, tapping his feet restlessly, his face flushed and sweaty.

I couldn't help but laugh when I realised what he meant, it was such an absurd situation, hard to take seriously yet understandable, and Olaf's guilty conscience was genuine. Obviously I'm going to tell her it's all nonsense, but at the same time, it's worked, it's like she's come to her senses, somehow. And even though I feel bad for tricking her, it's nice to see that she's pulled herself together and realised the gravity of the situation. Olaf, it's going to be alright, I said. Maybe you don't need to tell each other everything.

Olaf stopped popping over quite as often after that conversation, and initially I thought it might be a case of embarrassment, but then I realised it was because he and Liv were growing closer once again, as he had described to me on one of his last visits. It's not like it was before, he said, but maybe that's OK, it's more honest now in some sense. I nodded, swinging between feeling used and being pleased on their behalf – and realising that I couldn't relate to anything he was saying.

◈

'Is this you?' Anna asks, standing at Dad's bookshelf and looking at a large photo from our childhood where I'm standing naked between Liv and Ellen, each of them holding my hand on a beach in Portugal.

'Yes, Dad always says it's *very* me,' I tell her.

Dad thinks that my expression in the picture says a lot about my personality as a whole: smiling and squinting and sceptical and open all at once, as he puts it.

'What a lovely little boy,' Anna says, turning to Dad who is standing behind her and who accepts the compliment with a wide smile.

She's investing in me, acting like a girlfriend would, someone looking to the future, I argue inwardly, and I resign myself to the thoughts associated with this new, reluctant pathway. Anna strokes the picture of me, running her finger over my bare chest and my tiny scar.

'Did you know that Håkon was born with a hole in his heart?' Dad asks.

'Honestly, Dad!' I say, embarrassed, mostly because I've told Anna about my heart defect, the operation, the exaggerated melodrama, all in an attempt to impress her, or at least to arouse some interest or sympathy. Maybe even her maternal instinct. Oh God, this is hopeless.

'Yes, he's told me,' Anna says. 'An incredible story.'

Olaf looks at me, but before anyone has a chance to say another word, the doorbell rings.

◈

So concerned with biology, yet unable to cope with *this*, Anna said in my kitchen a few months ago. She dangled half a pepper in front of my face, the same one I'd impulsively chucked across the worktop with a frightened cry when I'd found what Anna calls a baby growing inside it. It's just a baby pepper, she said. That's not biology, that's a biological aberration, I replied. I couldn't even laugh, had to turn away as Anna removed the incomplete red clump from the core and ate it. OK, Adolf, let me check the rest of this veg for biological aberrations and get them out of your way before we continue, she said.

I'd invited her to mine for the first time, it was January – the day after Ellen had introduced us to Paul, and I felt as if her enthusiasm had spread to me. I was so nervous that all of my tiny neuroses seemed to flail with twice the intensity. Things were still straightforward at that point; I recognised the familiar tingling sensation, sweaty palms and quickened pulse in her company as signs of my interest and desire, just as I'd experienced with others in the past. There was nothing conspicuous about anything, nothing apart from Anna herself; I'd experienced all these inner processes and thoughts before now. I fall in love just like anyone else does, I told Karsten when he asked me whether I missed properly falling for someone. No, I don't think so, he said, falling in love paves the way for feelings of possession, you can't get away from that. You're wrong, I don't need to possess the person I'm in love with, I'd prefer that they're free, I replied. I meant what I said; until then I'd only ever experienced tiny flickers of jealousy in former relationships, nothing that couldn't be rationalised. Nothing like the dark hell that had now claimed me, seizing control of body and mind.

I met Anna at an event. I try to subdue the romantic side of the pre-destined nature of meeting in the way Mum and Dad did. It was a panel debate on female writers and male readers, and I'd reluctantly agreed to go with Mum – she can't attend things like this alone, it's an irrational handicap that she herself is well aware of but which, ironically enough, worsened both after the divorce and once things had ended with Morten.

It's not possible to discuss the fact that male readers prefer books written by men, I said. How are you supposed to discuss people's individual preferences? But that's precisely it, I don't think it's a matter of preference, it's about the fact that men almost subconsciously consider books written by women to be literature *for* women, while books written by men constitute *literature*, full stop. And stories written by men with a male protagonist satisfy the interests of everyone, while stories written by women about women are only of interest to other women, because they focus on women's themes such as emotions and children and can't be considered to have any other overarching themes beyond that – take male authors who write about their fathers, for instance, they're supposedly writing about something more universal, Mum said almost without drawing breath while rolling her eyes. Ugh, it's an old-fashioned problem, as we'll see. For some reason, the literary world is lagging behind in the race for equality, she said. Maybe it's a matter of art and freedom of choice, perhaps that's why it can't be controlled, I said. No, it's just old prejudices that are to blame, Mum said. That and a bunch of old gits, she added.

It was Mum and Anna who were first to meet. Anna had been engaged throughout the debate, I'd noticed her sitting in her seat in the row in front of me and squirming with irritation, shaking her head with such fervour that her curls brushed the face of the man sitting next to her on numerous occasions, and groaning loudly at poorly constructed arguments. For what it was worth, her physical objections suggested we saw eye to eye on things, and I was pleased to hear her sigh and groan in all the right places, pleased that someone was expressing my own thoughts on the matter. All the same, I thought to myself, she's one of those sorts, the kind to make longwinded contributions at events, and if there's anything that drives me mad, it's that. The kind of person who just loves the sound of their own voice, who refuses to withdraw from a list of speakers even when they know their arguments have already been made, or who can't contain themselves at the close of a meeting or a lecture when in reality everybody has packed up and is perched on the edge of their seats waiting to leave, thrusting their hand in the air to pose a pointless question in spite of the fact that the event, whatever it is, is already running five minutes over. But Anna didn't pose pointless questions, she made a concise comment at the end that kept to time, focusing on the role of publishers, the media and critics, questioning who was given space to air opinions, who was taken seriously – and she closed with a well-aimed jab at the white, middle-aged male domination of the literary scene that caused at least five short-haired heads in the front row to freeze.

Mum's eyes shone with enthusiasm after the event and she elbowed her way through the dense crowd to grab Anna before she disappeared. When I found her again, she was out on the steps with Anna, smoking, of all things. It looked so forced, but it always looks forced when you see your parents doing something that somehow initiates you into a confidential adult world, removing the divide between parent and child by revealing their own fresh, hidden sides. Perhaps it also looked forced because as far as I know, Mum hates smoking. Come and meet Anna, Mum said. This is Håkon, my son. Anna smiled, switched her cigarette to her left hand and wrapped her strong, cold fingers around my own as we shook hands.

We stayed behind after Mum had left. I like your mum, Anna said.

Yeah, she's intense, I replied. I don't know if that's exactly the word I'd use, Anna said, she's engaged, it's so nice to meet people with opinions, people who say what they're thinking. I can see the same thing in you, too, I said, smiling. And what about you? Anna asked, simultaneously replying to her own question. I laughed, but since then I've been preoccupied with showing Anna the clarity within me, that I have the highlights with which she's so concerned.

◈

Two weeks and three meet-ups later, I invited her to mine for dinner. In contrast to the other women I'd met, with whom I'd introduced my thoughts on freedom and relationships as early as possible to avoid any misunderstandings, I hadn't brought it up with Anna quite yet. We hadn't actually talked about ourselves in that way at all, she hadn't even asked if I was single. It was a new experience. Earlier processes with vastly different women had followed the same introduction: map the other person in relation to yourself, explain things in the correct order and at the right speed, reveal and surprise with a sense of good timing. I hadn't realised I followed such a set pattern before meeting Anna, who wasn't concerned with talking about herself *or* about me at all – not unless it fitted into a larger context, such as providing an example to prove a point, or as part of a self-ironic joke. After meeting her twice, however, I felt I knew her better, that she'd shown me more of herself – and perhaps more important sides – than if she'd regaled me with me a chronological tale of her life and break-ups and childhood.

She looks like you, Karsten said when I showed him a picture of her. No, wait, she looks like your sister. Which sister? I asked him. Both of them, he said. Have a think about that, he said, laughing. I don't think she's much like Ellen or Liv, not in terms of her appearance or personality, but it struck me that there was something familiar about her, something safe and comfortable, something recognisable, all while being totally different and exciting. It's almost impossible, I said to Karsten, I can't put my finger on it. You can't put your finger on what love is, that's kind of the point, he replied.

In my intoxicating anxiety and anticipation, I'd spent a few days planning how to introduce the theme over dinner, since I had a strict rule not to sleep with potential partners or even with obvious one-off flirtations before I'd clarified my own standpoint. That's stupid of you, Karsten told me once, nobody else goes around and flags up the opposite – nobody inclined to being overly dependent or desperate or possessive goes around telling people they're never going to stop calling you if you happen to sleep with them. Either way, it's neater this way, I replied.

But Anna didn't make way for an intimate conversation over our pepper-less curry, in spite of the candles and the roaring fire, the soft music, she wouldn't allow things to affect her, her temperament seemed to be the same, regardless of her surroundings. After three glasses of wine I grew impatient; the less interested she appeared to be in me and my feelings, the more pressing it became for me to tell her that I was opposed to entering into monogamous relationships.

So, what about you? I asked, interrupting her at completely the wrong moment, in the middle of a sentence. What do you mean, what about me? Anna asked. What's your situation, or however I should put it, I said, taking a large gulp of wine to hide the fact I was blushing. Anna started to laugh. My situation? she repeated. Yes, let's be honest, I don't know much about that, I mean, I know how you feel about most things, from literature to politics to refugees to interior design, but I still don't really know much about your life. Well, you know that I live in Major-stua, I'm a freelance writer for various newspapers, my sister calls me a lot, Anna replied. That's true, though your phone is suspiciously silent today, I said, but I was thinking more about relationships, beyond this so-called sister of yours, I said, smiling, feeling sweat oozing from the pores at my hairline, hoping it wouldn't start to trickle.

Aha, Anna said, leaning back, it's *that* conversation. She seemed resigned, but even so, I regretted what I'd said almost instantly, I felt ordinary and banal for bringing it up, entirely lacking the highlights she held so dear. No, no, I protested, this isn't any kind of conversation, I was just curious. Forget it. No, I don't want to forget it, it's fine, this is the infamous fourth date, after all, she said, and I melted a little when I heard her describe our meetings as dates. I thought it was the third date that was infamous, I said. Aha, of course, Anna said, laughing. Well, I don't know much about that, in truth – I don't know much at all about traditional relationships, she said. What do you mean? I asked her. Well, I've tried all that, several times over, but it's not for me, she said. So, I just need to be honest and tell you I'm not looking for anything serious, regardless of how clichéd that might sound. I held my hands up to demonstrate how unclichéd it sounded to me. In reality I wanted to ask her what she meant by serious – I was more serious than I'd ever been – but I let it go. What about you, Anna asked, what kind of relationship do you have with relationships? I believe in free love, I said. Romance or friendship – every relationship should be free, if you ask me. What do you mean by free? she asked. Free from the straitjacket that society forces us to adhere to, I don't believe collective external structures have any place in emotional relationships. I think it should be up to individuals to define how they want to relate to a partner or spouse. For me, it's also about the fact that I don't want to promise something that I don't believe in, I don't think it's healthy or constructive to vow that you'll love someone for the rest of your life, for instance – how could you? Why shouldn't a person look at every unique relationship they have and say: this has a value of its own, regardless of how long it lasts. If it ends tomorrow, whatever has passed between us has held significance for me, I replied, and realised that I was partly talking as if on autopilot, afraid of things ending with Anna before they'd ever really begun. That's interesting, Anna replied, but how does it actually work in practice? At the risk of belittling your theories, we're talking about what most people refer to as an open relationship, wouldn't you say? she asked, smiling slightly. You might call it that, I replied. I don't believe in monogamy, I don't believe that humans were created to be monogamous, and I think we take it too much for granted that we should live in a way that other people decide for us, I carried on. But it can probably still work, even though we're not created that way, don't you think? Anna asked, now leaning across the table with an earnest curiosity. Yes, of course it can work, but what if something else could be even better? I replied, and it knocked the air out of me a little to see Anna agree with my arguments; I wasn't used to being met with a nodding, enthusiastic smile. The principle is the whole point, I added, and noted how important it was for me to state my final argument. There's no point in going around sleeping with other people for its own sake. Quite the contrary, I said, and flaring up within me I felt the same reluctant, unfamiliar need for something I didn't want to explore, something I had no desire to feel but which had caused cracks to form within me over the past few years. Have I told you I was born with a hole in my heart, by the way? I said.

◈

Dad makes his way quickly into the hallway, picking up the entry-phone and pressing the button that opens the front door to the block of flats. I can hear Ellen's footsteps in the stairwell, the rattle of her heels as she clicks up the stairs.

'Happy birthday, old man,' she says, embracing Dad as he opens the door to the flat.

Dad laughs slightly half-heartedly and takes Ellen's coat.

Liv emerges from the kitchen again when she hears Ellen's voice.

'Would you taste this for me?' she asks, blowing gently on a spoonful of sauce before popping it in Ellen's mouth.

'Very nice,' Ellen says. 'A little bit more lemon, maybe?'

Ellen isn't a particularly gifted cook. More often than not she adds too much salt and lemon to anything she does make, but Liv doesn't ask Olaf, Dad, Anna or me to taste it, homing in on Ellen instead. I console myself with the knowledge that it's a gesture on Liv's part, intended to normalise things, but even so, it hurts a little to see my two sisters in such a seemingly natural interaction with one another, just as it has always done, with me on the outside looking in.

On the whole, I function as a replacement if one of the two can't be there for the other or doesn't want to be, for some reason, such as after the divorce, when I seemed more important to both of them – but when Liv believed that Olaf had been unfaithful to her, and when Simen walked out on Ellen, they found their way back to one another. I don't feel as if either of them felt there was anywhere else to turn *but* to one another. At the same time, there's nowhere else I'd turn other than to them. I know they love me, and I don't doubt that I have a better relationship with my sisters than many other people – not to mention the fact that we're more alike than any of us would actually ever admit. I can see myself in both Liv and Ellen without looking too hard, catch glimpses of myself in their expressions and gestures, the way they think, talk, laugh – as well as the things they laugh *at* – but even so, throughout my childhood I often wished for a brother, not instead of, but in addition to having them both.

Ellen walks into the room, hugging everyone, including Anna.

'It's so lovely to finally meet you. I've heard so much about you,' Ellen says.

It's like being trapped in a bad comedy where everyone consistently and unintentionally makes comments that embarrass me. What's happened to our family's sense of tact? We used to be quite good at feeling our way forward, knowing what should be said when and to whom and how it should be formulated without needing instructions in advance. But then, I've never been quite as conscious of what people think or believe about me or my family, never quite as much as I have with Anna.

'I've heard a lot about you too,' Anna replies, and it's true.

I feel a little guilty about how much I've already told her about Ellen, the fact that I've more or less intentionally used Ellen's situation to scare Anna into something I've not managed myself. I'm just aware that I want her to know that Ellen tried for a long time to have children. But it was too late, I said, yet again drawing my own conclusion, that Ellen's age was to blame for her issues.

Nobody has actually concluded anything of the sort, no one but Ellen herself.

◈

Ellen lived with Mum for two months after her break-up with Simen. She was too unstable to work, and so depressed that Mum and Dad and Liv and I looked after her in shifts. I'm still not sure it was necessary to babysit her in such a way, she was matter-of-fact and controlled, her line of argument was logical: if you don't view yourself or anyone else you know as anything other than an organism, the only meaning to be found in life is in procreation. When that proves impossible for you, meaning disappears – a person becomes an aberration. I'm abnormal, the kind of thing you're so averse to, Ellen said, chuckling under her breath. No, this falls way outside of that, I said, though that wasn't entirely true.

But Ellen, you believe in lots of other things, I said. You believe in society, in relationships, in everything that occurs between people, there's meaning in those things, I said, doing my best to recall several of Ellen's arguments in the past. No, that's just filler, Ellen said, filler and excuses. You can't use my old arguments to convince me, nobody has any less conviction in the old me than I do. Anyway, this is the theoretical side of things, but the practical consequences are almost worse, knowing that I'm going to be alone for the rest of my life, she continued. You don't need to be alone for the rest of your life, even if you can't have children, I said. No, I know I can probably find a man who'll make do with me, but that's a poor consolation. I'm talking about a different kind of loneliness, she said, the kind that could never be understood by those who have become parents themselves – the loneliness in knowing that there's a deeper kind of attachment and meaning you'll never come to experience. Those with children don't ever need to ponder the meaning of life in the same way, she continued. You know, I'm sure that Mum and Dad and a lot of other parents would attest to the fact that what you're saying isn't quite true, I said. Then they're either spoiled individuals or terrible parents, Ellen replied.

Even though Ellen, strictly speaking, didn't require looking after in such a way as far as I was concerned, it became a kind of collaborative project that the entire family could contribute towards. I think the others also understood the slightly exaggerated nature of the situation, but everyone, even Ellen herself, seemed to be glad to have a joint task, something collective and reconciliatory. We didn't have to talk about anything other than Ellen, or to wonder what lay beneath people's words and actions; self-obsessed hang-ups and accusations were forced to yield, everyone was concerned solely with what was in Ellen's best interests, exceeding one another in their well wishes. In spite of the slightly contrived nature of this episode, it brought Liv, Olaf, Mum, Dad and me close together once again, returning us to something that resembled what had once been so normal for us.

Ellen eventually grew tired of being looked after and more frequently decided to deviate from Mum's schedule when it came to who'd be looking after her – instead she'd organise things directly with Liv, who was only too glad to hear from her, happy to accept the normalisation this signalled. She helped Ellen to move out of her flat in St. Hanshaugen when it was sold. Simen initially offered to buy her out. He came to Tåsen one evening when Mum, Ellen and I were sitting in the living room watching a film. He'd phoned her to talk about the flat, and as she previously would have done, she'd invited him over to talk about things properly – something everyone saw as a good sign – but when he suggested that he could buy her share of the place, she grew frantic. You can't live there with someone else, she screamed, what will you use the room for? What will you use the room for? And Simen backed off immediately. We can sell it, of course, he said, we'll do that, Ellen, we'll sell it. It was a stupid suggestion, he said, and I remembered how much I liked Simen in spite of how little I knew him. The flat was sold, and Ellen rented a place Liv found for her, which was close to her and Olaf. That pulled her out of her hibernation, as if she'd taken stock and decided to forge ahead. Mum's schedule of visitors became redundant, and one evening when I popped by to check on her only to find that she'd gone out to see a friend – without telling anyone – we grasped with mixed feelings that our project had come to an end.

◆

I didn't realise that I'd spent all of the past year unconsciously imagining that Dad would move back into the house in Tåsen; it was such a fully formulated thought that even I was surprised when the realisation hit me. It almost moved me to laughter, but it was so revealing and painful and raw. I hadn't realised that my positive feelings around Ellen's so-called breakdown were a result of such expectations, so I was similarly unprepared for the pain that followed when they gave way.

The summer that Mum and Dad started living separately, both took pains to demonstrate that everything was to be different, all while taking care to show consideration for one another. Both refrained from visiting the cabin during that first summer holiday, for instance. It'll actually be quite nice to do something different, Mum told me, to get out of a rut, I can't recall the last time Sverre and I spent any less than half the summer in Lillesand, it's funny what creatures of habit you become without even realising it. Dad went to Finnmark on a fishing holiday; it was fantastic, he said when he got back, nothing compares. Even so, last summer they were both extremely keen to spend a few weeks at the cabin. You can arrange it between yourselves, Liv said. It ended with Mum taking Liv and spending the first week there, Dad joining them for the second week, and after a few days together, Mum driving his car back – with Ellen driving Dad back home again the following week. I spent half a week with Mum and half a week with Dad. It reminded me of the previous year's planning, one of our typical Sunday dinners in the spring during which Dad had pulled out a pen and piece of paper to note down everyone's wishes and the logistical challenges to be worked out. He's always had a knack of working things out so that nobody gets their way, but everyone feels satisfied nonetheless.

Hopefully it won't feel too forced, Ellen said before leaving. It didn't, and the days the family spent together were lovely, natural and intimate, perhaps much like they used to be, right up until the night before Mum was due to leave. We sat outside and enjoyed our traditional meal of crab; it was a bright and mild evening, and I felt more agreeable and tranquil than I had in a long time, even managing to overlook the slurping noises Dad had made as he had tried to draw the moist meat out of the crab's claws.

Do you remember tipping over the pan of crabs that summer, Liv? Dad asked. It wasn't me, it was Ellen, Liv replied, laughing. Yes, Ellen was busy trying to kill Håkon, Mum said. Håkon? Liv and Ellen said in chorus, where were you? I was sitting right beside Dad, I replied, but before I managed to point out the striking fact that nobody but Mum had remembered me even being there, Dad interrupted to say he'd had a text message from an estate agent. Look at this, Torill, this is way above what we thought. Have you had a valuation? Liv asked. How much, then? Ellen asked.

I think everyone assumed that one of the others had informed me that the house was to be sold. I don't think it was done on purpose, they couldn't know about the hopes I'd had, I wasn't even aware of them myself, but suddenly I felt as crushed as the crab's claw that Liv loudly crunched. I shrank back in the face of both the noise and the realisation.

◈

Mum and Dad bought the house in Tåsen just before Liv was born. It was white at first, but Mum painted it various different shades at regular intervals over the years after Ellen was born. I needed something to do while I was waiting for you to come along, Mum said to me once when we were looking through old photos of Ellen and Liv, posing together on various occasions – under the sprinkler on the lawn, on the way to school, with a sled under their arms – and the house behind them changed colour at least three times in five years. Very little changed indoors; they've reluctantly switched out white goods when Dad has had to give up on repairing the old ones, reupholstered the sofa and chairs a few times, always in the same colour, and swapped out the yellow curtains with the crocheted linen they inherited from Grandma – beyond that, anything else has been added rather than swapped out, and now it's full, in truth, I said to Mum as she tried to make space for a lamp Dad was given by Liv on his birthday a few years ago.

I lived with Mum and Dad until I finished university. Too old to still be living at home, but only in theory and for the purpose of making self-ironic jokes among friends, because in practice it worked like a dream. I can't recall feeling as if I was missing out on the experience of living by myself; why would I? I had all of the benefits of living at home along with complete freedom to do as I liked. It's almost like living in a commune, I told Liv, who just laughed and said she'd gladly live in a commune where her cohabitants paid the full rent, cooked all of her meals and did her laundry for her. It's more like a hotel, I'd say, she added, stroking my cheek condescendingly.

Liv and Ellen might have a closer relationship with one another than they do with me, but I have a much closer relationship with Mum and Dad. You're practically an only child, Karsten said to me once, who grew up with three brothers close to his own age. You've had your parents all to yourself, while still having siblings, *that's* a result if ever there was one. I can see it that way now, but when Ellen and Liv both moved out, it didn't feel quite so much fun having Mum and Dad to myself – I'd have preferred to have shared them with someone. When Ellen travelled to the US after high school and I could no longer hear a single sound from her room, which was just below mine, I cried myself to sleep every night. After a while I got used to things, and Mum, Dad and I entered into a new day-to-day existence in which I received all of the attention and care that had previously been split three ways.

It was horrible moving away from home, so horrible that I couldn't tell a single soul how I really felt. I was a twenty-three-year-old who was sick with longing for his mum and dad – both of whom lived in the same city, no less. I moved out with the greatest reluctance, only because the external pressure proved too hard for me to resist – after a while the stigma of telling friends and partners that I still lived at home without a valid excuse as to why that should be was too much for me to bear. It wasn't consistent with being a well-informed, independent person with purpose, there must be something wrong with a man my age who lived at home, sleeping every night in his childhood bedroom. I don't know, it just clashes with everything you stand for, a female friend commented, you fly the flag for freedom and independence while your mother still takes care of your laundry for you. I moved out three weeks later.

Both Mum and Dad must have been prepared for the fact that I'd move out, we'd talked about it, joked about it, Dad would even show me property listings from time to time, but still it seemed to take them by surprise when I eventually left. They were both still in full-time work at the time, both had a large network of friends and acquaintances and numerous hobbies between them, but still Dad remarked on how the house felt terribly empty, as he put it.

I suddenly have so much time on my hands, he said to me once when I popped back home – something I did several times a week in those early days. Don't be daft, I said, it's not like I took up that much of your time when I lived here. It's just a feeling you have, I continued with a combined sense of egotistical relief and guilty conscience. In that case I think you underestimate how much time Dad and I have spent on you and in being there for you – wondering where you are, if you'll be home for dinner, conversations, questions, mealtimes, clothing, keys, noise, all that and more. You have to remember that you take up more space in our lives than we do in yours, Mum said, smiling. I was fairly certain she was wrong about that last part.

At the same time, my guilty conscience caught up with me. With the privileged, self-centred attitude of a child, I hadn't thought about how this would affect them. I had only thought of myself and the pain I felt at reluctantly having to tear myself away. Suddenly it struck me that I was also leaving something behind, that naturally this would change something for Mum and Dad, as well as for me. A phase of my life had come to an end, but an even more crucial stage of their lives was over too – something they'd poured virtually every ounce of their effort, determination and love into ever since the moment Liv was born more than forty years ago. The emptiness that Dad spoke of was suddenly so much easier for me to understand, it was about more than just me.

Such is life, sadly enough; change is painful, Ellen said gently when I tried talking to her about it, and I felt indignant at how unfair it was that both she and Liv had escaped without having to deal with any of this; back then, they'd been able to break away in the knowledge that I would be there for Mum and Dad, small and dependent, entrusted with dealing the final blow.

All the same, I couldn't get my head around the idea that Mum and Dad wouldn't somehow find their way back to one another without Liv, Ellen and me around, or perhaps find something new in one another. I don't think the thought even occurred to me.

Neither had it occurred to me that they would sell the house. That they could. Even after Dad had moved out, the thought was completely alien to me. It was my childhood home, my house. Nowhere else felt quite as much like home, even after I bought my own flat and decorated and furnished it with all of my own things. I still called the house in Tåsen home. *I'm just popping home for a visit*, I might write in a text to Mum. I still don't know what's worse, the acknowledgement of the finality of their separation, or the fact that the house itself was gone.

But honestly, didn't you realise that's what would happen, Mum asked over our crabs last summer, after I fell silent and felt the blood drain from my face. My cheeks and lips prickled. Her reaction wasn't sufficiently strong, none of the other faces around the table revealed the slightest hint of the bottomless pit I felt open up within me. I get that it's sad, Håkon, Dad said, I find it distressing on a personal level, you know how much I love that house. But you're grown adults with your own lives now, Mum and I can't keep the house for the sake of memories of things that have passed, he carried on. And we still have those memories either way, Mum added. I couldn't answer.

Don't you at least think they ought to have asked us first, I said to Liv afterwards, and she gave a slight shrug. It's their life, Håkon, she replied, and Dad's right, neither of them can or want to stay in the house by themselves. I couldn't understand how she could take it so lightly, not given that this time last year she'd been out of her mind over the divorce – and that made it all the worse for me. There had been something comforting in Ellen and Liv's reactions and the ensuing turmoil, it had made it simpler for me to distance myself and to be the one to maintain a mature, matter-of-fact approach to the whole affair, bolstered by sound arguments. Without Liv and Ellen's resistance, my arguments lingered as if suspended in mid-air, suddenly aimless.

❖

'This is from Paul and me,' Ellen says once she's said hello and hugged everybody present, looking around as if there's a hug she's forgotten to give before placing a gift on the table in front of Dad.

'Thank you,' Dad says. 'How's it going with your chap in...?'

'Dubai,' Ellen says. 'It's fine, just six days to go now.'

'And what about...?'

'Thea? Things are slowly improving,' Ellen replies.

Ellen started seeing Paul around New Year, two weeks after meeting him through a dating app. Liv had downloaded it onto Ellen's phone against her will six months after things had ended with Simen. It's time you got back into dating, Liv said, nobody's saying you need to get married to the first man that comes along. It's the most superficial thing I can imagine, Ellen said at the time, swiping right and left and judging people's appearances in that way without speaking a word to them. How can you make that judgement without hearing their voice? Not to mention everything that you can tell about someone from observing their body language, she said. Two months later, she told us over a few beers that she'd met Paul. There was something about his expression, Ellen said, and it turned out that in addition to this expression, Paul had a deceased wife and three young children.

To begin with, Paul's eldest daughter Thea made things hard for Ellen. Liv was worried and she called me, afraid that Ellen would have a relapse – that Thea's rejection would trigger new, irrational thoughts in Ellen about her ineptitude as a mother. But Ellen did everything right, she allowed Thea to take the lead on things between them, she didn't put any pressure on her, she kept her distance and asserted the fact that she wasn't trying to be her mother in any way. I'm not trying to be your mother, Thea, I told her, Ellen said to us, a new warmth in her voice and her cheeks and her expression.

'Have you spoken to Mum?' Ellen asks me now, as Dad laboriously unwraps his birthday gift from her and Paul.

Dad straightens up, his good ear in our direction quite by chance. I don't know how to respond, what the right thing to say might be. I have spoken to her, she's on a singles holiday in Hardanger organised by the Norwegian Trekking Association, but you don't need to tell the others that, Mum said to me before leaving. Especially not your father, she added. You're divorced, you've got the right to meet other people, I said. Yes, but you know, it's Dad, she replied. He'll take it person-ally, she added. I don't think so, for all you know he might have met someone himself, I replied. What are you talking about, who has he met? Mum asked. I don't know if he has, I'm just saying he *might* have done, I replied with a smile. I was still childishly pleased to see she was so concerned about Dad. He might have done, of course, Mum replied. That's nothing to do with me, she added. But this is still new to us, isn't it? Well, it's been two years, it can't really be called new any more, I said, but maybe the years feel shorter when you get to your age. Don't be so ageist, you cheeky so-and-so, Mum retorted wryly.

'She's walking in Hardanger, stopping at various cabins,' I reply.

'With...?' Ellen asks, not knowing when to give up.

'Auntie Anne,' I say.

'Anne? Well I don't believe that for a second,' Dad said, laughing. 'The last time I saw her, she wasn't far off needing a Zimmer frame.'

In recent years, both Mum and Dad have mastered the art of remark-ing on everyone they know who shows any signs of ageing with thinly veiled triumph, as if it were some kind of competition. Perhaps it is, too, but there's something odd about them emphatically pointing out that one's friends and contemporaries are growing old, while actively suppressing one's own age.

'Maybe there were others, I don't know, I don't know everything

Mum's up to all the time,' I say, then find myself saved by Liv, who emerges from the kitchen brandishing Mum's tea towel – goodness knows how it's ended up at Dad's – telling us that dinner is served.

◆

You shouldn't be caught up in the middle of all this, Mum commented last autumn as we cleared out the house, as if I were any old child of divorce. She and Dad disagreed about the division of their things, and in his anger, Dad had hopped on his bicycle and pedalled away. You can't always have it all, Torill, I heard Dad say as I stepped into the hallway. What did you imagine? That you could carry on with life just as it was before, with all of the same things, the same habits, the same financial situation, and that the only difference would be that you'd be rid of me? he continued, his voice loud. Rid of you? Mum replied, I don't think I need to remind you who it was who found himself wallowing in a ludicrous crisis, who exactly wanted to get rid of who to begin with. No, now you're being unfair and you know it, egotistical and self-centred as usual, something that says a lot when all of this is actually your fault, Dad replied. My God, Sverre, just take the collection if it matters more to you than your decency, Mum said. Everything fell silent before I heard Dad making for the hallway; he spotted me and threw out his arms in infuriation, walking past me out of the door and jumping on his bicycle.

It was good, in a way, to finally witness something that testified to there being any kind of confrontation between them. In spite of several situations over the past six months suggesting things weren't quite as simple as they made out, like Mum's anxiety attack and Dad's escalated fervour for physical exercise, there had been strikingly little friction between them. In the presence of Ellen, Liv and me, they'd been polite and calm, discussing and addressing one another neutrally and with good intentions. I gathered after a while that much of this was rooted in pride, that they felt they had to prove something to us, and perhaps to everyone else – things had to go without a hitch, there wasn't anything strange about divorcing at the age of seventy, it was the right decision, something they both agreed on, look how straightforward and good and right this can be, and so on – but even so, it was a relief to witness a small part of what unfolded when nobody else was listening, when they weren't conducting themselves as if they were always being watched and judged on how they were dealing with the situation.

The plan was for all of us to clear out the house as if we were still a functioning family unit, but Ellen, who had only just met Paul at this point, sent her apologies and said she'd come and take whatever of hers was left in her room later. Liv and Olaf popped in and took a few cardboard boxes from Liv's room before disappearing again. It was Mum and me who stayed behind and cleared the place. We stacked Dad's things in one corner and Mum's in another, and it seemed that Mum experienced a pang of guilt, placing the record collection in Dad's corner.

Ugh, you shouldn't have to be dealing with this, Mum said more than once. Maybe so, I replied, but I'm here anyway. Maybe there's something therapeutic about it, Mum suggested hopefully, I'm sure you remember how much you regretted not seeing Grandad when he died. No, I regretted not going to see him the day I'd thought about doing so, not that I didn't see him laid out in his coffin, you need to stop reimagining things all the time. Anyway, this is hardly comparable, I said. This is a loss too, Mum said, before having to sit down.

Dad eventually returned, wrapping an arm around me, thanking me for my help, it's not always easy, he said to me, though really he was speaking to Mum, who was standing with her back to us out of consideration. It's not just a case of sorting through furniture, it's an entire life together, isn't it? There are a lot of emotions involved, he continued, and was forced to swallow. It'll be alright, I said. He moved the record collection to Mum's corner and they resumed their polite cooperation.

I lay on the bed in my old room, listened to the house, smelled it, felt it, and wondered how many confrontations and determined amends had been made over the years between Mum and Dad without me ever having known a single thing about it.

◈

Ellen thinks Mum and Dad are getting a divorce because they've never really been close, Liv told me a few days after we'd cleared the house. She'd started getting in touch with me more often, once again using me as a kind of substitute for Ellen while Ellen herself was so caught up with Paul for the time being.

I can't recall them being cold, not in front of us, but perhaps they were around one another? she mused. You know what I think, I replied. No, Liv said, looking genuinely curious. I felt irritable about having to repeat myself yet again: They're getting divorced because it's the only natural thing they *can* do, I replied, feeling like a robot, because it's completely crazy to live with the same person for so many years, and now they've realised the absurdity of it without children around to take into account. You might be on to something there, Liv said, to my surprise. It must have felt terribly empty in the house when you moved out, I can't imagine what it'll be like when Agnar and Hedda aren't getting under my feet all day long. And if I were to give up working too, and every day it was up to Olaf and me to give our days substance ... I can understand how things might feel empty, to put it bluntly, Liv said.

I think there's a void there to begin with, I replied, and all romances are miscalculated attempts to fill that void, to be understood, but it doesn't work, not in practice – because at the same time, you need emptiness and a sense of *not* being understood in order to maintain a necessary longing for the other person. People are always longing for someone who can fill something within them, longing to be fully understood, to access some sort of higher plane with another person, but at the same time it would kill every relationship stone dead if that wish were actually fulfilled. If you stop longing, you stop loving, I said, yet to meet Anna at that point. I was certain that Mum and Dad had never felt that about one another, that they longed for one another, to be understood by the other. The emptiness that Liv was talking about was another kind of emptiness, practical and almost physical.

Liv looked at me. I didn't think you believed in love, she said. That just goes to show how little you all actually listen to what I have to say, I replied, feeling short-tempered. I've gone over this a thousand times, I probably believe more in what you call love than you and Ellen and Mum and Dad and everybody else put together, but I don't believe in regulating it, I believe that it has to exist without rules and without being forced into shapes that others impose upon us. Still, there needs to be room for longing, I continued, but by that point Liv had already stopped listening, always so ready to reject anything that might challenge her own decisions. Say hi to Olaf for me, I said, feeling puzzled to find that my own arguments on rules and norms for love no longer held the same resonance for me.

◈

'That was really wonderful, Liv,' Anna said, making eye contact with Liv across the table.

She always uses people's names in a meaningful manner, even when she's only just met them, which has a disarming and intimate effect in most contexts. I've always felt that people who use my name without knowing me are being invasive and almost cheeky, that there's something false and condescending about it, but Anna seems genuine – and it's one thing about her that I suspect Ellen will pick up on and approve of.

My need to impress Liv and Ellen is never-ending, even as an adult, and if I can't impress them, then I at least need to feel that I have their approval, and that goes for everything from my studies to work, clothing, activities, music and friends. The problem is, or at least has been, that they're so different, and have such different preferences, that the same thing never impresses them both; Liv isn't concerned with Anna's manner of addressing people, for instance, she probably doesn't even notice it, other than the fact that it registers somewhere in her subconscious as a positive. Ellen, on the other hand, doesn't pick up on Anna's personality and mood, her intoxicating charm, while Liv does, acknowledging it with the briefest, slightest change in her facial expressions.

'Thank you. It's my grandmother's recipe,' Liv says. 'Anything I manage to make is usually a result of following one of her recipes,' she says, laughing apologetically in our direction.

'You do that lamb casserole that my mother used to make too,' Dad says, smiling, clearly keen to provide some balance.

'Of course,' Liv says. 'Both of our grandmothers were good cooks. I'll never be able to cook as well as they did. It's like they both had some sort of secret ingredient at their disposal.'

'The fact you were a child is probably the secret ingredient,' Anna says, and it feels so natural having her here, she fits right in. 'I remember my own grandmother's food as being fantastic too, but as an adult I realise that it can't have been as amazing as I remember it, there must have been something about the ambience too. Sitting in my grandma's kitchen as a child, everything felt fun and safe and lovely – and then there was the simple fact that her food didn't taste like Mum's,' Anna adds.

Dad nods animatedly.

'Not to say that your food isn't fantastic,' she adds looking at Liv, then laughs, and Liv's expression and gestures soften upon receiving praise, as is her way.

'So, how long have you two been *friends*, then?' Ellen asks Anna, doing her best to imitate the trill of Grandma's Hardanger accent.

Anna looks at me and furrows her brow. Does she really have to think about it? And doesn't she have any reaction to being described as a friend?

'We've known each other for ... what, three months now?' she asks me.

'Three months, four days and...' I reply, looking at the clock, pretending to joke about what I know with all-too-great precision, 'and nineteen hours.'

'I'm actually living with Håkon now,' Anna says.

Everything falls silent. Everyone looks at me; Liv has inherited Mum's ability to appear hopeful and sceptical all at once.

'Just for a week, that is, while my bathroom is being done up,' Anna adds and laughs, satisfied at the response she's received.

It was my suggestion, it seemed natural to offer when she said she had to find a place to stay while the builders were in her flat, but Anna's reaction revealed that it didn't seem quite as natural or obvious to her. Won't it be a bit strange? she asked, almost suspicious. Why would it be strange? You're not moving in, I said. It's just a friendly suggestion, I added, realising I'd crossed a line that Anna was nowhere near reaching, and in spite of the fact that I was aware of her position, I'd subconsciously interpreted all of the time we'd been spending together and our conversations and our closeness and Anna's arm in mine and the introductions to friends and family as *progress*. Without spelling it out too explicitly, I'd felt like things were going somewhere.

Then I accept, Anna said. As long as we're still in agreement about what this is. Relax, my outlook on things is crystal clear, not even you can rock its foundations, I replied, frustrated both that I felt a need to compete with her detachment – look at her, coming here and warning *me* against becoming too attached to *her* – and uncertain that there was any truth in what I was saying at all.

'Haven't you ever lived with anyone else?' she asked me on her first evening at mine. I was so thoroughly content in Anna's presence, surrounded by the things I'd so eagerly anticipated seeing – her suitcase in the bedroom, her laptop on my desk, her shampoo in my shower, her toothbrush in the glass by the sink – I'd been looking forward to it all for days. I lived on-and-off with an ex for a year, but she still had her own place, and she spent a fair bit of time there, so perhaps that doesn't count, I said. What happened between you two? Anna asked, and I saw it as a good sign that she was finally asking me about my previous relationships, about something personal, about me. She wanted children, but not as part of an open relationship, and she issued me with an ultimatum of sorts that I couldn't agree to, I replied honestly and somewhat urgently, possibly even with a hint of defiance in my tone. But as usual Anna wasn't curious, she didn't take the bait. It's a strange idea, embarking upon a relationship with someone only to try to change them, she said, I've never managed to get my hea around it.

'But you're a couple, aren't you?' Agnar asks us at the table at Dad's.

I'd barely noticed he was there, even though he takes up a disproportionate amount of space at almost six feet tall and with limbs he's yet to fully master manoeuvring.

'No, we're not a couple, Agnar,' I reply, beating Anna to it. 'We're just good friends.'

'*Oh*, OK,' Agnar replied, then laughed. 'Just friends.'

I forget that he's sixteen, because in spite of his height and his broad shoulders and the shadowy beginnings of facial hair just visible along his jawline, Agnar is a child in my eyes – perhaps because he and Hedda are, for the time being at least, and perhaps for evermore, the sole representatives of the next generation. Agnar, on the other hand, regards me as a buddy of sorts, an ally within the family, and he often calls me to ask for my advice – whether about girls or friends or Liv and Olaf. Mum wonders why you never have a girlfriend, he said a while back when he was over at mine playing on the Xbox. She knows the answer to that, I said, and anyway, that's not true, I've had more girlfriends than your mum has had boyfriends. Dad says it doesn't count because you always have several on the go at once, Agnar said, he didn't dare look at me, just stared at the screen, clearly curious and a little embarrassed. He's half-right about that, but I think it counts all the same, I said. Agnar turned to look at me, couldn't maintain the façade any longer. How does that work? Is that even allowed? he asked. Only you and the person you're with can decide if you're allowed to have more than one partner at any given time, I replied. But don't they get annoyed at you? he asked. These are the kind of things you have to work out for yourself, Agnar. But just look at how many people are getting divorced these days, look at Grandma and Grandad, what do you think the reason for that might be?

The following day Olaf called, clearly on Liv's behalf, asking me to refrain from spreading my propaganda to Agnar, since he'd now got it into his head to dump his girlfriend and live as a free man.

'I agree with quite a lot of Håkon's theories and points of view on relationships,' Anna says now. 'To be quite honest, it's liberating to meet someone so ... well, liberated.'

'What do you mean?' Liv asks, I can see that Anna's response has stirred something within her, whether reminding her of the propaganda I had exposed Agnar to, or perhaps arousing a need to defend herself.

'I thought you'd told them all about it?' Anna says quietly, cautiously.

'Don't worry about that, everyone knows, it's only my lovely sisters who fail to listen or take anything I say seriously,' I reply, smiling at Ellen and Liv in the full knowledge that they disagree, that both are no doubt keen to point out that I'm the person in the family whose voice is always heard above all others.

'But surely it's not the case that you don't believe in relationships?' Olaf asks.

'No, of course not,' I say, and now I'm not certain how to continue; I don't want Anna to taste blood, to provide more arguments for her to agree with, not when I'm starting to feel uncertain about how I feel about them myself. At the same time, I can't go back on what I've stood for all these years, not in front of Ellen and Liv, and especially not in front of Dad.

In the chaotic hours after Mum and Dad announced their divorce – before I properly got a grip of myself and anchored everything in the unfeeling acknowledgement that this was an obvious course of action – I felt infinitely let down by them. They had broken the contract I'd done my bit to keep. I'd conducted myself like a responsible son should, while remaining dependent on their care, and for their part they should have played the part of accepting, protective parents. No matter how thoughtful and mature I could be among friends, partners and colleagues, this entire sense of independence disappears in the presence of family, and I automatically become caught up in the role of younger brother and youngest son; should I ever attempt to break free, it's seen as insincere and gently mocked, or in the best-case scenario, regarded as 'cute'. The fact that Mum and Dad could apparently so easily abandon their own roles was impossible for me to get my head around.

For a while I put all of my energy into rationalising things, suppressing the sense that someone had pulled the rug from under my feet. This is totally natural, I told Dad, and it helped to say it out loud as often as possible. It's crazy to think you might have spent your whole life with Mum, I said again and again. He and Mum had previously been sceptical, wondering if my philosophy on life was simply a form of protest for a generation so fixated on the individual. But in the wake of the separation they both showed a greater interest in my theories than ever before, and I no doubt exaggerated in order to underline how natural this was, not just to them but also to myself, harmless and unthreatening, not something with the capacity to rock the foundations of my entire existence.

It's impossible to go back on it, I have to stand up for what I've said. God, this entire situation has turned into a bloody nightmare.

'Of course I believe in relationships,' I continued. 'Healthy relationships in which we establish the rules for how they ought to work based on what makes us happy.'

'So, what, an open relationship?' Liv asks, she seems genuinely curious, not defiant or provoked, glancing every so often at Anna as if she's asking in order to help me to clarify something to her, but I'm still convinced that this has nothing whatsoever to do with Anna.

'You could call it that,' I say.

'What would you call it?'

Dad, Olaf, Ellen and Anna are following with interest, Dad is leaning back in his chair as if he's watching the football on TV.

'I call it a relationship,' I reply. 'It *is* a relationship, it just doesn't fulfil the same expectations that you and society have about what that concept means, there's more to it for me.'

'Well, sure, you can be in a committed relationship and reap all the rewards of that, while sleeping with other people,' Liv says casually, her expression neutral.

'That's not the point,' I reply, starting to tire of the way things always eer off in this direction. 'Sexual freedom isn't primarily what I'm talking about.'

'So, it's not a case of having your cake and eating it?' Liv says, and I detect something else in her tone, something harder.

'No, it's about the freedom to live the way you decide, obviously in agreement with a partner,' I reply. 'For me it actually means that I'm able to connect with someone on a more intellectual level, I don't have to devote all of my energy to living up to the expectations of others where my private life is concerned, expectations that result in most people spending a lot of their time suppressing their natural instincts.'

Anna looks at us, nodding enthusiastically at me, she couldn't be more on the same page, and I regret my words, our conversation, especially when all of *my* instincts are crying out for Anna, crying out to me to pin her down, crying out about the wonder contained in all that she is, that I am, that we are, the soft, thrilling, threatening, steadfast nature of the entire situation. But the acknowledgment plays out the contrasts within me, and in the next instant, in the silence that has fallen around the table, I carry on talking:

'I think everyone should think more about how they do things and the way they live their lives, the rules they choose to live by.'

'So, everyone should live by their own rules, basically?' Liv says.

'More or less,' I reply.

'OK, but have you given any thought to all of the systems and rules required in order for society to function? What would things be like if everyone just pleased themselves, ran red lights, stopped paying their taxes, stopped working, even?'

'I have thought about it, but it's not like I'm suggesting complete and utter lawlessness, and obviously I agree that there are plenty of fundamental structures that function remarkably well. I just don't think that marriage is one of those, I think that love rooted in duty over desire is something that we, as modern, liberated individuals, ought to ... well, free ourselves from.'

'Has it occurred to you that duty and desire aren't mutually

exclusive? Or that one might naturally lead to the other in a hea
relationship?' Liv asks, her cheeks flushed.

'I don't think that's healthy,' I say, and I want to bite my tongue, but
I've also become intent on winning the argument. 'Duty kills any sense
of spontaneity and joy and freedom, something that any relationship is
dependent on in order to survive.'

Liv gazes at me. She pauses for a moment.

'You know that Sartre and Simone de Beauvoir had a terrible relationship,' she states loudly and scornfully after a few seconds. 'This is
all based on nonsense, de Beauvoir was so jealous that she didn't know
what to do with herself. Sartre was an egotistical bastard. Don't come
here with your undergraduate-level philosophies and think you can
apply them to real life,' Liv says, now half-standing up from her place
at the table.

'It makes no difference what kind of relationship they had,' I tell
her, but that's not quite true, it reveals a slightly uncomfortable divide
between theory and practice, but I forge ahead regardless: 'The important part is what they thought, their theories.'

'Sure, the theory that you can go to bed with whoever you like is
ground-breaking stuff,' Liv says, then sits back down, resigned.

Silence falls. Dad looks amused, Ellen yawns. Anna is leaning
forward where she sits.

'Shall we call it a tie?' I ask, as we so often do when we want to bring
a conversation to a close without it ending in a disagreement, and at
this point I have every desire to end this one.

Liv smiles.

'No,' she says. 'Half a point to me.'

Nevertheless, Anna looks proud, as if I've won an important battle.
I want to wrap my arms around her as much as I want to punch her for
making me doubt everything I've ever believed in and stood for.

A few days ago, on the evening after Anna had occupied the flat
with her sounds and her smells and her routines and everything else
that I grew used to and dependent on in the space of just a few hours,
she was sitting on the sofa chatting to someone on Facebook for a few

rs. With every persistent ping of her phone or computer, I felt my body tense with the uncomfortable, petty urge to have her all to myself, started having obsessive thoughts without even realising that they were over-the-top and – *yes,* quite frankly – paranoid, I pictured her naked body pressed against someone else, I imagined that it was this very scene that was being described or perhaps planned with each of the pings I heard; after a while I became convinced that they were talking about me, too, about how she was tricking me in order to be able to stay here, perhaps, while I, in my blind naivety, believed her to be in love with me.

I was surprised at myself, at what my body and mind had activated in such a short space of time, when Anna suddenly turned her laptop around to show me a string of messages between her and her sister. Do you think we look alike? Anna asked me, pointing at the picture on screen. I nodded and laughed with relief, yes, you're both really similar, I said, wanted to tell her everything that had been running through my mind for the past hour, but luckily I was interrupted by Mum, who called to explain that she was feeling nervous about her trip to the Hardanger Plateau with people she didn't know. I mean, who actually goes on trips like this? And isn't it a bit too much like I'm trying to make a point, leaving just as Sverre's birthday comes around? she asked. No, I said in response to her final point, even though I wasn't entirely sure. Think of it as exposure therapy, you've always said yourself that you should seek out the things you fear in life.

◆

I'm sitting on Dad's balcony after dinner, the temperature is mild, it's dusky. Anna had somewhere else to be, and all of a sudden I had no desire to return to the flat without her. I held her for a little bit too long as we hugged in the hallway before she left. I'll see you later on this evening, she said, chuckling when she eventually found herself having to writhe free from my grasp.

'She seems nice,' Liv says, appearing in the doorway all of a sudden; I've no idea how long she's been there.

'Do you think so?' I say, pleased.

'Down-to-earth and genuine. Different,' she says.

Karsten and several others have often reacted to the fact that n. sisters and I can talk about things, often apparently heatedly, as if we were arguing, only to speak to one another later on as if nothing has happened. For me it's always felt natural, and I've come to understand that it's the result of discussing a whole range of issues, as well as being thoroughly confident in the knowledge that we are there for one another, regardless.

'Yes, she's very different,' I say.

Liv comes outside and sits at the opposite end of the table. She looks younger in the candlelight, just as she did when I was a child. I haven't ever thought about the fact that she's changed before now, I feel as if she's looked the way she does my whole life.

'Are you in love with her?' she asks with the faintest hint of a smile.

'Yes,' I reply, swallowing.

'It's fairly obvious,' Liv says. 'I've never seen you get so stressed over dinner before.'

I say nothing.

'Isn't that a little bit contradictory, maybe?' Liv asks.

I nod slowly.

'There's nothing odd about wanting something to cling on to, Håkon, when everything that's always seemed so secure has come undone,' Liv says.

◈

Karsten's gaze is fixed on me. I told him earlier on that if he gets too nervous, he should look at me, find his own calm within my expression. Now he's staring at me with such intensity – rather than looking at Cecilie, standing before him in her white dress – that I have to give him a brief nod to indicate that he needs to compose himself, just so it doesn't appear that the groom might prefer to be marrying his best man.

...ten marries Cecilie six weeks after Dad's seventy-second birth-
...He proposed two years ago – that's something I find more absurd
...an marriage itself, just going around for two years or more, promising that you *will* marry someone – and asked me if I'd be his best
man the day after popping the question. I'd only just returned from our
fateful family break in Italy.

After all, you're my best friend, Karsten said. And to be completely
honest, I think you'd have been offended if I hadn't asked you, somewhere beneath all of your principles, he said. I laughed. My principles
don't pit me against the idea of you two marrying, obviously, I said to
them both, I only hope it's *your* decision. Of course it's our decision,
Cecilie said, I can't think of anything more romantic than demonstrating to friends and family that I've chosen Karsten, that we're
committing to one another. I bridled: Everyone says that, that com-
mitment is romantic, but why, I asked, other than because someone
has taught you that sacrificing something and offering it up is a romantic gesture in its own right? Cecilie was offended. What do *you* find
romantic, Håkon, hmm? Sleeping with as many people as possible?

No, the most romantic thing I can imagine is living with someone
in full freedom, and this person choosing to spend their time with me
because they want to, mind, body and soul, not because they committed to doing so twenty years ago in front of someone or something
they don't even believe in. The whole idea makes me want to laugh! I
can't understand why any modern individual would voluntarily choose
something so reactionary, something founded on a fundamental tradition of oppressing women, regardless of whether it's a religious or
a civil affair, I continued, unable to stop myself. Nice choice for best
man, Karsten, Cecilie said before upping and leaving us both.

I had to promise Karsten that I would limit my outbursts in the
lead-up to the wedding if I wanted to remain his best man. She was
the one who asked, I said in a somewhat insulted tone, but my obvious
need to assert myself in such a way had left a slightly unpleasant taste
in my mouth.

Mum and Dad, who have been like an extra set of parents to Karst.
ever since he cycled his way into our garden and my life when we were
four years old, are sitting together in the third row at the church. Mum
hadn't met any promising candidates on her trip to the Hardanger
Plateau, and in fact seemed relieved to have escaped the prospect. These
men bring a lot of turmoil with them, after all, she said to me a few
days after arriving home. Once you reach a certain age you have a lot
of habits, don't you? she continued defensively while rearranging her
bookshelves in line with the change of season. And a person's aptitude
for change is limited for the same reason, I said, laughing. Anyway, it's
lovely not to have to change, she replied. There's actually something
very nice about finally being able to just be myself, not someone's wife
or someone's mother all the time, if you see where I'm coming from, she
said. I could, I knew what she meant. Family members are never truly
able to see one another completely clearly, only ever through the veil
that their relationship draws over things, I said. And there's nothing
wrong with that, Mum said, it has to be that way, of course, but that's
not to say that it can't be liberating to step away from that slightly, to
get a sense of who you actually are, just for yourself, she added.

Anna is sitting beside Mum looking radiant in a pale-yellow silk
dress with thin straps that cross over her tanned back, impossible not
to touch. Do you want to be my no-strings date to Karsten's wedding?
I asked her a few days ago. A few weeks had passed since the discussion
with Liv on Dad's birthday, and we hadn't spoken about the conversation or us since then. She had moved back into her flat once work
on her bathroom had been finished, and without Anna there, the
place had felt empty all of a sudden, less like a home than ever before.
We continued to spend a lot of time together, but mostly over at her
flat, and I interpreted the silence on the subject of us as a good thing:
everything was fine, there was no hurry, and I could joke about keeping
things simple, just as I did in reference to Karsten's wedding. She took
longer to answer than I had anticipated she would, I thought she'd

out it more, perhaps say that yes, she'd come, as long as it was a no-strings affair – but Anna only gave the briefest hint of a smile ore asking when it was. Two weeks on Saturday, I said. Yes, I think I'm free, she said.

I've actually always liked churches; in spite of the fact I dislike most things to do with religion, there's something about the space and acoustics that I find soothing. Karsten has also calmed down, his gaze resting on Cecilie as the priest asks if, before God and the witnesses here present, he takes Cecilie, if he will love and honour her, be faithful to her until death they do part. Karsten responds with a loud, resounding yes. Both smile widely with such happiness and relief and love for one another when the priest pronounces them man and wife that, in spite of the reluctance that had built up within me, and the aggravating nature of the priest's words, I need to blink away the tears that have welled up, touched by the moment in a way that has escaped any internal filter.

I can hear Mum's unmistakeable, squeaky sniffs from the third row, and out of the corner of my eye I see that both she and Dad are red-cheeked and shiny-eyed. Only Anna appears unmoved, but she doesn't know Karsten, I think to myself, and for a moment I allow my thoughts to dwell on the idea of Anna in a white dress, kissing me with the same heartfelt intensity and delight as Cecilie appears to feel now, kissing Karsten; she doesn't want to let him go, she's making a point of it, clutching on to him, and Karsten lifts his hands in the air, seemingly helpless – they laugh together, mouth-to-mouth, as applause breaks out among their guests.

◆

I've spent a lot of time thinking about my speech for Karsten. I've even humbled myself to the point of asking Ellen for help – she read and discarded the first draft, which I'd been working on for several months. This is just full of your own reservations, it's plain as day that you're jealous, Ellen said when she called me to provide feedback.

Jealous? I cried. Either that, or that you don't have a clue what you want to say, Ellen replied somewhat disarmingly. You and Liv are the same when it comes to this kind of thing, when you don't know what to say you start blabbing away about yourselves. This speech is about Karsten, am I right? And about the woman he's marrying. You have to be sincere. If you can't say anything genuine about marriage, then find something you *can* talk about with sincerity, something you have an opinion on, and that way everything will be rooted in Karsten, rather than in your own stance on things.

Every word I stand here saying to Karsten now, about love, about the sense of connection and security, every word is rooted in me and in Anna. Throughout the entire creation of this speech I've imagined her, considering the fact that she'll hear it, that she'll feel it, that I'll cast glances in her direction, knowing looks laden with meaning. But Anna still appears unmoved, she smiles enthusiastically in my direction, laughs at all the right moments, but it's obvious that she has no idea it's all about her, me, us.

◆

My right hand on Anna's bare back, the muscles and bones beneath her skin, her breath in my ear, her long, cold fingers in my left hand, the smooth fabric of her dress over her stomach and hips. I'm overwhelmed yet again, pull her close to me, totally unaware of the others around us on the dancefloor. Together we are one, I want to whisper in her ear, my hand starts trembling at the mere thought, at the drop height that has been revealed to me, at how intensely and genuinely I want her, don't want to want her, don't want to miss her, don't want to fear – I just want to have her.

◆

'We agreed we'd be honest,' Anna says, apparently genuinely surprised at my reaction. 'Keep things simple.'

I can't speak. I picture myself grabbing him by the throat and squeez-ing, feeling the tendons pulled taut beneath his skin, then watching as his gaze, which has wandered greedily over Anna's naked body, loses focus. I picture his body tensing with the lack of oxygen before it no longer puts up a fight, and he dies at my hands.

'Håkon?'

'It's OK,' I reply eventually, swallowing.

'But I don't want to stop seeing you,' Anna says. 'I think we're good together.'

'Just not good enough?' I reply, unable to let it go, crossing my arms, right over left, across my heart.

'More than good enough,' Anna says, wrapping her arm around me in a friendly fashion. I want to saw her arm off, but her presence feels so right at the same time, so much so that I soften in this false sense of security. 'It's not about being good enough or not, you know that, this is your approach too, after all.'

Perhaps she just wants to demonstrate my own theories in practice, I think to myself, introducing a glimmer of hope. So I can understand that she's the only one I long for, that she longs for the same thing. To live with me, us and us alone, our whole lives through.

'You don't want to end up like your parents, after all,' she says, smothering any sense of hope.

❖

I leave her flat in Majorstua, then stand behind a tree and watch the front door of her building for what must be an hour. Paranoid and fit to burst. How about dinner tomorrow? she asked, kissing me unbear-ably briefly on the lips before I left. Maybe, I said, smiling, pulling my shoelaces tight with such speed that my shoes almost went up in smoke. I punch my clenched fist against the tree trunk four times, but I'm all that breaks, and I can't deny how much it hurts.

I call Liv.

❖